Snowflakes, Iced Cakes and Second Chances

ALSO BY SUE WATSON

The Ice-Cream Cafe Series
Ella's Ice Cream Summer
Curves, Kisses and Chocolate Ice-Cream

Snowflakes, Iced Cakes and Second Chances
Love, Lies and Lemon Cake
Snow Angels, Secrets and Christmas Cake
Summer Flings and Dancing Dreams
Bella's Christmas Bake Off
The Christmas Cake Cafe

Fat Girls and Fairy Cakes
Younger Thinner Blonder
We'll Always have Paris

Snowflakes, Iced Cakes and Second Chances

SUE WATSON

bookouture

Published by Bookouture
An imprint of StoryFire Ltd.
Carmelite House, 50 Victoria Embankment,
London EC4Y 0DZ
www.bookouture.com

ISBN: 978-1-78681-299-5
eBook ISBN: 978-1-78681-298-8

Happy Christmas and a wonderful
New Year to readers everywhere.

Chapter One

Jimmy Choos and Turkey Tiramisu

I felt like I was walking in an enchanted forest, tripping through a Scandinavian landscape of silver birch trees, ice-blue skies and snow drifts. I gazed through the silvery twigs at the lonely princess dancing on ice, platinum hair flowing behind her as she turned slowly on the glittering frozen pond. And peering further into the cavernous space, I gasped at the beautiful sight before me – the most *divine* pair of Jimmy Choos I'd ever clapped eyes on. They were hanging from a branch to her left. Long, spiky heels, lashings of cranberry-red glitter and a dangerously pointed toe that could take a man's eye out with one kick.

'Want!' I said under my breath, almost licking the store window and spotting my reflection. In truth, I felt just like the lonely princess in the Christmas window display; I could so relate as she went agonisingly slowly round and round on the bloody circle of ice with no real purpose or destination. At least she had the prospect of a pair of Jimmy Choos, which was a damn sight more than I had just now. Yep, this was me – a

lonely princess on life's squeaky treadmill: my marriage was over,
I lived alone, Christmas was weeks away and I was dreading
it. I had nothing to look forward to, no one to go home for,
no gifts to buy, no Christmas dinner to share, just me in my
lonely princess tower – or to be more precise my little flat in
Clapham. There was no prince to sweep me off my feet and no
scrummy Jimmy Choos to pluck down like a ripe berry from
a nearby tree either.

I was really feeling sorry for myself as shoppers rushed past
me on that uphill climb towards Christmas. Everyone else was
bustling around, whizzing past with presents to buy, places to go,
and people to see. And as everyone lived their lives and hurried
by, it seemed that mine had ended before it even started.

I was standing outside Harrods lusting after expensive shoes for
a reason. Yes, I like shoes; I'm female, it's in my DNA. But I was
gazing at the Christmas windows because I was trying to pluck up
the courage to enter those hallowed portals of festive excess and
fabulousness. I was about to begin a two-week freelance stint as
Christmas Marketing Consultant here, which I was delighted to
do because it would be a lovely, Christmassy job. But like most
lovely things in life – it came with a price.

I moved away from the windows and headed for the entrance.
Holding my breath, I pushed through the doors and entered the
glitzy Christmas interior. My mouth was dry, and my heart was
performing a vigorous little dance, because here, in London, in

Harrods Department Store, at Christmas, was the place where it all began. Almost twenty years before, as a young marketing assistant, I'd met the rudest, most self-obsessed, arrogant man I'd ever known – and reader, I married him.

Gianni Callidori was an Italian chef whose unusual dishes had caught the eye of a Harrods boss who'd decided to package and sell them for Christmas. And if on our first meeting anyone had told me I would fall in love with this awful man, I wouldn't have believed them. I was in charge of making sure the right products appeared in the right spaces in the right windows, and was happily doing this when I first encountered him.

'Take your feelthy hands off my Christmas puddings!' was the first thing he ever said to me, and he'd yelled this in a thick Italian accent. Not the most memorable or romantic opening line, but as I was to find out, this was classic Gianni. As assistant to the brand manager, one of my tasks was to help find a prominent place for Gianni Callidori's Christmas collection, 'a new and exciting range of fabulous festive dishes for the discerning foodie'. I was shocked to be spoken to in this way, and I didn't care that he'd just been featured in a double spread in *Vogue* and was December's 'Culinary Hunk', in *Festive Food* magazine. All I saw was rude and difficult and I tried to ignore this grown man having a toddler tantrum, swearing at everyone and anyone about everything.

This was almost twenty years ago, and back then I hated him on sight – and sound. How dare he storm into the Harrods window where I was creating a wonderful display for his products and start shouting at me.

'Holy horses, don't bloody put them there,' he had carried on shouting and demanding some kind of response, so I turned quickly round and shouted back.

'Where the hell do you want me to put them then?' I'd picked up two of the clementine and clove Christmas puddings from his 'Callidori Christmas' range and thrust them at him in what must have seemed a rather aggressive gesture to those passing by.

'Not in the bloody sodding window,' was his charming, and heated response. 'They must be in dark, they mustn't see the light,' he'd said, grabbing a handful and clutching them to him like they were overexposed newborn chicks.

'Oh I'm sorry, no one told me your puddings were to be treated like vampires,' I snapped, 'perhaps you'd like me to avoid sprinkling holy water and garlic near them too?'

'No, there is already garlic in the bloody puddings,' he'd snapped back, which left me a little surprised that a) he didn't get sarcasm, and b) there was garlic in his Christmas puddings!

Before I could stop him, he began piling them on a table behind a turkey the size of a small child where they'd never be seen by shoppers.

'There, you see, she needs to be kept in shade, no light, no light,' he was waving his arms around. 'Put them here,' he said angrily, pointing aggressively at the table.

'I know where I'd like to put them… and they won't be exposed to light up there,' I muttered. His sodding puddings weren't selling and needed to be on display, not hidden at the back of the window. My job was at stake here.

So as he stood there, all 6 foot 4 of him towering over me with his hair all curly and tousled and his brow furrowed, I explained about 'marketing' and 'visibility' and moved his puddings back to where I'd originally put them. Then, after a few seconds, he gasped in apparent horror at my rudeness, said something about 'holy asses', and stormed out of the store window.

When my friend Cherry later showed me the article in that month's *Vogue* with him sitting on a chair back to front Christine Keeler-style, I had to laugh. Described as the '*enfant terrible*' of Italian cooking, he was clearly the next big thing and apparently Harrods were delighted to be selling his slightly crazy culinary Christmas. Oh God, I thought, I might lose my job over this. I fully expected to be hauled before the bosses for not hailing the king and offering to push his puddings up his arse.

'No one wants to work with him,' Cherry said. 'That's why you're on the account, you're new and the bosses don't want the hassle.'

I was annoyed that I'd been handed the poisoned chalice, but wanted to do a good job because I was conscientious. What I *didn't* want was to be shouted at by a rude Italian who hadn't even had the manners to introduce himself. I told him this the following day when he turned up without warning as I titivated the 'Christmas at Swan Lake' window.

'Who are you?' he said.

'And who are you?' I responded, from behind a giant swan. 'I'm sorry but you can't just barge into windows and make demands about where stuff goes. You were very rude yesterday.'

'And so were you,' he huffed. 'I will speak with the bloody management.'

'Okay, you complain about me, and I'll complain about you,' I said, hoping he didn't take me up on this. I was pretty sure management would be quicker to get rid of me than him; after all, I just moved the swans around – anyone could do that!

He just stared at me and I stared back, and this stand-off continued for some time, until he muttered 'holy horses', and swept out of the window.

I'd always been good at reading people until I met Gianni. I thought I knew what people were thinking and could often out-think them. I was used to handling difficult personalities in my job, but here was someone who was quite unreasonable. This was a double-edged sword for me, he was annoying, arrogant, his behaviour unfathomable and alienating – yet from the outset I was intrigued. He had this amazing energy, he was untamable, often unreachable, and yet after a while I somehow managed to communicate with him on some level. I worked for several weeks on his festive feasts, placing them in prominent positions throughout the store, especially the windows, attending promotion meetings and coming up with sales ideas. I referred to his range privately as 'Callidori's Crappy Christmas', and had little hope of any success given the concoctions he'd produced. I would smile bravely when he popped in to ask how things were going, and when I gave him the sales figures he invariably erupted like a firework. He complained bitterly about the lack of sales and had the bloody cheek to ask me what I was doing wrong. He had the ability to send me from 0–100 in a matter of seconds and we always ended up arguing. It wasn't always anger that drove our conversations, sometimes we'd chat about food and whatever else was going on at the store. It was usually small talk, but it was in those moments I saw a different man, someone who was reachable. I sometimes detected a twinkle in his eye but this was often followed by him teasing me, or a full-blown row.

He was pretty impossible to work with, but I stuck to my guns and if I wanted the turkey/crackers/Christmas puddings in a certain place, and he didn't, then I'd insist on it. Often I'd come back the next day to discover he'd moved them, and I would move them back. I didn't always get my way, but then neither did he.

It wasn't until I stopped working with Gianni and I was sent to 'Dog Comestibles', that it dawned on me that I missed him turning up unannounced and finding something to 'complain' about. After a while I'd realised it was all surface, and Gianni actually seemed to enjoy the combat, which had become more flirtatious as the weeks passed. I loved the way his eyes twinkled with hidden mirth, and the way he looked at me when he thought I wasn't looking, and rolled his eyes in mock frustration when I contradicted him. I had to admit I actually looked forward to him sweeping in and making ridiculous demands about placing his puddings in a prominent position or complaining about the way I was showing his panettone. And I knew he was always waiting for my outraged response, my own eye rolling under fluttering lashes (okay I flirted back, I was young). And sometimes, just sometimes, we'd catch each other mid-combat, and both laugh, shaking our heads at the other's apparently ludicrous viewpoint. But we both knew we were laughing at ourselves, and the exciting spark developing between us.

I was fairly happy in 'Dog Comestibles', and had become quite creative with the doggie Christmas stockings and ribboned marrow bones, but when Gianni 'demanded' I be returned to his festive collection, I made like I was doing everyone a favour. I pretended to be upset that I was leaving behind a life of horsemeat treats and a Christmas tree decorated with bones, but inside felt irrationally delighted. I secretly missed the play-fighting and flirting, and the days when we would just chat, like 'normal' people. I found him fascinating. On quiet days, he could be more pensive, less flamboyant, and talked about his family home in Tuscany, his mother's amazing cooking and his father's wine, made from grapes grown on their own small patch of Italian countryside. This would be sandwiched between the daily combat, him the villain and me the stroppy princess in the pantomime we played out.

'You not always bloody sodding right,' he'd mutter, his lovely Italian accent and dubious grasp of English creating a delicious cocktail I loved to listen to. Despite the chilly exterior, I soon realised his bark was worse than his bite. He'd sometimes thrust one of his famous Italian iced cakes at me – a beautiful box containing the most divine cake I'd ever tasted and, in my view, one of the few edible things in his collection – and say under his breath, 'Take this home to your mama.' I didn't want to spoil the gesture by telling him she'd died several years before, so I would graciously accept his gift. I wasn't going to turn down free cake! At those times, a faint smile would hover on his lips, and I could see it pleased him to give me things. This belied the rather grumpy, unfeeling image he liked to project to the rest of the world. It also made me realise there were hidden layers to this man, and I wanted to be the one to know what lay beneath – and keep it for myself.

There was always lots of bluster but Gianni never really lost his temper, just shouted and complained about everything with various swear words thrown in at random points to emphasise the strength of his feeling. As he was still struggling with English, these swear words often ended up being lists of expletives with no real context, which offended many, but I found amusing. He may have been stroppy and argumentative but I learned early on that the way to his heart was through food and I could always calm him down by asking about his 'Nonna's garlic bread' or his 'Mama's pasta sauce'. It was only then that the real Gianni would emerge, misty-eyed for the Italian cuisine of his childhood. 'Rich tomato sauces laced with the fresh garlic from the field,' he'd say, 'and the cheese, Chloe… ah the bloody wonderful Italian cheese.'

He'd left Italy at nineteen to find his way in the world, and though he'd settled in London, he said he'd never found anywhere that served food like 'back home'.

Around this time, a TV company began to show interest in making a documentary all about Gianni, this new kid on the block who made pasta like mama used to make it. His dishes were traditional Italian, with a modern twist, and along with his cutting-edge Christmas range he was famous for his blue cheese cannelloni and lemon and walnut pasta. But during an early encounter with a food critic who'd dared to criticise the consistency of his turkey tiramisu (the consistency was the least of its problems!) Gianni didn't like what the critic was saying so pushed his face into a large gateau and his TV career was over.

He was disappointed, but as I told him back then, it wasn't for him – he had to ignore the offers of TV fame and fancy dishes and stick with his principles of simple, Italian food. I mean, who wanted to eat turkey tiramisu anyway? Yuck!

Despite branching out into weird and wonderful ways with offal, his star began to rise and the more we worked together, the closer we became. I knew he liked me the way he baited me with cheeky comments about my outfits (when I dared to wear yellow, he said I looked like a 'bloody banana'). I wasn't offended, it was meant in jest and reminded me of the way the boys had teased girls they fancied at school. Clearly Gianni Callidori wasn't as sophisticated as the Sunday supplements would have us believe. All the lovely black and white shots of him in the kitchen, or sitting cross-legged with a huge carving knife and a twinkle in his eye, were just a pose. I saw the awkward teenager and the vulnerable man hiding just underneath the surface. I secretly warmed to his rather gauche attempts to gain my attention, and sometimes I wished he'd abandon the façade and just kiss me right there behind a pyramid of his special Christmas sausages.

Cherry had spotted the chemistry between us too. 'Whenever you're around, the miserable sod has an almost smile on his face,' she'd laughed. 'It's the only time he *ever* smiles.'

One morning, when I was working on a PR campaign for his Italian iced Christmas cake (the title was quite a mouthful, and the cake was the best mouthful I'd ever tasted), he wandered into the office.

'Morning,' I said brightly, 'look at the poster we've made.' I stood up and held up the glistening photo of the delicious cake.

Gianni had explained to me that Italian icing is made with egg whites and is essentially a form of meringue, and the light, fluffy texture against two layers of deep, warm velvet chocolate chilli sponge was truly a match made in heaven. I knew this because he'd given me a whole cake to 'take home to my mama' earlier that week and I'd eaten it all in two days. It was delicious; the sweet heat made my jaw ache in exquisite pain and the lacing of alcohol in the delicate crunch of sweet icing turned each mouthful into Christmas heaven.

'This is my favourite product in your range,' I said, my arm now aching from holding up the poster for his approval, waiting for a response. Gianni didn't really respond, he was being his usual self, not saying very much, just looking at the photo with a shrug.

'This iced cake reminds me of you,' I added, catching his eye.

'Me?' he said, with a frown.

'Mmm the frosty icing makes me think of your frozen heart.' I was goading him, wanting a reaction. But what I didn't tell him back then was that I knew the sweetness of chocolate and the warmth of the chilli were also there underneath his frosty exterior.

He stood a while, without taking his eyes from mine, obviously thinking about what I'd said.

I wondered if perhaps I'd gone too far. It was a joke, but he was a client and it may have been a little too near the bone.

Eventually, he dragged his eyes away from mine and looked at the poster, before returning to me, unsmiling. 'And I think you might be the chilli that warms up the frosty icing and my cold heart.'

I hadn't expected this and felt a surge of chocolate chilli run through my veins as he leaned towards me. I looked at him as he lifted his hand and touched my cheek with the tips of his fingers. We both looked into each other's eyes for a long time, and it dawned on me that finally something was happening here. But as I braced myself for a kiss, he pulled away and said 'Good work Chloe, I like the poster.'

I'd been confused by his rather abrupt departure. Was he shy, a little embarrassed about taking things further with me, or did he simply see me as a colleague to tease and nothing more? I didn't see him for a few days after that and was more disappointed each day when he never appeared to admonish me or cause a rumpus about his pretentious Christmas cardamom puddings. As I created pyramids of his puddings and helped the window dresser set Christmas dining scenes with all his crazy stuff, all I could think of was the way his fingers felt on my cheek. Again and again, the thoughts swirled around my head: why had he just walked away, and where was he now? Had my surprise seemed like rejection, or had the spark between us scared him? Even if he wanted to, could this outwardly cold man thaw whatever was in his chest?

I continued on with my work, trying not to think of him but seeing his face in every reflection of the Christmas store windows, imagining every man walking past on the bustling streets was him.

Then, just when I thought it wasn't going anywhere after all, and it had merely been a moment between us that had passed, something happened. It was Christmas Eve and I was finishing off the January sales campaign for when we returned after the holidays. All around me the air was tingling with other people's excitement, but I'd spent the day trying not to cry because my little cat Freddie had run into the road and been killed by a car the previous evening. I was so upset I didn't want to be in work, but as I was merely an assistant, I'd got the short straw and doubted anyone would give me compassionate leave for a cat.

That morning, Gianni came thundering in complaining about some trivial matter. It was bad timing, I was too distraught to be pleased to see him and though he was ready for friendly combat with me, I couldn't respond in my usual way. When he started shouting about how his smoked paprika mince pies hadn't sold, instead of saying 'I'm not surprised, because they are awful,' I just burst into tears. I was devastated about my little cat Freddie but strangely relieved to see Gianni, which had brought all my emotions to the surface. I had this almost irresistible urge to put my head on his chest. I longed to lean on him, and have him put his arms around me and tell me in his lovely Italian voice that it would all be okay. But he was cool at the best of times and I had no intention of throwing myself at his frosty mercy. Even through my tears I saw his face drop, he stopped shouting and his huge shoulders slumped – he had absolutely no idea what to do with a crying woman.

'I sorry, so sorry, I was teasing with you...' he was saying.

'No, no, it isn't you,' I said and explained about Freddie. As I looked up from my tears I saw such tenderness in his eyes it almost stopped me in my tracks. He continued to stand by me for a few minutes as I sobbed, looking at me awkwardly, his arms at his sides. Eventually, I dried my eyes, looked up and he'd gone, clearly unable to deal with the emotion. I decided not to care, I wasn't wasting my time or emotion on someone who couldn't feel, he couldn't cope with those feelings, so I carried on working and tried to push him from my mind. But when I came to leave for home that afternoon, I stepped out into the dark, rainy street and bumped right into him walking into the store. I gasped in shock, and started to laugh, it was a strange and embarrassing combination of delight at seeing him and fear at feeling so vulnerable around this man. I knew in that moment, I really, really liked him.

'Ah Chloe, I come to find you,' he said. He was walking strangely, his overcoat closed like he had something under there.

'Gianni, what are you doing? You look like a shoplifter,' I laughed. 'Or a flasher.' I blushed slightly at this.

'I don't do the flashing,' he said, looking confused, 'is this something you English people do?'

'No – it's not a national pastime anyway,' I giggled and shook my head.

He was moving shiftily, standing in the doorway looking guilty of something – I wasn't quite sure what.

'I bring you a present, a gift for Christmas,' he said, and slowly opened his coat gesturing for me to come closer. I was now a little concerned, what the hell was he about to do in Harrods' doorway on Christmas Eve? It might not be a British pastime, but perhaps flashing was an Italian one, they just had a different name for it? I looked at his face uncertainly, but he was smiling (yes actually full-on smiling) so I readied myself and moved towards him. My worries that he might be about to expose himself disappeared as I got closer and breathed in the intoxicating scent of aftershave and garlic. I'd never been this close to him and it felt good, comforting and exciting at the same time. As he put a hand inside his coat, I felt a flood of warmth (and it has to be said relief) as he pulled out the most beautiful little furry animal with two of the biggest blue eyes I'd ever seen. It was love at first sight.

'A kitten?' I asked, like it could be anything else.

'For you, to stop the crying for Freddie,' he said, still smiling, hopeful of my response. He gently put the tiny little white kitten in my arms, as her pink mouth opened to squeak her first 'hello'. I just gazed from her eyes to his and felt the world stop. That moment, outside Harrods, the snow began to fall and, despite everything that happened in the later years, it will always be the most beautiful, perfect Christmas memory for me. Nothing or no one will ever smash that bauble.

Chapter Two

A Ravishing Redhead and a Cottage by the Sea

I spent my first Christmas with the kitten sleeping on Cherry's sofa. She was in between husbands and we'd decided to spend the time together in her little flat, both enchanted by this fluffy little thing that would sit in the window and try to catch the snowflakes as they fell outside.

'That's what I'll call her,' I said. 'Snowflake!'

Cherry said she couldn't believe Gianni had given me such a thoughtful gift.

'He is just so closed off to everyone,' she mused, as we drank mulled wine and ate warm mince pies (without smoked paprika!). 'I think he's fallen for you,' she said.

'I just wish he'd say something, ask me out…' I sighed, knowing I wouldn't see him for a couple of days and dreading the time without him.

'I reckon Gianni Callidori is the type of guy who gives his heart away once, and once only… he won't rush into it, he has to be sure.'

I liked her theory, and hoped she was right, because as he'd put little white Snowflake into my arms in the doorway of Harrods, I'd secretly handed him my heart in return.

'Never thought I'd say this, but he's a keeper,' she smiled, giggling at Snowflake dancing under the tree, launching sudden attacks on the gift ribbon round the brightly wrapped presents.

The following year, Snowflake did the same, only this time it was Gianni and I smiling at her as she chased the tinsel up the tree.

By then we were living together in his cramped flat. Sadly, his Callidori Christmas wasn't bringing in much money and we were saving up for a business, the restaurant he'd always dreamed of owning. I was working full-time at Harrods and he was working on his dream, but we always found time to be together, and it was wonderful. Gianni would cook the most amazing dinners from nothing: his carrot soup tasted like lobster thermidor, cheap cuts of meat were transformed into the melt-in-the-mouth consistency of fillet steak. And for me a bottle of cheap wine shared with him tasted as wonderful as champagne.

'That man can make vegetables sing,' I remember saying to Cherry.

'Ah, what a man,' she'd laughed. 'May your cabbage always sound like Pavarotti.'

That first Christmas we'd bought a tiny tree and dressed it together, with much help from Snowflake who felt the need to be involved in anything that twinkled or dangled. Once we'd finished, Gianni lit the fairy lights and we both sighed at the beauty of our little two-foot tree. To us it was even more spectacular than the seventy-foot Norway spruce in Trafalgar Square.

As we sat together cuddling Snowflake and sipping on sparkling wine, I spotted a glass bauble that hadn't been on there before, and on closer inspection, I could see there was something twinkling inside it. I reached out, looking from the bauble back to Gianni, who was watching me and smiling while stroking Snowflake.

'What's this?' I said, curious, my heart doing a little skip.

'Open it up and see,' he smiled.

So I took the bauble down, opened it and inside was a beautiful diamond ring.

'Marry me Chloe, there's no one else for me,' he said.

I couldn't speak, I was overcome with love and happiness and the word just wouldn't come out.

'Just bloody say yes… yes?' he said, looking slightly worried now.

'Yes… yes, please,' I nodded.

'Thank God,' he said loudly, relief sweeping over his face. 'I thought Mummy might just say no for a moment,' he said to Snowflake, now rubbing her head up against his chest. He was teasing, he knew I wanted what he wanted and I loved the sound of the word 'Mummy' on his lips. Even now the memory of him placing the ring on my finger makes me tingle with love and Christmas. But we didn't know what lay ahead and the road is never as smooth as we perhaps hope it will be.

The last Christmas we spent together was not magical. We'd been married fourteen years, and so much had happened. Gianni came home drunk very late on Christmas morning, and this time I cried with rage and sadness and disappointment. The rows, the hurt, the blame were all whipped up into a Christmas cocktail that dampened any sparkle we'd once shared. I'd hoped we were for ever, I couldn't ever imagine loving anyone else but Gianni, and I couldn't imagine or bear to think of him with anyone else but me.

I'd tried to reach him, but that Christmas I realised we couldn't even talk to each other any more. He stormed off to bed saying I didn't care, when I really did, but he wasn't listening to me – again. So, with a heavy heart, I packed an overnight bag, and headed off into the dark of an early dawn, snow twirling around my head, my heart breaking as I walked away from my husband, my little cat and my life.

Leaving gave me a chance to think about everything that had happened and I realised we'd spent the later years of our marriage drifting apart. We'd both spent time away from home and each other, using our careers as excuses to hide from what was happening, and while life continued, we lost each other. Gianni was running his big London restaurant and I was an international events manager. On the surface, we appeared to be the couple who had it all. Our lives seemed so glamorous, the fiery Italian chef married to the globetrotting PR girl who launched parties on yachts, royal garden parties and all kinds of celebrity-infested celebrations.

While I had been on the other side of the world organising soirées for Saudi princes, Gianni had been lauded around London. His photos had been in Sunday supplements, wearing his chef whites, looking moody and broody. The accompanying interview often hinted at his 'difficult nature', his 'genius' and his 'cutting-edge' food. I remember reading an interview about him once on a plane journey and thinking 'This is my husband, but it's like I'm reading about someone else.'

This Christmas was my first as a single woman. It had taken me a long time to adjust, I had once liked being married, I loved sharing my life with someone, and though the sharing part had ended several years before, I think I'd been too scared to let go. And as crazy as it might seem, I was still scared of life without Gianni. It wasn't like I hadn't tried to embrace my new status, but after a few half-hearted, disastrous dates – I felt committed to being single.

And here I was back at Harrods to launch a brand-new champagne. Walking back into the store mid-December, I was slightly nervous, not just because I was meeting up with the champagne team – I rather liked the idea of being part of this, the fizz and sparkle of champagne at Christmas was just what I needed – but because I was returning to the place I'd first met my husband almost fifteen years before. I was torn between feelings of warmth and nostalgia, which would suddenly flip to heartbreaking sadness, and despite this being a great, well-paid freelance job, I was conflicted.

Just walking through those doors reminded me of Snowflake and Gianni's garlic-laced Christmas puddings. It brought back so many bittersweet memories from those early days in our relationship, and I mourned the loss of what we'd once had. There was so much promise, everything had sparkled, and I asked myself for the millionth time, how did it all go so wrong?

I suppose the physical separation mirrored the emotional one; in the early days of our marriage, Gianni and I had made it a rule that we were never apart for longer than a fortnight, and never ever on Christmas Day. This rule wasn't always easy to adhere to with our busy, independent lives and sometimes meant me getting on a plane, travelling halfway across the world and then helping out in the restaurant just so that we could spend the day together. But then one year I took a long-haul flight back on Christmas Eve, I was jet-lagged and just wanted sleep, the last thing I felt like doing was waiting around the kitchens of my husband's fancy restaurant until he'd finished sweating at the pass. So I went straight home, opened a bottle of wine, and went to bed, alone. This was the first time either of us had broken the rule, but looking back, the spell was also broken that night. Gianni had also been exhausted from a busy Christmas Eve and I doubt he even noticed my absence that night. After that we both agreed that it was impossible to make promises to each other about where we'd be and when, but now I could see this is what marriage is about, just being there. In effect, we gave ourselves permission to do exactly as we pleased, with no consequences. But life has taught me that there are always consequences. Ironically, this year I would be in London from the middle of December, plenty of time to prepare and celebrate Christmas at home. But it was too late for me and Gianni to be together; besides, I'd heard he'd left the capital and was planning on opening a restaurant somewhere else. I planned to spend Christmas Day home alone… probably with a magnum of vintage champagne.

Since becoming single, my whole life had been a bit 'home alone', and even in hotel rooms in Dubai, and at royal palaces in Paris, I felt lonely. Being away I didn't miss him on a day-to-day basis, I could perhaps subconsciously pretend nothing had changed. But then, in the middle of a pitch, the beginning of an important event, it would hit me that Gianni wasn't waiting for me back home. I remember working for a royal wedding in Spain, and as the bride walked down the aisle I remembered I would soon be divorced, and it totally crushed me. I had to pretend I had a migraine and leave it was such a physical blow.

Those first few months of the year had been hard, but according to Cherry, I was now in the latter stages of grief, which involved love, fear, tears, hate and everything in between. It also involved me checking Gianni's Instagram, Twitter and Facebook accounts far more than a healthy, separated woman should. Okay, I was obsessed. And despite finding only pain, resentment, regret and longing, I kept going back there like a drug addict visiting their dealer. I checked his Facebook page regularly because it was there that some of his personal stuff was posted, and I even saw a photo of Snowflake (who'd stayed with Gianni) and it set me back weeks. In the past, this page would be filled with photos of the two of us with our cat, our friends, or on holiday in our little cottage in Devon. But now, instead, I caught a glimpse of my husband's new life, and it hurt like hell. One photo posted in early autumn provided a nasty shock that sent me straight to alcohol – a whole bottle of wine in less than an hour. The photos were of Gianni at an awards ceremony where he was presenting an award for creative offal dishes. Gianni had a thing for offal, and would often lament at the dismissive way it was treated in the press. I didn't share his passion for gizzards, but I tolerated it – and sometimes even tasted it, but decided I wasn't a girl who relished organs, if you'll excuse the expression. In the photo, Gianni was dressed in black tie, and I was horrified to note I still found him devastatingly handsome, which annoyed me, but further perusal (okay stalking) of the timeline led me to a more horrific revelation. Gianni had a girlfriend! It had taken him less than a year to find my replacement, and I was beside myself with jealousy, hurt and an irrational desire to sleep with someone, anyone – just to get back at him.

I'd had to catch my breath when I arrived at the photo, the stunning woman was draped over his arm like a bloody fur coat. She was a redhead – I might have known; he'd always fancied Ginger Spice, something that made me absurdly jealous in the early years of our marriage. Years later this nameless redhead was causing the same green-eyed monster to pop up and I had to remind myself we were separated. I had walked out, so this wasn't a betrayal. Oh but it felt as sharp as one, and as I feverishly clicked for more photos, inviting the searing pain in via the screen on my phone, I tried to remind myself how much I hated him – even though that black tie turned my heart into raspberry jelly every time I looked.

The woman with him, described as 'my new girlfriend', was covered in diamonds, and smiling like the cat that got the bloody cream. She was also wearing a tight black dress that I could only dream of squeezing into. Obviously, I hated her instantly.

I'd been surprised at how much it upset me, but as Cherry pointed out: 'You can't blame him for moving on. You left him, not the other way round.'

'Yes, but he didn't fight for me to stay, and he's still my husband, and you're the one who said once he gave his heart to one woman that was it.'

'Don't blame me,' she said. 'Besides, we don't know if he's given her his heart, perhaps he only gave her his penis?'

'That makes me feel so much better,' I sighed. Seeing him with someone else had made me question myself, I was jealous of something I'd once had and walked away from. Why couldn't I just have been grateful for the wonderful life we'd been lucky enough to live?

About a week before Christmas, I headed home from Harrods determined not to spend the evening stalking Facebook like a hormonal teen. And what better way to take my mind off the fact that my husband had found love, than to decorate my Christmas tree. I was contemplating this when I arrived home and my phone rang.

'Is this Chloe Callidori?'

'Yes.' I hadn't divorced Gianni yet and still had his surname – to change it would make my working life difficult. Besides, I liked the alliteration, and the suggestion that there might be more to me than fair hair and pasty skin. I hoped the surname might suggest I had an exotic, Mediterranean back story; that's what I told everyone anyway, but I also found it hard to imagine myself as the Chloe before Gianni.

'I'm Fiona Langden,' the voice on the phone said, 'I'm the manager of a new restaurant, and I'm ringing to ask if you'd be interested in some freelance work over Christmas?'

My instinct was to say no, I'd been so busy the past few years, never taking holidays, going from one job to the next. I also needed a break from work to give myself time to heal and decide what I wanted to do with my life now I was single with no white picket fence, no husband and no 2.4 kids.

'I'm sorry, I'm planning to take Christmas and the New Year off,' I said. 'I may even continue into February, so I wouldn't be able to do it.'

'Oh that's such a shame,' she said, 'the owner specifically asked for you.'

'Oh I'm sorry...' I had to admit though I was intrigued; had Gordon Ramsay been asking for me again?

'We are so keen to get you on board, is there anything that would tempt you? It's a beach location, we'd provide somewhere to stay, and all your expenses would be covered.'

'Oh, it's not really about the money...' I said, thinking about the cranberry red Jimmy Choo shoes I'd lusted after in Harrods' window, 'I'm planning to take a break, I can't face another flight for a while,' I said, imagining a beachside restaurant in Monte Carlo, a pop-up in the Maldives, Raymond Blanc demanding my presence in Paris by 8 p.m. that evening. The prospect was tempting, but no, whoever and whatever it was I didn't have the energy or the inclination. And I didn't need a pair of £400 shoes... Come to think of it, who does?

But Fiona Langden wasn't letting this one go. 'This won't involve air travel, it's UK based and given the kind of work you do, Mrs Callidori, it would be very simple, very easy for you. You could combine it with a Christmas holiday?'

'Call me Chloe,' I murmured, 'I'm not Mrs...' But I tailed off. I had no intention of saying yes, but I was curious. UK based, eh? I hadn't heard of any chefs opening a seaside restaurant recently, unless Jamie Oliver was opening another one in Cornwall. I thought of the rocky beaches, the beautiful Cornish scenery in winter and I quite liked the idea, I hadn't worked with Jamie for a while, it might be fun. 'Could you give me some more details, where is it... what's the name of the restaurant?'

'Il Bacio in North Devon,' she said this very quickly, too quickly, almost like she was hoping I wouldn't hear.

My heart did a little jolt. Oh surely this was too much of a coincidence? 'Erm, Il Bacio?'

'Yes, it's a new Italian restaurant with a fresh take on Italian food... it's in Appledore,' she said, sounding like she was selling the concept in a TV ad.

I felt my stomach churn.

'Does this have something to do with my husband... I mean Gianni Callidori?' I asked.

There was an awkward silence on the other end of the phone.

'Yes, it's his new restaurant; he's left London,' she said quietly.

'Really?' I muttered, my head now working its way around the information.

Gianni and I had always talked of running away from London and buying a restaurant in the little Devon fishing village. We'd had so many happy holidays in Appledore, and even spent our Christmas honeymoon there – to live and work by the sea had been a dream for us both, to escape our hectic lives and spend some quality time together... just us. Now it looked like he'd abandoned his life in London and chased our dream on his own – and despite being separated, I felt a little pang of regret that we never did this together. Perhaps if we had things might have worked out differently? Like any married couple we often talked about our dream in some detail – the little restaurant by the sea, time to enjoy the sunsets, walks along the beach. We'd even bought a holiday cottage there to get away from the hustle of London and spend time alone together. It was the very beginning of a bigger plan, the first step in our escape – and now he was doing it on his own – or worse still, with another woman. I tried not to think of the photograph of Gianni and the glamorous redhead and forced myself to remember what a pain in the arse he was to work with. So I took off the rose-tinted spectacles and continued the conversation.

'So my husband asked you to call me?' I said, surprised because the last time we'd met, in an attempt to arrange the divorce, things hadn't gone well. I'd ended up throwing a large glass of Merlot over his head and stormed out of the restaurant, leaving him to scream a string of unrelated expletives after me.

'Gianni mentioned you, he said you helped him with his very first restaurant.'

'I did, but we were married then, I'm sure you're aware things are different now,' I said, wondering if Fiona was just a manager. Oh God, was she the redhead in the picture? If so, what a hard-faced madam she must be, I thought, bristling at the very idea of her asking me to work on 'their' dream.

'How dare you build your tawdry little dream around the ashes of my life,' I said, melodramatically.

'I'm sorry Mrs Callidori, I'm doing this on behalf of my boss, I don't have any tawdry little dreams.'

'Tell me something, Fiona, do you have endless legs and long red hair?'

'No… I'm afraid I don't; in fact I'm quite short with black hair as it happens,' she snapped.

'Oh I…' I didn't know what the hell to say, this clearly was a genuine enquiry and not the supermodel winding me up. 'Oh… sorry, I just thought – your voice, sounds like you have long legs and red hair, I'm fascinated by… voices,' I tried. She didn't answer. She clearly thought I was mad.

Whoever she was, I had to smile at the fact Gianni was approaching me to work for him via a third party. For all his Italian machismo, he was afraid of rejection and admitted that was why he'd been so awkward around me when we first met. But I wasn't the little PR assistant he first met, nor was I the wife abandoning my own dreams to help him achieve his. I felt the rush of familiar anger and resentment that usually accompanied my thoughts about Gianni, like lemon on pancakes it came, the inevitable bitter aftertaste. He was probably thinking that I'd feel guilty because I was the one who'd walked out and so would rush to help him. Or perhaps he wanted to flaunt the redhead and her diamond collection in my face? No, I wasn't playing that game.

Meanwhile, Fiona was still talking and I'd barely heard a word she'd said; 'I'll be honest, I'm running out of options,' she sighed. 'We open in a week, we have no staff and Gianni has locked himself in his office.'

'Oh how typical,' I said, imagining the drama no doubt unfolding in Appledore, as I sat safely in my new living room. 'So, let me guess, Gianni has upset every person you've employed and there's now not a single soul who'll work with him?'

'I think it would be fair to say he's had a few issues with the launch of the new restaurant.'

I had a vision of the bodies of staff lying all over the floor and Gianni, the Godfather, standing over them, his gun smoking.

'As you were involved in the launch of his first London restaurant which was a success, it made sense to come to you,' she was saying, clearly trying to flatter me. It wasn't working.

'Yes, but as I said, I worked with him then because I was married to him. It was before my own career took off and I helped out with everything in that restaurant. To be honest, it was the only way I ever got to see him,' I said with a hollow laugh. 'I wasn't involved at all in his second restaurant, the one with no name.' I tried not to think about that time, recalling the long, late nights, the empty double bed and the sheer loneliness of my marriage. He hadn't been there when I'd needed him most, so why should I be there for him now? 'So why does Gianni want me now?' I continued. I'd said I never wanted to see him again as the Merlot landed from a great height on his crisp white shirt and I'd swept out of the restaurant at our last meeting.

'Erm, I think at this stage he would be glad to have some support... any support... he said you would be perfect for Il Bacio.'

I tried not to let this soften me; I agreed, I'd be perfect for this, and I can't deny the idea of a lovely little Italian restaurant on the North Devon coast was appealing. I'd done so many huge corporate events this year and something like this would be a complete change. It would be small, the world's press wouldn't be watching and I could just get back to that grass roots PR involving food and real people – and it sung to me. I was also possibly the only person in the whole universe who could work with the stroppy, irritating, megalomaniac that was my husband.

In the absence of Cherry to give me some perspective, I gave myself a talking-to. I couldn't take a freelance job where my estranged husband was handed the opportunity to boss me around and rub my nose in the dirt for what he saw as me ending our marriage, let alone watch as the bloody redhead paraded around like Lady Callidori. At the same time, I was nosey enough to want to know exactly what was happening in his new venture, so implying I might be vaguely interested, I asked Fiona for details. She explained that the restaurant had held an 'open evening' the previous week, and mysteriously alluded to a 'fracas' with one of the local food critics. She said the original plan was to open by Christmas, but this was fading fast and they needed someone to help oversee the design, the opening... and Gianni.

'I am desperate,' she said, so I asked for a ridiculous amount of money expecting her to say 'no' and for me to say 'goodbye'. But to my horror and amazement, I heard her say: 'Okay.'

I couldn't believe it. I'd never imagined she'd agree. She went on to say I'd be expected to work two weeks over Christmas, oversee the restaurant launch, help out with any other PR matters like I'd just agreed to do the work. I suppose in effect I had, I'd named my fictitious, over-the-top 'Louboutin' price and I was well and truly booked. Not only did I now have a restaurant to open, I also had to babysit my out-of-control husband in the fragile early days of the opening.

'There's a cottage... Gianni's cottage... he said you can stay there,' she added, before I could find any more obstacles.

'Seagull Cottage?' I asked, remembering the place we'd shared so many happy times together. The open fire, sand from our toes on the wooden floor, warm scones fresh from the oven, simple, easy days with no work, just the two of us being... us.

'Yes, you have the opportunity to stay there...'

'Alone? I don't want to share with Gianni... and whoever...'

'Oh he can stay in the flat above the restaurant while you're working...' she said, refusing to offer any information on his personal circumstances.

'So, I won't have to pay rent?' I asked, knowing this would be the ultimate insult and I could say 'no way'.

'No rent, all free accommodation,' she was clearly so fed up and desperate she'd have thrown in a weekly crate of vintage champagne and dancing boys if I'd asked. I didn't, I had my own champagne, and was too tired for dancing boys.

Whichever way you spun it, and as much as I didn't want to, there were lots of reasons to take this job, not least of which would be to perhaps touch base with Gianni. Despite our love turning to hate, I'd always admired couples who divorced but remained friends and I wondered if one day we could do that. I couldn't exactly see me having girlie nights with the redhead, but I had to be a grown-up and being in his company might be a way for me to accept he had moved on, and for me to move on too. But there was the fundamental question: could we ever get over our mutual resentment and bad feeling to have a basic, business-like conversation, let alone a working relationship? Would I be able to resist dousing him in wine and would he be able to refrain from calling me a bloody bitch whore, or whatever other nonsensical string of swear words came into his head in the heat of the moment when we'd last met? In essence, could either of us ever grow up?

I ended the phone call saying I'd get back to her with my answer. I was a little unnerved by the past coming in on me unexpectedly and went straight to the kitchen where I poured myself a glass of Merlot and allowed everything to sink in.

So he'd opened 'our' restaurant had he? I quickly Googled it for signs of a woman's name or a co-owner and was relieved to find it was solely his. Perhaps the redhead wasn't even in his life any more? There weren't many women other than me who could put up with him, you had to be stupid, or in love – and where Gianni was concerned the two were inseparable. I'd been 'stupid' once and said yes all those Christmases ago, as he'd opened up the glass bauble and placed the diamond on my finger. I thought about it again now, as I dragged the big cardboard box stuffed with Christmas decorations through the room. I was peevishly annoyed that he got to move on and start a new life, perhaps even a new family – but I couldn't, at the age of forty-five my days of having a family were long gone. But I wasn't allowing that to define me, I still had a career, my own flat and my motto has always been that as long as there is good food, good wine and good friends there's a hell of a lot to live for. I needed to practise what I preached and stop wishing for a life that never turned up – I had to take pleasure in other things now, Gianni was the past and I would leave him there. I would dress my lovely tree, embrace Christmas alone in my flat and forget about the silly job offer – it just wouldn't work.

I continued the tree trimming, dragging out dusty old tinsel and loving every second. I enjoyed digging out the decorations, and greeting them like old, familiar friends who visit once a year. 'Oh there you are, sparkly ballerina,' I said, picking out a rather tired old lady who had once been young and perky – she'd lost one of her glass legs several years before. 'I know how you feel love, but let's keep on dancing like no one's watching,' I said out loud, trying to ignore the fleeting dip in my chest, recalling how years before I'd bought the glass ballerina for the little girl I hoped I would one day have. I remember hitting my thirtieth birthday and as I blew out the candles on the cake it was my dearest wish to have a daughter. Of course I'd have been equally happy with a son, but I just loved the idea of passing on all my 'wisdom', sharing perfume and gossip as I had with my mother. And until I reached the big 3-0, it never occurred to me that this might not happen, that I might not meet someone in time. So, when I met Gianni a few weeks after that birthday, I really believed that wishes came true. How wrong I was.

I finished decorating the tree and switched on the pretty lights and was just about to close the now almost empty cardboard box when I noticed I'd left the silvery green glass boat in the bottom. This was a memento from our honeymoon in Appledore, and just gazing at the glittery blue and green sails made my heart lurch.

Thinking about that honeymoon in Appledore now I felt sad for who we'd been back then. We were naïve but happy in that little cottage behind the seafront shops, where the future lay before us like the big, grey sea, just waiting for me and Gianni to dive in.

How could we imagine the disappointments, the pain ahead of us? When we had first married we'd had little money, but he had a dream, and I shared that dream, so everything we earned was going towards owning our own Italian restaurant. Gianni wanted a legacy for our kids, a 'proper family business,' he used to say, 'where we cook like home'.

We'd talked about our future on honeymoon, on the snowy Christmas Eve drive down to Appledore, our wedding night greeted with swirling mists and snow. Arriving outside the rented cottage we'd one day own, we climbed from the car, and I gasped at the frosty air in my face. Straight off the sea, the air was cold and biting and we laughed as we tried to put the key in the lock of the cottage door. It was too dark to see and Gianni's hands were so cold his fingers shook, and for a moment he abandoned the lock and pushed me gently against the front door. My back was on the holly wreath, but I didn't care as he kissed me in the darkness, snow swirling around, sea crashing in the near distance, the taste of salt on his lips. And despite it being so cold even inside Seagull Cottage, we couldn't wait and tore each other's clothes off in the hallway. He lifted me up and I wrapped my legs around him as he carried me upstairs, my fingers running through his dark, curly hair, eager to love him as his wife. I adored Gianni, and the strength of my feelings surprised me afresh each time I looked at him. He was traditionally handsome, but I loved him best when he was unravelled and delicious at the end of a long day. And at the end of that long drive to Appledore he was exhausted, his hair tousled and I loved him all over again. Sometimes I think we were both surprised at our feelings for each other, I recall him once telling me he'd do anything for me and my happiness was his happiness. And I felt just the same.

Our honeymoon had been the first time I'd ever been to Appledore, and it turned out to be the perfect, romantic winter escape. The following morning as we gazed out at the sea together from the upstairs window I had to catch my breath, witnessing the sheer beauty of white sky meeting pale waves, caught through a mist of snow, was overwhelming. Gianni brought me fresh, warm croissants and called me Mrs Callidori. I'd never been so happy, and it made my eyes damp now as I sat alone in my flat.

Of course the first thing we planned after the marriage was babies and we'd talk for hours about our imagined children, one of each, Anglo-Italians, bilingual, intelligent and very beautiful.

'They have to have my humour and your height,' I'd said.

'But I am very good to be funny too,' he'd say.

And I'd laugh; 'Yes you are, Gianni, you're very good to be funny, but sometimes only I see that you're "funny".'

'We have our bambinos now?' he'd suggested, only half joking, on our wedding night, and I'd nodded and hugged him and we'd made love again. Now we were married, we had a bright future, everything was in place, the children could come and we were ready. Neither of us had even considered this might not happen.

The little ornamental boat brought back the happier times, the sheer hope and optimism that shone through everything back then. And despite everything that had followed, I smiled to myself now remembering Gianni in those halcyon days, the way he spoke, that lovely accent that would fill my head with Tuscan vineyards drenched in sunshine, and fields of vibrant yellow sunflowers. It spoke of Italy and another place, but I'd had to learn to translate 'Gianni', because what he said and what he meant didn't always come together.

'Where do you see your life going?' I remember asking him early in our relationship.

'I love bitches,' he'd said. I turned to look at him, surprised. What? Had I completely misread this man?

'What did you say?'

'Leeving by the sea… I love bitches.'

'OH, beaches… you love beaches?' I said, relieved.

'That's what I said,' he'd nodded, clearly unaware how his pronunciation may have sounded to the untrained ear.

'The fresh, local produce,' he'd continued, his eyes misting over at the thought. 'Straight from the sea… I love just sitting on the bitch…'

'Yes.' I didn't want to embarrass him by pointing it out, so I said, 'I love the *beach* too,' trying to emphasise the correct pronunciation so he'd hear it. He never did, and on more than one occasion he'd announced to assembled friends or customers how much he loved 'going down on the bitch'. I'd always stepped in quickly saying, '*beeeeach*', but God knows what happened when I wasn't around.

He worked hard in those early days, his Callidori Christmas at Harrods had brought some interest, but given the weird concoctions, it was more a macabre fascination. Consequently, he wasn't invited to create any more Christmas lines for the store and by the time we married he'd found work as a chef in a big London restaurant. But all the time he talked of owning his own little restaurant and so when we'd been married a few months I said, 'Let's give up our jobs and go for it.' I was happy at Harrods, but I wanted to be with him and help him achieve his dream; besides, I would soon be pregnant and if we lived over the restaurant and I worked there too we could spend more time together with our baby.

So we took out a scary loan to start up the restaurant in London, our dreams of Appledore were for the future, he wanted to make it in the capital first. We lived off our nerves those first few weeks before opening, the rent was high and we could barely afford the food for the first night. I'd taken freelance work with a small company writing PR copy in the day, and at night I was decorating, sawing wood, helping to make the restaurant ready. Meanwhile, Gianni had called in favours from friends and written I owe yous to everyone just so we could get the restaurant on its feet. We painted the inside and outside ourselves, it was a deep red, warm and cosy, and with no money for extras we raided skips for old Chianti bottles to put candles in. The restaurant was tiny and dark and by day it was nothing, but when those candles were lit and the oven was on the place was transformed.

We'd talked about a name for the restaurant and though Gianni offered to call it 'Chloe and Gianni's', I declined. 'This is your food, your dream, this is "Gianni's",' I said. And so 'Gianni's Italian' was opened one sunny July evening in the back streets of Islington. The air was permeated with warm garlic and red wine, the waiters were Italian students and locals who needed the work but loved the food. They were paid in pennies and pasta and real Italians said it was just like being back in Italy when they walked through the door. Critics raved about the Italian comfort food, praised the 'honesty and tradition' of Gianni's cooking and within a few months queues were forming outside every night and we had to extend the opening hours. It was such a happy time, our journey was beginning, and for a while it looked like the sun was shining on us and everything was going to work out. But life has a way of sneaking up on you and back then we'd never imagined things turning out the way they did.

Chapter Three

Dr Who, Mr Spock and a Cosy Selfie

As the wine and the memories of my marriage to Gianni took hold, I allowed myself to drift back to Appledore again. We stayed there as much as work would allow, renting Seagull Cottage and never imagining in our wildest dreams that one day we'd have enough money to own it. There had been a lovely cafe there called Caprioni's that sold the most amazing ice cream, real home-made, fruity, creamy stuff like nothing you ever tasted. It was owned by an Italian woman called Sophia, who had a lovely accent similar to Gianni's. I adored the sundaes drenched in hot chocolate fudge sauce and sprinkled with nuts and cherries, and he loved the unusual flavours like rhubarb, lemon sorrel, elderflower or white chocolate. When we stayed in Appledore we visited most days for hot chocolate in winter and a kaleidoscope of ice creams in the summer. We both loved it there and Gianni was delighted to speak to Sophia in his native language for a while. He and Sophia would chat away about her home in Sorrento, where apparently the lemons were the size of a man's head. Gianni would talk to her about his own Italian birthplace in Tuscany, describing those rolling hills, vineyards and endless fields of sunflowers. They'd both become misty-eyed and though they tried to speak in English to include me, their excitement about their homeland (particularly the food) often spilled over into Italian. I'd just hear the odd word, 'winter truffles', 'Puglian grapes', 'and the cheeses, ahh the cheeses'. They would both sigh together before embarking on another Italian frenzy of words. I loved the melodious sound of this beautiful language and, while on honeymoon, asked Gianni to teach me some words. We had been lying in front of the open fire, the Christmas tree twinkling as his lips formed the word slowly, 'Bacio.' 'It means kiss,' he said and then he demonstrated, saying it again and again, covering my body in kisses.

Sitting by my tree in my little flat, clutching the little green boat now, I wondered if Gianni remembered those early days. Or had all those feelings he'd once had for me died years before, never to be resurrected?

We'd had some of our happiest and saddest times in Appledore, and when he sold Gianni's, the first London restaurant to open a bigger one, Seagull Cottage went up for sale. It was a bit crazy, but we loved the place so much and worried if we didn't buy it someone else would and we wouldn't be able to stay there again. We'd planned to spend even more time together there because the second restaurant had an army of staff, but somehow Gianni still had to be there. Appledore seemed like another life, another time, the world was young, and so were we. In those days everything shimmered with promise, until reality shattered everything. How could we survive after all the heartache we'd been through? Seagull Cottage had been the place we thought we'd one day escape to and live in for ever. A place we would raise our family, and build a better life – but that dream was never to be.

Now Gianni had a new life in our Devon cottage, and judging from what Fiona said, it didn't sound like he'd changed much, being stubborn with staff and customers and demanding his own way. With me he was different – still stubborn, often cross and loud and dramatic, but also kind, gentle and funny, particularly in the early years of our marriage. Then later, after all our problems, he became detached, and on the rare occasions he was with me, emotionally I felt he was somewhere else.

I suddenly realised I was sitting cross-legged in the middle of my living room clutching the toy boat, tears streaming down my face. No, I couldn't take the job… could I? I had to make a new life without him. I could form new relationships, perhaps even find a new partner one day. Following my ex to the place we'd loved wasn't going to help me do that. After we'd parted I'd been a mess. I'd spent the first three months unable to function outside work. But now, I'd licked my wounds and it was time to face up to a different future, and who knew what that might be?

Despite giving me almost all the money from the house, Gianni had offered to help me with the rent on the flat too. He was a proud Italian male and even though we weren't actually together any more he was keen to 'look after' me. But I wasn't prepared to let that happen. On paper we were still married, but if I was going to start a new life, without Gianni, I would have to be independent. With the house sold, our only link had been Snowflake our cat. I had to travel with my job and though it broke my heart to leave her, it seemed the kindest thing for her was to let her remain with Gianni. She was 16 years old, which must have been about 120 in cat years, so we didn't want to uproot her.

Cherry said Snowflake was a tug-of-love-cat and joked that I should probably be paying maintenance, which made me laugh, but it also made me cry – I really missed her. When Snowflake died just a few months after we'd parted, one of Gianni's assistants called and told me and I burst into tears. It hurt all the more because Gianni hadn't even bothered to take the time to call me himself. Snowflake was a part of us and he knew how much she meant to me. Gianni must have no feelings for me to allow someone else to break the news. He'd been the same about our marriage when it was limping along, refusing to face it, unable to talk through our problems, not wanting to hear about my pain. Like Snowflake's death, it would have been kind of him to acknowledge the end of our marriage, and deal with it together. I know I hurt him, and because I was the one who ended the marriage, who finally had the courage to say, 'I can't live like this', he owned all the pain of being the one left behind. But long before I walked out the previous Christmas, he'd already left me. So many times I'd tried to talk to him and ask how he was feeling, to work out a way we could survive, but he never heard me. If he ever managed to squeeze me in between meetings and shifts, he blamed my unhappiness on something else, trivialising my emotional state by attributing it to 'hormones' or 'tiredness'. But it had been about so much more than that, and it had eaten away at us both for years, until one of us had to be strong enough to leave. On the day we sold the house I cried, it felt like the final nail, a strange commitment to being apart for ever. I called him, but he didn't answer, so I left a message, but he never got back to me. I'd wanted a final reassurance that we were doing the right thing, that this really was a hopeless case… perhaps I was still looking for a chink of light? But Gianni obviously wasn't interested in any kind of friendship or rekindling, and I had to accept that.

I'd tried to open myself up to new possibilities, and had been out on a couple of weird dates with friends of friends, but it never felt right. It was never like it had been with Gianni. Despite his surface arrogance he had the ability to make me feel wonderful, special. He said he'd never really loved anyone until me, and I felt the same. I knew it was futile to try to recapture those feelings with anyone else, but when a lovely guy called Nigel asked me out, I felt like I should at least give it a go. I'd been doing some work for a big hotel in Brighton, and Nigel was in the hotel bar attending some sci fi convention. He was wearing Mr Spock ears at the time, which was an ice breaker, and we got talking. I told him I was in PR and marketing and he explained he owned 'Nigel's Deli' in the Lanes and said, 'I need someone to brand me.' Once we'd established he meant branding in the marketing sense (and not the masochistic one), he asked if I'd take a look at his air-dried salamis. It was an offer I couldn't refuse. He was good-looking, witty, intelligent and after I'd created a European woodland for his autumn launch, complete with hanging flanks, he asked me out for a drink. He was also good fun, and as Cherry pointed out, 'what's not to sleep with?' I was flattered by the attention – it had been so long since Gianni had even noticed me – and so I went out with him. He was pleasant company, but there wasn't much of a spark and when, after the third date, he filled me in on all six series of *Game of Thrones* with actions (some elaborate and quite detailed), I said things were going too fast for me. And I wasn't talking about the plot.

Cherry reckoned I wasn't giving it time, I was being too choosy and just because he was into box sets didn't make him a nerd.

'No, but it makes him a bloody stalker when he turns up on your doorstep with a *Star Trek* collectors' special,' I'd said, referring to his impromptu 'gift'. I'd made the mistake of telling him that Gianni had stopped giving me presents during our marriage, so Nigel took it upon himself to present me with a box set comprising of SIXTY DVDs, which when put together, he excitedly told me, formed a mosaic picture on the spine.

Standing on my doorstep proffering his 'gift', Nigel had misinterpreted the sheer horror on my face (at the prospect of over 100 uninterrupted hours of *Star Trek*) as a look of sheer joy.

'We're not watching them all at once, missy,' he warned, waiting for my crashing disappointment. 'We'll ration them, too much of a good thing and all that.'

In truth, it was all self-inflicted. I'd tagged Nigel in a few photos that I hoped would let Gianni think I was having a big, hot romance. I wanted to get back at him for the redhead, but in doing this, I'd obviously given Nigel the wrong impression.

Cherry had roared with laughter when I'd told her this story, and how I'd kept Nigel on the doorstep for half an hour.

'I pretended I had a flood and couldn't let him in,' I said, feeling a bit mean.

'Did he leave?' she'd asked.

'No, he insisted on taking me to a restaurant instead so we could discuss an episode in season 7.'

'What happened?' she asked.

'Well, apparently Worf pulled out his phaser and pointed it at the view screen and Picard used the moment to give Worf a chance to verbalise his thoughts, irrational though they apparently were. But according to Nigel, this scene is fundamental in that it differentiated the Picard character from Kirk in a profound way. Apparently, Kirk would have never done that in a million years,' I laughed.

'I didn't mean what happened in bloody *Star Trek*, I mean what happened when you went to the restaurant with him?'

'Oh God, you see? That's what Nigel does, he gets inside your brain. By day he's a harmless deli owner, but by night he turns into Nerd Man, and it's infectious. As for the dinner, I was hungry, so I didn't mind, but he insisted on trying to spoon-feed me chocolate mousse,' I added, 'at the table. Gross!'

Cherry laughed. 'I can think of worse things.'

'You weren't there. It was revolting, especially when I physically fought him off with my own spoon,' I continued. 'It was like some kind of weird spoon duel, chocolate mousse everywhere, and me shouting for him to stop. Then the waiter asked if I wanted the police involved, and people were filming us on their iPhones,' I added, reliving the whole embarrassing drama. 'I guess I'm just not ready for any kind of intimacy, and feeding each other is akin to sex as far as I'm concerned.'

'Chocolate mousse and sex on a restaurant table, sounds like bad porn… or good, depending on what gets you through the night,' she said. 'But you can't deny he's attractive?'

'Yes, he's very attractive, but then he speaks.'

'Don't listen.'

'He's just not what I'm looking for.'

'What are any of us looking for?' she said her hands up in the air despairingly. 'All you need is to make an appointment with passion, unlock your inner porn star and you'll be off. Trust me.'

'Thanks Oprah, but I'll give it a miss,' I said. 'The walls of his bedroom are probably covered in Mr Spock and Dr Who, which would be very distracting, if not unnerving… *in flagrante*. I don't know about an appointment with passion, an appointment with a psychiatrist might be more appropriate for Nigel.'

'Look, Chloe, you need to loosen up, and let in the superficiality. Be shallow, see him as a good-looking guy who you can sleep with, and forget all the other stuff.'

'Like his major personality disorder?'

'Yeah, forget all that. Just put on your best underwear, drink half a bottle of vodka, and pretend he's Brad Pitt, before Angelina and all that trouble on the private plane. Go for it. You'll thank me in the morning.'

She had a point. If my husband was moving on with Miss Redhead then so should I. Maybe sex with someone I didn't love, who couldn't hurt me might just be the start I needed. What was there to lose?

So, with Cherry's words of encouragement echoing in my ear, I set off for the fourth, and as it turns out, final date with Nigel. He'd invited me for dinner, and I arrived at his flat by taxi, having drunk the requisite half bottle of vodka as recommended by 'Dr Cherry'.

He opened the door, delighted as always to see me and I walked on shaky, vodka-infused legs into his lovely home to soft music and even softer lighting. So far, so good. I behaved coquettishly, leaning on his kitchen worktop, batting my eyes seductively, and trying to convince myself a night of unbridled passion with Nigel would be good for my emotional and physical health, not to mention my self-esteem. And as the vodka melted into my veins, I became less horrified at the prospect of a naked Nigel and was even considering the kitchen counter as a starting post. But then he invited me into his well-appointed living room and the veritable treasure chest of DVDs lined up on the coffee table, from *Dr Who* to *Game of Thrones*. He talked of Jon Snow as I clung to the vain hope of a 'normal' evening, trying hard to ignore the fact we were drinking from his 'Thrones'-style goblets. I tried not to think of the DVDs waiting in the other room, the *Dr Who* posters lining the wall and the way he laughed hysterically at everything I said – even when it wasn't meant to be funny. It was awful, but if nothing else I could get a few selfies of us cosying up together to add to Facebook and drive Gianni wild with jealousy (though I feared he might be too loved up with the redhead to notice). Then, just when I thought it couldn't get any worse and I might need to ingest vodka by the gallon to get through this (even the cosy selfies), he said: 'Hab sos Liquch.'

I just looked at him. 'Are you okay, Nigel?' I said, in my calmest voice, convinced he was speaking in tongues and now torn between downing more vodka and screaming for help – and if I did, would I need a doctor or an exorcist!

'Yes, I'm speaking Klingon, Chloe,' he laughed, like I was the mad one. 'I just said, "Your mother has a smooth forehead."'

'Oh.' What the hell was I doing here? Nigel was irritating at the best of times and now he was talking about the smoothness of my mother's forehead in a made-up language. I stood for a few minutes trying to do as Cherry had suggested and concentrate on his quite attractive face. I was also trying not to hear him address me as 'my queen' in Klingon and just concentrated on the image I had of Gianni's face when he saw the photo of me with a good-looking guy. I was just thanking God that Nigel's 'Nerdness' wouldn't show up on camera when he popped upstairs and returned sporting a pair of Dr Who lounging trousers and the Spock ears he'd been sporting when we first met (I should have known back then). I felt bad, but knew it wasn't going to work. Ever. So I kissed him on the cheek, told him I had an emergency and disappeared into the night, for ever.

Since then I'd steered clear of any kind of romantic entanglements, Facebook photos or new romances; perhaps Cherry was right, I was too choosy.

And until I could erase Gianni I was always going to be comparing whoever else I might meet to him. I was seeing him through rose-tinted glasses and perhaps the answer was to go back there, work with him and put the past to bed. This way we could finally, properly say goodbye to our marriage and each other – and I could move on.

Chapter Four

A Klingon Christmas

The day after the call from Fiona, was my last day working at Harrods. I'd thought seriously about my options and though I'd initially considered it a terrible idea, was slowly coming round to going back to Appledore. I skyped Cherry at lunchtime to tell her about the offer, I needed her honest advice – and I got it. 'No, No, No,' she yelled from her bed in Sydney. She'd landed a contract in Australia and I missed her like hell, but thanks to modern technology she was just a click away – even if it was the middle of the night.

'Oh I was thinking it might be good for me, I'd love to go back there and...' I started.

'Jeez, it's a lovely place... but think about the absolute shit you're going to have to go through working with Gianni again. Why would you do that, Chloe?'

'I know, he broke my heart and ruined my life.'

'Erm... and he's a total dick?'

'There's that,' I agreed. 'And I don't know what I'd even say to him.'

'Don't go then.'

'But I love the place and I'm on my own this Christmas because my best friend abandoned me,' I joked. 'And then there's the fact that I hate the animosity between us. Gianni and I have things to sort out and perhaps we could patch it up and be friends again?'

I was surprised at myself, the more Cherry sensibly told me it was a mistake, the more I felt I should go. By the time I'd finished talking to Cherry I was metaphorically packing my bags; sometimes just talking to someone and disagreeing with their advice tells you what you want to do. Gianni and I had once loved each other, we'd been through a lot together, shared happiness, pain – and even a business. I wanted to prove to him that I was over him, or perhaps I was trying to prove it to myself? Either way, he had moved on, and I wanted to show him that so had I – even if it was a work in progress. If I wanted to look at this more objectively, I wasn't staying in London on my own in a flat for Christmas, I was going to the seaside to help out an old friend. I had to think of him in those terms or I would feel an endless bitterness and anger for Gianni that I didn't want to carry for the rest of my life. Before I could change my mind again, I decided to call Fiona.

'My answer is yes if you still need me there,' I said.

'Thank God,' she sighed, and it came from the heart.

I told her I'd head down in the next few days and when I put down the phone I sent an email to Gianni with a list of things I would need, which included his suggested guest list, the names of local restaurant critics and businesses.

He didn't respond, he never did. Same old Gianni, I thought, wondering if he'd ever change, and if we could ever get back to the people we were before we fell in love. I was about to find out, and just hoped I hadn't made a huge mistake by deciding to go back to Appledore.

On the way home from my last day I stood on the busy tube, trying to hold on and stay upright and avoid landing on someone's knee as I had on several occasions. Cherry said I did it deliberately for a cheap thrill, but trust me, a lap dance for a stranger on the Piccadilly line wasn't my idea of fun. Or theirs!

It was particularly mad that evening, filled with office workers freshly soused from their Christmas parties. I watched, fascinated, as a group of young girls in full war paint laughed loudly over nothing, their phones permanently poised for selfies. I wondered if a daughter of mine would have been like that? Or would she be more studious? Would she have looked Italian like her dad, or would she have been fair-skinned and blonde like me? I found it comforting to think about what might have been, to slip into another life, like sliding doors, different choices, different outcomes. Would things have been different if I'd met Gianni when I was younger?

I was just pondering this when I heard someone calling me and turned around to see Nigel, of Klingon and air-dried salami fame.

'Chloe, it's so good to see you,' he said, hurling himself towards me and holding me just a little too tight and too long. I heard a few suggestive cheers erupt around us from those in the festive spirit, but just ignored them.

I smiled and reciprocated the greeting, but tried to keep him at arm's length once I'd extricated myself from his grip.

'Happy Christmas,' I said, trying not to look in any way seductive or alluring – which wasn't difficult given that I'd just spent twelve hours working in an enclosed space, my hair was matted and my make-up had left long ago.

'Chloe, it's just so lovely to see you. Oh I do miss you,' he said, grabbing my hand and standing slightly back to survey me like I was a fine sculpture.

'Oh,' I mumbled without looking at him.

'So what are you doing for Christmas?'

He knew I had no family to speak of with Mum and Dad both gone and no siblings.

'I'm going away,' I said quickly, afraid he might be about to suggest a 'Klingon Christmas together.

'Oh it's a shame you're going away,' he said, pulling a theatrical 'sad face'. 'I was going to say, if you're staying in town we could get together, grab lunch on Christmas Day?'

I felt bad, he obviously had no one to be with, and he'd cottoned onto the fact that neither did I. Even if I wasn't going away, Christmas with Nigel was not on the agenda. I suddenly had an unwelcome vision of the two of us in masks with pitted foreheads and long straggly hair and Nigel speaking gibberish whilst I filled my mouth with Brussels sprouts.

'Mmm that would have been lovely, Nigel, but I'm away in Appledore, in Devon, for Christmas, I'm working at my husband's new restaurant.'

His face dropped and I thought he might burst into tears, this wasn't what he'd wanted to hear. 'Oh I didn't realise...'

'We're not together,' I said, I couldn't lie about that, and I really didn't want to hurt him any more than I had to. 'I'm just working there, it won't be easy,' I said, honestly. 'I'm staying in our old place, Seagull Cottage, and it'll be good to get away.'

'That sounds nice,' he said, unconvinced.

I really didn't want to hang around any longer, because I could just tell he was about to ask me out there and then. So I lied and said this was my stop and as I tried to make for the door, he lunged at me for a hug. But I was ready this time and moved like a panther avoiding any body contact and threw myself out into a large group of passengers waiting to get on.

As I extricated myself from a man's thighs and a lady's umbrella, I realised I couldn't wait to escape London and everything that came with it. I climbed up from the underground and walked home, just imagining that sea air, blustery walks along the front and mugs of warm hot chocolate topped with melting mallows.

As soon as I arrived home I began packing my case for Appledore. I was excited but nervous about this venture and had almost forgotten that Christmas was just around the corner. I usually loved this time of year, it began with a slight glimmer on December 1st when the first advent window was opened, building up to gift buying, food ordering excitement and, until the last few years, romantic anniversary loveliness on the 24th. When we were first together, I was like a child and by Christmas Day I'd reached a crescendo of excitement worthy of a five-year-old with a mega box of that year's Lego. Gianni liked a day off and I was happy to step in with the turkey basting, stopping every now and then to sip on sweet sherry. Recent years had been more subdued, less happy, and this year, Christmas was very different, because I would be alone, yet I would be back in Devon. Of all the things I'd expected to be doing, driving a few hundred miles through snow to our old cottage wasn't one of them.

After a long, snowy journey punctuated by snarl-ups, I arrived in Appledore early evening. The snow showed no signs of stopping (as the song goes) and I carefully pulled through the dark little street along the front. I couldn't see the sea, just a picture of blackness framed by the grey snow along the pavements, but I could imagine it.

Heading up through the windy roads, my satnav finally found my destination, she'd been the only voice I'd heard all the way here, and I was strangely grateful to her for guiding me along the treacherous winter roads in darkness. Her clear, no-nonsense manner had focused me, I just wished there was the equivalent to guide one through life and stop us making the wrong turns. Okay and I admit in the absence of anything interesting on the car radio apart from bloody Christmas carols, I did share my life story in some detail with Ms Satnav. She didn't judge.

'Thanks for listening, Sarah,' I said, pulling on the handbrake.

I had a momentary wobble as I sat there, the engine now dead, and wondered if I'd made the right decision to come here. Was

I walking back into the eye of Gianni's storm? And if so, why? It wasn't about the money, although the huge salary he was paying me would be nice. But this reunion was about something more. It was about tying up loose ends and coming to terms with everything that had happened between us. The pain we had been through together. The loss of our dreams of beautiful babies, olive-skinned and dark-haired like their father. I mourned for the never to be first words, first schools, making sandcastles on the beach – and Christmas. Oh the Christmases we would have had, carrots for Rudolph, mince pies for Santa left on the hearth, and the tangible excitement on Christmas Eve, shining eyes and hope for what tomorrow would bring. Perhaps I had to do this in order to let go – of those precious babies, but also Gianni? I had no idea, and neither did the satnav, who started to blink and suggest I turn off her power.

I climbed out of the car and stood in front of the tiny fisherman's cottage, a place where, fourteen years before, my husband and I had started our lives together. It was just like our wedding night; snowy and cold with a light wind causing flurries of flakes and sharp minty blasts of chilly air. The moon was full so I could see the cottage clearly despite it being dark – it was just the same, tiny, with four windows and a little door, like a child's drawing. Covered in snow and moonlight it seemed magical, like a silvery white ghost waiting for someone to live there and bring it back to life. Perhaps one day someone would, but in the meantime, how fitting that I was now back here to say goodbye – I liked the neatness of it all – a full circle.

I wandered to the cottage next door where the keys had been left for me and as the door opened the warmth of family hit me in the face. It was the Saturday before Christmas, and I could hear *The X Factor* on the TV, could imagine the big tin of Quality Street being shared between the family members sitting on the settee and Simon Cowell's smug face. Standing on the doorstep, I felt like the outsider hearing soft laughter, and a waft of warm meat and alcohol danced down the hall from the kitchen. I suddenly felt very alone and my dearest wish was to move into this woman's spare room and become part of her family immediately. As this suggestion might at best alarm her and at worst have her reaching for her phone to call the police, I played safe and just asked for the cottage keys. She left me at the door and went over to a little dresser in the hall, which gave me time to think again about how scared I was and question what the hell I was doing here all on my own. My feet were frozen, the biting sea wind nibbled my face, and I just wanted someone, anyone to put their arms around me and tell me I was going to be okay. I'd gone from strong, independent woman to the equivalent of weak, snivelling girl in 0.1 seconds.

The woman smiled kindly at me and handed me the keys which almost caused me to burst into tears and hug her. I think she sensed something wasn't right when my shoulders began moving up and down involuntarily and she asked if I'd like to come in. But a stranger on your sofa crying over her 'wasted life' while the family tried to watch *The X Factor* final wasn't a great night in. I politely declined her offer, saying I needed to unpack, thanked her and left the golden glow of her doorstep for the cottage – which had more of a grey chill around it.

I opened the door and tentatively walked in, found a light, and while switching it on managed to fall over a line of wellington boots standing to attention against a floral wall. It made my heart twitch to see them, Dad's, Mum's and two children's sets of wellies, all waiting in the vain hope of walking beaches, hunting in rock pools and running along the craggy beach. I'd bought them in a winter sale many years ago, two adult pairs and two children's – how stupid of me to assume that one day little feet would walk in those boots. I had been as arrogant as Gianni, believing I could have anything I wanted. I felt a pang of sadness for the holidays we had here, and the ones we might have had with our children. I always imagined teaching them to swim, searching the rock pools for sea treasures and mythical creatures, and ending each day with ice creams and kisses. Was the answer really here, could I ever let go of the past by immersing myself in this sea of nostalgia and lost hope?

I took off my warm jacket, feeling the chill pass through me as I hung it up in the hall, and another pass through me as I spotted the four pairs of wellingtons in a line. I sighed as I continued down the hall, and wandered into the olive green farmhouse kitchen we'd had put in about six years before. I turned around and took in the living room, caressing the floral walls, Laura Ashley sofas and big, soft rugs. The sofas were topped with folded throws I'd had specially made in the right shade of sage green, the soft cushions, a gift from Cherry. It was as cosy as I'd remembered it; Gianni had changed nothing. I doubted this was in deference to my interior design, but more about the fact he couldn't be bothered. His view was, if you couldn't eat it, then why bother?

Back in the kitchen I spotted a basket filled with crusty bread, home-made jam and a bottle of wine. I felt a little lift at the sight of this, I hadn't realised I was hungry, and I picked up the note wondering if Gianni had left it. But on reading, I could see it wasn't from my delightful ex.

Good luck, you'll need it! Fiona x

This was lovely and accurate but Fiona didn't need to warn me, I knew just what I was in for. I just hoped I was up to it.

It was clear this was going to be anything but a typical Christmas. No gifts, no gatherings, just work and walks on the beach. But just because I was here to work it didn't mean I wasn't allowed the pleasure of an open fire, so I went into the living room and set about lighting it. And as the warm and flickering fire brought the room to life, I popped upstairs to choose my bedroom.

The master bedroom was lemon with pale grey walls and deep smoke carpet that my feet disappeared into, but I couldn't sleep in there. I'd decorated this room with us in mind. I'd bought the seagull grey wallpaper with Gianni several years before and even now, after a year apart, all I could think of was the many happy times we'd spent here together, sleeping in that bed. I lay down on it and let the sumptuous softness of the freshly washed linen absorb me, then I suddenly remembered the redhead. Had he ever brought her here? Had they slept in this bed? I shot up quickly and went straight to the whitewashed Scandi furniture and blowsy pink roses in the other bedroom, where, to my knowledge, no one else had ever slept. It had been meant for the children. I doubted even Gianni had been back here since we'd split. He'd be just as happy on a camp bed in his restaurant kitchen – he'd had plenty of those nights over the years. I put my bags on the bed, unloaded my stuff then lay on the blowsy roses before dropping off in an exhausted sleep.

When I woke later that evening I ate the crusty bread with a warm, tangy round of Camembert from the basket. Dipping the bread into the molten cheese between sips of full-bodied red wine was as comforting as lying in a man's arms... well almost.

Chapter Five

Offal Lollipops and Gwyneth's Jade Eggs

Despite the freezing temperatures the following morning, I felt wide awake and leapt out from under the rose-scattered duvet. I immediately walked into the main bedroom and over to the window, where I could see the sea on the horizon. It was grey and misty, but quite beautiful, like a charcoal drawing. It was funny to think of the years we'd looked out onto this view together and though we'd both changed, the view was still exactly the same as it had been that first time. The sea was still here pounding the beach, swirling like white molten lather, and the sky was still above, swollen and smoky grey, not the pinks and blues of summer but beautiful nonetheless.

As the snow showed no signs of relenting and I wasn't due in work with Gianni until the following day, I decided to go shopping for provisions. The cottage was only a few hundred yards from the seafront lined with cafes, pubs and one or two gift shops. So I braved the snowy walk, and stepping into my old wellingtons, and in some ways my old life, I left the cottage. As I made my way around the corner, I could see there were a few changes since I'd last been here a few years before. There was now a lovely deli that hadn't been there before along with a refurbished hotel but I was delighted to see the old Ice Cream Cafe was still standing. Last time we'd been here it had seemed a little shabby and forlorn, but it had been repainted and from a distance looked like a pale pink fairy in the snow.

I went into the local deli first and bought some winter vegetables to make a hearty casserole. I'd made quite a hole in the crusty bread so I bought another fresh loaf and a couple of bottles of red wine too. It was Christmas after all and a girl needed festive sustenance.

As I was leaving the deli, I tried calling Gianni, and just seeing his name on my phone as it rang made me feel a little nervous. I contemplated trying to call Fiona instead, but knew I was just putting it off and I had to face my demons or there would have been little point coming here. Gianni and I hadn't spoken for a while, the last time was a call I made before Snowflake had died, I asked how she was and if I could see her. I'd tried to keep it light, asking if I could take her to the park and then McDonald's like all the other weekend parents, but Gianni didn't laugh. I wondered then if I'd taken away all his happiness and left him with nothing when I walked out of our marriage. Gianni had never quite got his head round why I'd said goodbye and couldn't really believe there wasn't anyone else involved. 'But you can't just leave, you must be loving another man,' he'd said. 'People only leave for other people.'

I'd almost lied and told him there *was* someone else, it might have been easier on his macho Italian ego because to leave him as I'd had enough was unthinkable to him. It took a long time to convince him I'd simply wanted to be alone. I was keen to make sure he knew there was no one else because in those early days I'd wanted to keep the door open on our marriage and I knew he'd never forgive me for being unfaithful. But we were both so stubborn, neither of us would make a move anyway. Then as the months had gone on and I'd seen the photos with the redhead I felt he'd lost interest in rekindling anything.

I let the phone ring again and was just about to leave a message for him when it was picked up, answering with his usual monosyllabic greeting.

'Chloe?'

'Yes… it's me.'

'I am very busy. I'm opening a restaurant.'

'I know, your company employed me to come and work with you.'

'Oh I had not an idea of this,' he said, clearly pretending he hadn't been the one to ask for me, but Fiona wouldn't lie. It seemed Gianni's deep fear of rejection was still alive and kicking then. He was infuriating, and any sense of nostalgia I had for my life with him was quickly being obliterated by his arrogance.

'Fiona said you'd asked for me?' I said, determined to start this process as I meant to go on, with honesty and openness on both sides.

'Fiona?'

'Your assistant,' I said, irritated, he knew damn well who Fiona was.

'Oh *Fiona*… she is gone, she can't take the fire in the kitchen so I tell her you get out.'

Great, so my only potential ally here had been sacked already and in the first few seconds of our telephone conversation I hated him all over again. This was going well.

'Ah, so am I to take it that I'm not required to work for you now?' I said, my enthusiasm waning already and wishing he'd say I wasn't needed now.

'She give you the contract, Chloe?'

'Yes, she did. And offered a substantial fee.'

'Oh… we might need to discuss this.'

'Okay well, let's try to work out a plan and a fee that's acceptable to both of us,' I said, trying to sound businesslike. I really wasn't here for the money, but he wasn't getting me cheap either, because judging by his current mood, I would be earning every penny.

There was silence on the other end of the phone, I was used to this from Gianni, but now he was a prospective employer I wasn't going to put up with it.

'Before we agree to anything we will need to talk,' I said, assertively. 'There's no need for us to work closely together… we don't have to be in each other's pockets… but if I do come to work with you, we have to both be grown up about this if it's going to be a success and not drive us both mad.'

'It is difficult, I don't know if I can work with my wife who leaves me.'

'Likewise I don't want to be somewhere where I'm not wanted, but it seems to me that everyone has abandoned you.' I was torn between being angry and feeling sorry for him. He'd obviously asked for me and wanted me to help him, but his pride wasn't allowing him to say this.

'Including you, Chloe, you abandoned me too…' he sounded sad and I knew he would be adding a large helping of guilt to this Christmas cocktail.

'I'm talking about the business, I'm here in a business capacity,' I stressed, 'and from what Fiona said, she was the last man standing.'

'I manage my own restaurant. No one tells me you are here…'

'Look, just tell me, do you want my help?'

The silence spoke volumes.

'Gianni, we both have to move on,' I said into the silence. 'And you need all the help you can get if you're going to open soon.'

'Okay, okay,' he snapped.

'Good, so you want me to stay?'

Silence.

'Gianni, if you can't even say yes to that then there's no point in me being here.'

'Bloody yes. Arses.' I almost smiled to myself, at last I'd got him to admit he needed me, in his own inimitable way.

'Good. Can we meet up and make arrangements?' I asked, determined to keep this on a business level and ignore his sulking.

'I am at the restaurant, if you want to come over then you can.'

'No. I would like to meet…' For this first meeting, I felt it was important for us to meet on neutral ground, if he was going to be a total pig then I would simply hotfoot it back to London, sod the money, sod Il bloody Bacio – and sod Gianni Callidori. I looked around and the nearest place was the Ice Cream Cafe, 'At Caprioni's.' I knew he knew it well, we'd both had many happy times there, and it might even lighten his mood. Who was I kidding?

'I will be there soon,' he said.

'When?'

'When I am ready.'

I wasn't putting up with his stroppiness. Throughout his time in London he'd been allowed to play the hot-headed Italian chef who demanded perfection, and when he didn't get it he would start shouting. I knew as his wife that if you gave in to him it made him worse. From the very beginning of our relationship I would have no truck with his tantrums and just told him not to be so ridiculous, which always brought him down a peg or two. And now, the man they referred to as 'the *enfant terrible*' of the kitchen was more 'mid-life terrible', and I wasn't impressed.

'I'll wait in the cafe for ten minutes and if you don't turn up by then I'm going back to London,' I said, putting the phone down before he could reply, refusing to put up with his stupid games.

I moved through the freezing air and drifting snow towards the Ice Cream Cafe, and stood on the step peering in. Thinking of the times Gianni and I had spent in this cafe, I was surprised to realise it felt a little raw for me to go inside. Perhaps this wasn't such a good place to meet after all? Gazing through the windows made me think of the shared sundaes, the new, shiny gold bands, sandy feet, and hot chocolate with fluffy cream and mallows. I wasn't sure how I'd feel, seeing him in the flesh after almost a year, and my stomach twisted slightly at the prospect. Despite being in this lovely, nostalgic setting, I was sure that after a few minutes I might want to kill him and may well spill his blood on the shiny white floor. But there was only one way I would find out.

For a moment I wondered if Caprioni's was open; after all, this was an ice cream cafe and it was mid-December, but there were lights on and then I spotted someone behind the counter. This was as good a sanctuary as any on a freezing cold day, and a hot chocolate was just what I needed to take away the chill and that little twist of nerves in my tummy.

Entering the cafe, I could see it had been treated to a lick of pink paint inside too. The furniture was new, but similar to when we'd first come here, all pink and peppermint green with furry, candy coloured cushions on the seats, probably a winter addition. I loved being back here and wondered how it would feel when Gianni arrived. Would he melt like ice cream when he saw me in 'our' cafe? Probably not, but if he continued in the same vein he had on the phone I might be tempted to cover him in an ice cream sundae and see if that melted. In the absence of a large glass of Merlot, there was also a danger of me hurling a large milkshake over him instead. I was glad there weren't any customers in the cafe because when Gianni and I were together, things became quite heated! But that wasn't what I wanted today, I wanted a civilised conversation. I looked around, wondering idly if he'd ever got the red wine off his white shirt after our last 'civilised conversation'.

The woman behind the counter of the cafe wasn't the one I'd remembered when we last came to Appledore. She was younger, dressed in a red and green glitzy sequined top and Christmas tree earrings in the same colours. She leaned on the counter, seemingly engrossed in a crossword magazine, and as I walked in she looked up at me and said, 'Pig.'

'I'm sorry?' I said, a little surprised at this greeting.

'Oh luvvie, don't mind me,' she laughed, suddenly focusing and wafting her hand in the air. 'It's my crossword. Three across, seven letters, another word for pig,' she said, holding up the puzzle and shaking her head at her own madness. 'What am I like?' She laughed again and put the magazine down on the counter. 'What can I do for you, sweetheart?' she said, getting down to business.

'Porcine?' I said, in answer to her crossword query.

She looked puzzled. 'Sorry, love, we don't do that, got some lovely brioche though?'

'No, it's another word for pig and it's seven letters,' I explained and she laughed loudly at her mistake, asking me for the spelling and eagerly writing the word in with her little pencil. Then she sat back and surveyed the squares, delighted.

'You can come again,' she beamed.

'Oh it's easy when you see it fresh,' I said.

'I'm just confuscious,' she sighed. I doubted that but nodded in agreement, ordered my hot chocolate, and took a seat near the window. She eventually brought it over, and with great care placed it on a mat on the table. 'There you go, love,' she said.

It was very hot, but I was able to spoon out the melting mallows and the cold whipped cream as it cooled. I cupped my hands around the warmth, it was worth coming in here for this mug of Christmas magic.

From my seat I watched the crashing sea, looking out onto the freezing pavement, the wind was beginning to whip along the front, turning an umbrella inside out and causing a dog walker's hood to fly off. Making the most of my comfortable, dry vantage point, I observed the lunacy of winter weather by the sea and drank the warming chocolatey drink. It was like a soothing balm on my soul and I tried not to think about my meeting with Gianni, and just let it calm my insides. I wondered if perhaps I'd been a little too harsh with him on the phone, but he made me react like that, he was the spark to my flame. This combination hadn't really worked during our marriage, so who was to say this would work now? He might decide not to turn up and I contemplated Christmas back home but I didn't want to go back to big, lonely London, I wanted to stay here for now. I loved the seaside, and here was such a special place I just wanted to get lost in it for a while, the sheer peace and anonymity of a place like this made me feel relaxed, happier.

I looked through the window at the choppy grey sea and twirling snowflakes while savouring every comforting chocolate mouthful until the woman behind the counter interrupted my bubble.

'Are you here for Christmas, love?' she asked, from her stool at the counter, her pencil poised over the crossword, her head to one side, making it look like one of her huge earrings was heavier than the other and weighing her down.

'Yes. I'm a freelance events planner. I've come down from London to work here for a couple of weeks, it's nice to get away from everything.'

'Oh Christmas you mean? I love it, but I know there are people who run a mile.'

'I used to love Christmas, but… well, last year my marriage…'

With that she left her stool and was suddenly at my side, all ears. 'Don't tell me, he ran off with a… a tart!'

'No, no…' I said, shaking my head. Her kind face was now in mine and I was torn between pulling away and telling her my life story.

'My marriage broke up too – left me for a hussy. I wish I had a torture dungeon, I'd put all men in there and turn on the electricity,' she hissed, pulling up a chair. It was extreme, but we've all been there. 'I'm Sue,' she said and I told her my name, but before I could say another word she was filling me in on her story. This involved an errant husband who ran off with her neighbour, a toyboy on Tinder who ran off with her money and, more recently, a string of unsuitable 'gentlemen' who ran off with her heart.

I wanted to suggest she give up on men and eat ice cream all day, but it seemed she had no intention of giving up on the dream.

'He's out there for me somewhere, Mr Right,' she smiled. 'But in the meantime, I'm happy here, in Appledore, lovely place, lovely people. And I've made some smashing friends.'

'Yes, coming back here has reminded me of the happy times,' I said. 'Me and Gianni were happy then, but it all fell apart and I wonder what happened.'

'*What happened?* His penis is what happened!' she yelled, still apparently convinced he'd left me for another woman. Just as she said this the door was blown open by the wind, and standing there like an apparition was a huge figure in a hooded overcoat. Gianni.

Sue screamed and put her hand to her mouth, making me jump, and we both stared at him in the doorway, the biting sea air swirling in with him. He looked like the Prince of Darkness, standing there, the snow fluttering behind him, his unsmiling face looking straight at me. And I couldn't believe it, but my heart did a little leap; he was as gorgeous as ever.

'Oh sweetheart, come in and close the door, we'll catch our death in here,' Sue said, recovering quickly and straightening her short, wavy hair.

He shut the door, gave me a vague nod of acknowledgement and walked over to where I was sitting. I couldn't help but be amused at Sue's familiarity – Gianni could never be described as a 'sweetheart'.

'Hi Gianni,' I said.

Sue looked at me and whispered: 'This isn't him is it… your ex, the vile, disgusting pig?'

'Yes,' I said, 'this is my… this is Gianni,' I concluded, wondering what exactly he was to me now.

'Do I know you?' Sue asked him. 'You seem familiar, you've been on the telly,' she was looking into his face as he joined me at the table.

'I have been in the national press,' he said, softening slightly at the easy flattery.

'Oh… no, that's not you, I thought you were on the telly, but you look like the new bloke who works at the garage.'

He looked a little crestfallen and I almost felt sorry for him. Gianni hadn't been in the papers for many years, no one knew him outside of London these days.

'So you've come to say you're sorry have you?' Sue continued, as he settled down into the seat opposite me.

I stepped in, Sue was just trying to be friendly but I knew Gianni and he wouldn't see it that way. I didn't blame him, Sue was clearly taking out all her frustration on every man she saw, and Gianni just happened to be here. I was also a little embarrassed because it probably looked to Gianni like I was having a good old bitch about him to a stranger in a cafe. He was likely to tell her off any minute and I didn't want the poor woman humiliated, so I said, 'Gianni is my husband, we're estranged... he's done nothing to be sorry about, he's... a brilliant Italian chef.'

He glanced at me, and seemed surprised at my positive endorsement.

'Oh I bet you make all those fancy pasta dishes... I love pasta,' Sue started, his misdemeanours all forgotten at the mention of food. She leaned in and spoke directly to Gianni; 'I'm not so keen on that partisan cheese though, I hope you don't use too much of that,' she said. He didn't answer, he hadn't a clue what she was on about. I only just managed to translate her malapropisms, so God knows what Gianni made of what she was saying.

'So what can I do for you?' She was smiling now, pencil poised over her little waitress notebook.

'Black coffee,' he answered, sullenly.

Sue was waiting for more: an order for a slice of cake; an ice cream; a smile or even (God forbid) a please from Gianni. But hell would freeze over before Gianni gave any more than he had to, and after an awkward few seconds, she gave up and teetered off to get his order.

'So, Chloe, why the bloody hell are you here?' he said in all seriousness.

I looked at him incredulously. 'We talked about this, Fiona called me and I know you asked for me...'

'Yes, but I didn't think you'd come. So why are you really here? Do you miss me, you want to be bloody close by me?'

What an ego the man had! 'Oh God is it so obvious?' I simpered. 'Yes, I followed you all the way from London to Devon in the snow because I couldn't bear to be apart from you.'

He looked at me with amazement; 'You're doing the stalking to me?'

'NO, I'm being sarcastic, you arrogant idiot. I'm here to work.'

'I give you work because you struggling with the money. So no need to be a nasty ass with me.'

'No, I'm not being a...' I wasn't repeating that, it didn't even make sense. 'And I'm not "struggling with money", as you know I've always earned enough to keep myself,' I said, knowing this would piss him off. He'd always wanted to be the great provider, and I'd always fought for my financial independence in the relationship. Perhaps if we'd had children and I'd wanted to give up work things might have been different, but we didn't and it wasn't.

He looked at me and I realised in that instant that as much as I wasn't sure of him, he wasn't sure of me either. I was still refusing to play the role of adoring, submissive wife, so he could forget any kind of gratefulness for him giving me work. I didn't need his bloody job anyway.

'I'm good at what I do and we both know that's why I'm here, so please don't pretend it's you doing me the favour.'

We both glared at each other and for a fleeting moment I thought about the last time we were here together. Things hadn't been great, but unlike now, there'd always been a little sliver of hope and we had both been willing to try. So with this in mind, I tried a slightly different tack.

'I was sad about Snowflake,' I said.

'She was okay, it was sudden. She had no pain.' He said this matter-of-factly, but I knew him and could see by his face that Snowflake's death wasn't something he was comfortable talking about.

'Did she miss me?' I said, my throat hurting with the threat of tears.

'No,' he said, in his usual blunt way. He wasn't being harsh, he just hadn't mastered the art of conversation and seemed to struggle sometimes with empathy. I used to think it was the language barrier, but now I just knew it was the Gianni barrier.

'Snowflake loved this time of year, she used to get all excited about Christmas,' I said, trying to find a point of reference we both shared to engage him. Talking like this used to work when we were in love. I could lift those dark clouds that seemed to hang over him with a few funny thoughts, a cute story, but not any more.

'Cats do the eating, the sleeping and the licking. A cat has none of the feelings like happiness, excitement.'

'Neither do you,' I said, swirling my drink to unearth the chocolate sediment, angry at his barrier coming up and metaphorically hitting me in the face as usual.

The silence between us grew thicker, and I realised I needed to avoid the personal, be professional and treat this like the job it was. I just found it so hard, and when I looked at him I felt this disconcerting feeling inside. I was looking for clues but he was unreadable like when I first knew him, before we fell in love. I discreetly searched his face as he gazed through the window, it was still a lovely face with big brown eyes that defied the anger, that showed inside he was as soft as melting mallow. His chiselled features and thin lips that created that rare but beautiful smile caused something to flood into me as our eyes accidentally met. Was it the remains of love, like the chocolate sediment in the bottom of my cocoa? Oh God, I hoped this was just a temporary flush of something, a passing frisson because I hadn't seen him for a long time. Would these flickering feelings settle and let me get on with the job in hand? I hadn't expected to still have feelings for him, to be honest I'd thought a few minutes in his grumpy presence might just eradicate anything except resentment. So this was a surprise, and certainly not part of the plan. I mustn't allow myself to be seduced by the past, and I had to remember the bad times, and the loneliness of who we once were.

'So, you made the move. You left London and now you're living your dream,' I said, trying not to sound bitter that he'd done it without me.

'Dream?' he said, looking at me like I was mad. 'I come to the sea in the middle of the bloody freezing winter,' he turned to gaze out at the mist and snow like a voile curtain over the sea. 'I mean look at this rough bitch,' he said, his hand gesturing outside and also straight at Sue just as she minced towards him with his black coffee.

'I beg your pardon?' she said, stopping in her tracks, clearly shocked.

'Oh when he says rough bitch he doesn't mean you...' I said, opening my mouth, horrified at the misunderstanding. 'Gianni's

Italian, he's saying beach, not bitch,' I said, looking at him for confirmation, but the awkward bugger just shrugged.

Sue wasn't totally convinced and gave him a tight-lipped warning look as she plonked down his coffee before walking briskly away.

I smiled after her awkwardly, wondering what the hell would have happened between these two if I hadn't been around to translate.

'You really need to work on your pronunciation, Gianni,' I said quietly as she stomped off. I sometimes wondered if he mispronounced things just to be difficult, he had after all been in the UK for more than twenty years.

He raised his eyebrows, 'I have the English, they just don't understand. They are horse assbutts.'

Again, his grasp of English swear words rendered me speechless, so I didn't say anything. I wasn't in the mood for an argument anyway and he could be so stroppy I didn't have the energy to cover for him any more.

I finished my drink, enjoying the last of the deeply comforting velvet hot chocolate. 'So, let's talk business, how's it all going so far?'

'It isn't going,' he put his head in his hands. 'I have opening and no bookings, staff leave, the critics hate me and newspapers write vicious Devon lies.'

'Oh?' I doubted Devon lies were different to any other part of the country, but I didn't tackle this, just tried to be sympathetic. 'What's happened?' I asked, not really sure I wanted to know the full horror and the latest fallout. Gianni clearly hadn't mellowed in the months we'd been apart.

'My kitchens, my dining room, they are perfection, I sweating everywhere to bring my brilliance here. But they complain because of no menu, they say my food isn't beeeg enough. What are they, pigs in a trough?'

'You didn't say… that… to them… did you?' I held my breath.

He nodded. 'And now the newspapers are saying no,' he continued, 'critics all hate me and customers stop their bookings, say they can't drive through a leetle bit of snow. They are ass clowns. So I tell them to bugger you off.'

'Did you actually say that… the ass clown and bugger bit?' I asked, unconcerned about the grammar, but alarmed by the customer care. He had never been overfriendly with his customers, in fact he was often downright rude, but in London that gave him character. That kind of behaviour here, in Appledore, could alienate press and customers for years. Mind you, alienation and offence were his signature dishes, it's what Gianni Callidori served hot. 'Gianni, how many times have I told you… you can't say things like that to people. You're not in London now. They forgave you anything there, they saw your rudeness as part of your act.'

'Act? I don't act.'

'No, sadly not, I just wish sometimes you could smile through your anger,' I said. 'Your established customers saw you as a Gordon Ramsay type genius who swears and…'

'Gordon Ramsay? Now you swear at me… he is a monkey butt.'

'No he isn't and I wasn't comparing you, well perhaps I was – but my point is that, in London, your customers *expect* an expletive with their twenty calorie portions of overpriced dinner. They're used to your… colour and… vibrancy and bad manners. But here you're just another chef opening another restaurant, and people have to learn to like you before they fall for your food – which in your case is a big ask,' I added. 'Remember when we first opened Gianni's, we had no pretensions. It was good, simple Italian food, it made you happy.'

'I'm not happy.'

His honesty took me by surprise, he didn't like to talk about feelings, especially his own.

'You were happy once,' I said, sad to see him like this and keen to bring him round, 'when we were first married and opening Gianni's, you making your mother's sauces and Nonna's garlic bread.'

I saw the façade begin to crack and the Gianni I knew emerge slightly.

'I miss Gianni's,' he sighed. 'Everything seemed so easy then, but the second restaurant…'

'With no name because the food had to speak for itself?' I asked, with sarcasm.

'Yes… that one, she is closing and I open the Appledore one. I think this will be easy, like Gianni's, but now I'm at the end of wit.' He went on to explain that the opening of Il Bacio had been delayed due to bad weather and 'builder trouble'. Having spoken to Fiona, and hearing his account of the past couple of weeks, I knew there'd been some 'chef trouble' too.

Anyway, according to Gianni, the builders were 'lazy horses', and had been the start of the trouble by delaying all the work. But once it had finally been completed, Fiona had, the previous week, arranged a low-key press evening as a little taster before opening officially this week. Unfortunately, this had apparently been disastrous, with staff not turning up, Gianni shouting at everyone and Fiona storming off, leaving no one to calm 'the bloody guests'. I nodded calmly and listened to him retell the tale, barely able to imagine the carnage, but it got worse. Apparently Gianni emerged from the kitchen waving a knife at 'some pig-worm', whatever that was (I didn't establish if this fused life-form was staff or customer, but was just relieved the police weren't involved), and the guests all (unsurprisingly) walked out.

'Oh God, what a mess,' I sighed, 'I don't know why you behave this way, you never did this when we had Gianni's.'

'I know, but you were there…' He stopped talking and looked at me for just a moment, and I saw something from the past in his eyes, until he pulled himself together and continued to blame everyone else for his current predicament. 'Fiona, she just walks… and I have to have perfection, Chloe. You know this.'

'So when do you open officially?' I asked, ignoring this comment.

'Tonight… I open tonight and tomorrow and see what happens and then Christmas happens, who knows?'

'What? But Fiona said I start tomorrow?'

'Fiona knows nothing she is stupid bloody ass basket.'

God knows where he got these phrases from, but as a young man he'd learned to speak English by watching TV. He loved all the old films especially those with Italian actors like Robert De Niro, Al Pacino and Roberto Riviera. He'd also enjoyed sweary TV shows and 'ass' was a large part of his vocabulary. It had no meaning, but the word was bolted onto much of his cursing for added effect.

'So you're telling me you open tonight and have no customers?' He nodded his head slowly.

'Well you've got your work cut out,' I said. 'Shouldn't you be on the phone, or emailing around?'

'Who do I email? Jesus Christ?'

'No, I think he washed his hands of you a while back.'

He shrugged, he did that a lot, I never knew if it was an Italian thing, or a Gianni thing. Either way it was frustrating. I'm a 'doer', if there's a problem I solve it, I don't sit there stirring coffee and shrugging like he was now. God it was all coming back, this man was extremely frustrating, no wonder I walked out.

'I'm surprised you turned up today, having heard all this I would have expected you to be back at the restaurant screaming at your staff,' I said.

'I have the stropping and I scream before 8 a.m. each morning and still they sit with their phones and their coffee… now they quit their asses.'

'There are no staff at all?' This was worse than even I had imagined.

'No.'

'Wow,' I said under my breath. He hadn't acquired any charm in his year apart from me; in fact he seemed as insular and cold as ever and I wondered where was the man I fell in love with, as he went back to stirring his coffee and gazing into nothingness. Gianni's screaming and 'stropping' carried weight in his fancy London restaurant where ambitious young chefs and waiters wanted a slice of his celebrity buzz. But here he was nothing, and no one knew him. His Devon restaurant staff were doing a job, the same as any other job, the great Gianni Callidori meant nothing to them. Gianni was stripped bare in this little seaside town, everyone probably saw him as just some foreign guy who shouted a lot, and they wouldn't take it from him. 'You can't operate without any staff...' I started.

'Oh I'm thanking you for your bloody help, Chloe, I never knew that.'

'Oh Gianni, please don't do sarcasm, you haven't mastered the language well enough for that. Let's face it you were still going in the wrong toilets up to a year ago because you didn't know the difference between Ladies and Gents.'

'Stupid pictures on doors, it was the pictures of two cows... who can tell them apart?'

'There was a bull on the gents' door and a cow on the ladies', you don't have to be fluent in the language to know the difference between a cow and a cow with big bloody horns,' I said, my irritation levels rising and going red at the memory of him being hauled from the ladies' by security while women screamed and clutched their handbags to their chests like he was some kind of rampant sex fiend. 'So, your staff, is there anything you can offer them as an incentive?' I asked, dragging my mind from the terrible toilet scenes, reminding myself this was business and finishing my drink.

'I pay staff lots of money, I give them discount on my range...'

I'd heard he'd relaunched his Christmas range. If ever there was evidence that he had lost his way without me, the Callidori Christmas range was it. 'Mmm discount?' I said, expressing my doubts with a curled lip. 'I doubt low-paid kitchen staff would be enticed to work long hours in a sweaty kitchen at the prospect of owning a jar of snails in aspic retailing at £22.50 – with discount.'

'They are deeelicious, but these people are wild hogs and don't appreciate fine food!'

I sincerely hoped he hadn't shared this view with them, but most likely he had, which would account for the fact he now had no staff. Or customers.

'Fiona never sent me a menu over, do you have a copy you could email?'

'No.'

'You don't yet have a menu?' Could things get any worse with no staff, no customers and no menu?

'No, they don't need a menu… I tell them what to eat,' he said grumpily. 'The British can't choose their own food, they've ruined their palates with the supermarket plastic.'

'Oh I see. Well, whatever the problem is with the English and their palates, it looks to me like this Italian has problems of his own,' I said.

Looking back now I can almost pinpoint the moment when Gianni began to unravel. We were still in Gianni's our first restaurant, working together, having abandoned my own career to muck in. We stayed there for three years, but then investors read about him in the press and offered backing to move to bigger premises. This was when Gianni's star really began to rise, and the new nameless restaurant opened to a great fanfare. But I think he'd been flattered by the praise, blinded by all the promises of making it big and hadn't considered the stress involved with the responsibility of someone else's money. In those first few years I watched him slowly change from a relaxed, loving husband to a man running scared and unable to sleep at night for fear of failure. He'd been happy in Gianni's our first restaurant, making his home-cooked Italian food, but his ego had been swelled by the critics and the hangers-on and he started to believe the hype. He'd been seduced into believing that a bigger restaurant with no name and cutting-edge food would bring us everything we desired. As we couldn't build a family, he built a business instead.

In the meantime, I had become less and less involved in the business and more and more involved in my own fledgling career. I tried to be there for him, but I felt like I wasn't needed any more. I'll never forget turning up at the big, flashy new restaurant late one night and going into the kitchen to ask if Gianni was ready to come home. I opened the kitchen door and he was stood with Bianca, his new agent (yes, he now had an agent). They were both leaning on the kitchen counter, heads together, and she was telling him he needed 'to break out'. I also heard the words 'more restaurants'. I know it sounds dramatic, but it felt like a betrayal, like she was luring him into something he shouldn't do, that was against everything he'd ever wanted. These people didn't know the real Gianni, they only saw the one in black and white photos on the front of magazines. But I knew him, and I also knew that by embracing this brave new world he was turning his back on ours.

I went home alone that night and the next day I tried to ask him what he really wanted, but he said it was all about making money now. 'I want to buy you beautiful things,' he'd said. All I'd wanted was him, and to be back in that first little restaurant with the candles in the old Chianti bottles.

Gianni had abandoned the food he loved to cook and did what he thought was expected of him, dancing to everyone's tune but not his own. I once asked him what happened to a dish of warming pasta, why did he now cook with quails' eggs and weird Japanese herbs, and he said 'because if I don't keep trying, it might all go away '. I know now that no one can live under that kind of pressure 24/7, and I don't think even he really believed in the droplets of reconstituted tomato or deconstructed candy floss he 'created,' for his audience. He was swept along into a world that wanted spectacle, and celebrated his 'wild untamed genius'. But I knew that what really made him happy was cooking his mama's pasta sauce in a cosy little Italian. And as if to prove my theory, here he was, the London restaurant had been sold and he'd run away to the seaside to start again. But if things didn't change he wouldn't even have a restaurant to open.

Gianni had never found people easy – which is where I came in, I smoothed the way and made things easier all round. He'd never found the staff or customer care side of things easy, and as I knew only too well from my own experience working with him at Harrods, he could be rude. But once we'd opened Gianni's he calmed down and I dealt with all the customers and staff and he was left simply to cook, which was perhaps when he was at his happiest. If he was in a bad mood, we just ignored him. But after being feted in London for his rudeness, often described as 'quirky' by the press (which I reckoned was news-speak for 'a bloody nightmare'), he became even worse, some of it for effect.

'It's what they want, Chloe,' he'd said after a particularly tough night at the new restaurant when he'd thrown Simon Cowell out for daring to suggest the eucalyptus and aubergine puree paprika sugar tuile was a little 'over the top'.

Sitting with him now in the Ice Cream Cafe, I could see the old, untamed Gianni and I didn't think it was his genius that motivated him these days, I reckoned it was unhappiness. He'd now begun some diatribe about 'scum restaurant critics with the attitude' and 'customers who don't know the fine dining because they eat from the trough'. It didn't take a detective to work out that Gianni had, before the official opening, managed to alienate anyone remotely vital to his new business throughout North Devon and the surrounding parts – he'd pissed them all off. And even here, during an innocent meeting over hot drinks, he'd been unfriendly towards Sue the waitress – and was completely unaware of what he'd done.

I jumped in: 'Gianni, you have no empathy, you seem to have little grasp of the hurt and anger you cause.'

'I have not caused the hurt and anger… what are you bloody hell talking about?'

'Oh grow up and try to see things from someone else's point of view. I know you can be a lovely guy, but to be honest most of the time you're not.'

He looked at me properly for the first time, like he was actually listening.

'You think I am the lovely guy?' he said, almost flirtatiously.

'No… well, you can be but you aren't at the moment.'

'Yes, well I have the stressing. I can't be the "lovely guy" when I have no ideas what on the earth I bloody do now,' he was saying.

'I have the best kitchen. All the steel grey shades, and white, lots of the white tables and chairs, and plain and simple, the clean lines, metal, lots of clean steel…'

'Sounds lovely,' I lied. I had this immediate visual of a cold and uninviting room, white hygienic surfaces, lots of metal. And Gianni standing in the doorway brandishing a large cook's knife, like something out of a low budget horror film. 'And what are you planning to serve?' I asked, brushing the vision away.

'But of course. My famous squid ink shortbread with a timbale of rabbit. Offal lollipops with piquant meadow foam,' he started as my heart sank. 'And for the sons of monkeys that won't eat the animals, I provide the smashed quails' eggs on a bed of spinach with fermented cabbage, the toasting pine kernels and fava beans.' At this he licked his lips and I was immediately reminded of Hannibal Lecter.

'Fava beans?' I asked, but he was now engrossed in his menu, and describing how his offal lollipops had made Sting and Trudie cry.

'I can imagine,' I answered, deadpan.

As he talked excitedly about different kinds of offal, I drifted off. I thought about the day we'd found out I was pregnant the first time and how happy we'd been. We'd been trying for a couple of years and now in my thirties it hit me that it wasn't going to be as easy as I'd hoped. So when I saw that little pink line on the test I was elated, this was all I ever wanted, and though I'm not religious I sent up a little thank you to whoever, because this was truly a gift from heaven. I remember Gianni's face, he cried buckets and hugged me and told everyone, calling family in Italy, baking my favourite iced cake and opening bottles of champagne in the restaurant and coming home early every night to be with me. In those first few weeks I felt so cherished, like a piece of art, a Fabergé egg held gently, admired and placed on a pedestal. Which is why, when the blood came, I couldn't tell him at first. I didn't want to see his pain, watch his happiness flatten like bad soufflé. I felt if I didn't say anything it might not be true, but when he came home early carrying a pink, fluffy rabbit for the baby and found me on the bathroom floor, I didn't need to tell him. He knew. This seemed like a lifetime away now as we sat in the cafe. I looked for the softness in his eyes, the way he looked at me back then – but it was gone.

'I've also designed a new dish for Christmas...' he was saying.

I pushed away the memory and returned to the present.

'Oh?' I said, vaguely hopeful this might be something festive and edible at least.

'Crispy sweetbreads, with chickens' feet and winter jus.' He looked at me quizzically, then he seemed to realise, 'Ah I know what you are thinking...'

I doubted that.

'Do you? I'm sorry, Gianni, I feel bad saying it but...'

'Your mouth she is watering and you wish the restaurant were open now and you were tasting the crispy sweetbreads?'

'Mmm... yeah,' I half-smiled and lied in sync, I sometimes found it hard to burst his bubble, especially when he was so excited about something. Excitement wasn't an emotion he showed too often and I liked to see the fire in his eyes.

'You don't have to wish you were tasting them, because I have her there.'

'Who?'

'The ingredients, she is waiting in the kitchens and tonight I cook for you.'

'Oh… look I don't think that would be a good idea,' I said, unable to stomach the thought of this. We'd always cooked simple food at home, and he'd saved his 'special' dishes for work, but now I was working with him it was going to be hard to say no.

'I thought you were opening tonight?' I said.

'I am, and you should be there too. I will experiment on you, yes?'

An offer to be experimented on by my estranged husband wasn't the best I'd had this season, and I had no intention of putting anyone's crispbreads or feet in my mouth. 'Officially, I don't start working for you until tomorrow,' I said, determined to keep this professional.

'Ah, you have the date?' he looked deflated. I hadn't put any pictures of Nigel on my Facebook page for ages, so he must have known I wasn't seeing anyone. Knowing him, this was just his way of making me feel guilty about breaking us up so I would be forced to sample his crispy sweetbreads and chicken feet. 'Yes, my lover and I are spending a night of passion in Seagull Cottage before I start work tomorrow,' I said.

He looked alarmed for a moment and put down his coffee cup.

'I'm joking,' I sighed.

I watched him now as he finished his coffee, and he looked like he had the weight of the world on his shoulders. He was a couple of years older than me, but considering the amount he ate, the late hours he kept in his restaurants, and the fact he was perhaps on the brink of disaster with this new one, he looked good. He worked hard in the kitchens and his biceps and forearms looked like he was permanently in the gym. His face seemed a little more tired than it had when I last saw him, a few more lines had appeared on the map I knew so well, but somehow the 'lived in' look suited him, like he'd grown into his face.

'So, where exactly is the restaurant?' I hadn't seen it along the front, but then I hadn't explored the locale yet.

'It's further along the road, beyond the hotel, magnificent views of the bitch and the sea…' he said, pleased with his location.

'Sounds nice,' I said.

'Come tonight and see,' he said, getting up from his seat.

I was about to say no again, when I saw an almost pleading look in his eyes and wondered if perhaps I should go. After all I was going to start work there tomorrow and it would be useful to see the restaurant for myself.

'Okay, I'll come over to check everything out and be a helping hand if you need me. I don't need you to cook for me though,' I added quickly, but he didn't acknowledge this and I knew there'd be a steaming plate of animal feet and innards with my name on it that night.

'Tonight then,' he stood up, leaving the table without a second look and heading for the door, then just as he was about to open it, he said: 'Dinner is served at 8 p.m., don't be late.' And with that he opened the door and disappeared into the whirling whiteness outside.

I sat at the table alone in the quiet after Gianni's storm, but just as I was relaxing back into the peace, Shakin' Stevens started singing from the jukebox in the corner of the cafe and I took this as my cue to leave. I gathered my handbag and shopping bags and put my coat on and caught Sue's eye behind the counter.

'You off then, love?' she said. 'Got yourself a date with Mr Grumpy Guts?'

I smiled at the description – international chef of mystery distilled into two very apt words.

'Oh, it's not a date, you can't date your husband, can you? He's the owner of a new restaurant, just down the road,' I nodded my head in the direction.

'Oh I heard all about that… and him, didn't realise it was him who was opening the restaurant. He's upset a few folk around here, you know.'

'Oh dear, has he?' I said, hoping she'd elaborate; I'd only heard his side of the story – which in fairness wasn't very favourable to him anyway.

'Yes, he was very rude to the man who delivers all our fruit and veg, apparently he told him his plums were under-ripe and his avocados were foreign. And then he threw them all into the road and swore. Mouth like a sewer apparently!'

She was filling a container with straws as she spoke and held them aloft, waiting for my shock horror, but I just rolled my eyes.

'Gianni throws things and swears a lot, it just rolls off his tongue.'

'He's very good-looking, mind,' she added, like this was compensation for being a total sociopath. 'Is he a good chef then?'

'He's a brilliant chef. In fact, he makes a better chef than he does a husband,' I laughed sadly.

'I heard he made weird stuff, like that Blumen Hestanthal chap?'

I had to smile at this, I'm sure Heston Blumenthal would have enjoyed it too. 'Gianni's simple cooking is lovely, but in recent years it's become a little... modern,' I said, for want of a better word. 'I worry people round here might think it's a little pretentious.' I don't know why I was confiding my fears to this woman, but I felt she was a good listener. I was surprised to hear myself rooting for Gianni after everything that had happened between us, but I couldn't help it, I wanted people to know he had a lot to offer. He could be annoying, rude, conceited – but he was also talented and his iced chocolate cake was to die for. The first time he made it was for my birthday and we ate it in our flat above the restaurant. We'd only just opened and money had been ridiculously tight, but he'd saved some ingredients and he'd made it just for me.

'Chloe's cake,' we called it, and every time something special happened in our lives – birthdays, Christmases and good news – he'd make and ice 'a Chloe cake'.

'Doesn't he do that fancy food, all smoke and foam?' Sue asked.

I smiled, 'Yes, his food is certainly different.'

Then she stood back slightly and looked at me like she'd seen me for the first time. 'Ooh, I think you still have feelings for him, don't you?'

I suddenly felt a little exposed – did I still have feelings for him? Had an almost stranger just spotted something I hadn't admitted even to myself?

'No, I care about him, but that side of things is over for me,' I said, thinking if I said it then it would be true. I was bound to be all types of confused, after all I'd just seen my husband for the first time in a year, of course my emotions were running havoc, that was all it was, surely.

'I bet you'd still like to spend time with him though, share a meal? Then you could talk and, well, before you know it you'd be ripping off his clothes…' she started. She was getting carried away and before she turned my life into a steamy novel, I made it clear there would be none of that.

'No, not at all,' I said a little too sternly. 'It's just business, strictly business.'

She nodded; 'Oh don't mind me, love, I'm only teasing. I just love a bit of romance. We're all looking for that special person, aren't we? Just wait until you meet Gina, she's one of the owners of this place. She knows all about romance, she's slept with film stars and presidents, and lived quite the life,' she said as another woman popped her head up from behind the counter wearing earphones. She was older, in her seventies probably, but very well preserved with dyed hair and full make-up. I hadn't realised she was here, she must have been behind the counter all along.

'Oh hello, love, I'm sorry, didn't see you there,' she said, taking her earphones out. 'I'm just listening to Beyoncé, the woman's a musical genius, *Lemonade* – ooh the furious glory of a woman scorned,' she sighed. 'She's finally telling it like it is about Jay-Z, isn't she? I've been telling her for years to dump him and as if one wasn't enough, now she's tied down with twins. THREE kids,' she stressed, holding up three fingers. 'What a silly girl.'

'This is Roberta, her daughter owns this place, along with her niece – Roberta's on the Twitter,' Sue explained and introduced me. 'She gives relationship advice to all the stars, don't you love? She's like a celebrity agony aunt.'

'Yes, but they don't all thank you for it,' she said, shaking her head. 'I'm seventy-nine you know, I've been through a lot and could share all kinds of wisdom with them, but will they listen? Will they hell.'

'She tried to help Chris and Gwyneth, didn't you sweetheart?' Sue said, cueing up her friend's story, lips pursed.

'Yes, but Gwyneth's a lost cause; all she does is drink probiotic smoothies and put jade eggs up herself all day. Then she goes on about how hard it is for working mothers. What would she know?'

'Well it *would* be very hard for a working mother with jade eggs up there,' Sue said, folding her arms indignantly. 'I bet they jiggle about something rotten.'

Roberta nodded; 'Well quite – I said to her on the Twitter, "Gwyneth," I said, "no wonder you and Chris are having marriage problems if you're doing that." The poor lad must have wondered what the hell was up there!' she added.

I wasn't quite sure how to respond. I felt like I was in a parallel, celebrity universe – with a twist, so tried to ground the conversation by asking about Sophia who owned the cafe the last time I'd visited.

'Sophia was my sister,' Roberta said, 'she died earlier this year.'

'Oh I'm so sorry.'

'Thank you, her daughter Gina and my daughter Ella run the place now.'

'Oh that's nice, keeping it in the family,' I said.

She nodded. 'Anyway, lovely to meet you, Chloe, I'd better get off to my office, Tokyo just woke up,' she said, like that meant something.

After she'd left I looked at Sue, who filled me in, I had a feeling she might.

'Roberta's doing the stocks and shares,' she explained. 'She says the footie's down 33 points and the markets have been rocked since Trump and Brexit... makes her nervous,' she added in almost a whisper. 'She's amazing – when she's not investing in pork bellies and shouting "buy, buy, buy", she's sexytexting handsome strangers. We're all looking for someone, aren't we love?'

'Quite,' I answered, noncommittally, still in shock from the idea of a seventy-nine year old sexting and Gwyneth Paltrow's apparently intimate relationship with jade eggs.

'Will you be okay, love?' Sue asked me as I paid for my drink... and Gianni's, who had left without paying for his, as usual.

'Yes, I'm only round the corner, in Seagull Cottage.'

'No, I meant will you be all right tonight with him? Don't let him feed you any of that weird foam, will you? I mean, he might be a serialised killer...'

I laughed along with her, 'No it's fine, thanks, he looks a bit mad, but it's just the wild hair and the accent. He's a bit of a pain in the arse but I don't think he will kill again,' I added with a wink.

For a moment, she looked shocked, then realised I was teasing and laughed. 'Well whatever gets you through the night as they say, you just make sure you enjoy yourself, love,' she smiled as I waved goodbye while having a fight with the door and the wind. 'And if I don't see you before, happy Christmas!'

I eventually managed to close the door and headed back to the cottage where I lit another fire and spent the afternoon with my book and several cups of Earl Grey tea, bracing myself for whatever faced me at the restaurant that evening. Then I started to imagine Gianni was with me, like he used to be on the other easy chair, drinking tea and reading in companionable silence.

This had been our sanctuary and when we stayed here it felt like we were the only people on earth – just big grey skies, heaving waves and me and Gianni wrapped up in each other. On winter nights we'd light a fire, cook wintry comfort food like pasta and bake scones, which we ate with cream and jam washed down with mulled Devon cider.

But that was my past, and though we had some good times, there was also the disappointment, and the tears, the exquisite pain of losing something you never had. And I knew that to dwell on that now was where madness lay.

After a few hours of reading, I looked at the time and realised I had to drag myself upstairs to have a bath and get ready for the restaurant opening. I was warm and cosy in the little cottage and the last thing I felt like doing was venturing out into the snow storm outside. It was getting worse, and I seriously considered calling Gianni and crying off because of the bad weather. But what if no one else turned up? Surely even here someone must have heard of Gianni Callidori? And a small part of me suspected that, despite his arrogance, he might genuinely want me there for support that night. There weren't going to be many people there, but perhaps the Real Housewives of North Devon would turn up and make Gianni feel better.

Women loved Gianni, with his film star looks, culinary genius and brooding manner. One (female) food critic, who'd ruined bigger and better chefs than Gianni, once wrote that 'Nasty Gianni is to the kitchen what George Clooney is to the bedroom.' (That was in the early days, when Gianni was feted and George was single.)

People went to his restaurant because it was 'the thing' to be seen there and verbose critics and footballers' wives loved to Instagram their plates and let everyone know where they were. I remember taking Cherry to the restaurant once and trying to explain to her the philosophy behind the all-white interior even though I didn't really buy it myself.

'Gianni wants the food to speak for itself. He doesn't believe in fuss and won't allow anything, or anyone, to distract from his food, he even sees menus as a distraction and wants the full "theatre experience",' I told her. But Cherry said it looked like a dentist's and was as painful and expensive, which made me laugh – she could always burst my bubble - but back then no one burst Gianni's.

I thought about his new venture here in Appledore and I couldn't help it, I felt protective of him, like I had when we were married. I knew Gianni didn't deal with disappointment well, and if things didn't come easily, he sometimes found it hard to cope. Like now. I wondered if he'd survive this, or just give up and walk away.

So, with a heavy but hopeful heart I headed off into the snowy night. It was freezing cold, the wind was horrendous, and the sea was hurling itself over the top and spraying me in my face as I walked. I asked myself not for the first time what was I doing, but just kept walking. Funny where life takes you when you don't even think you want to go, isn't it?

Chapter Six

Dirty Kitsch and Nasty Sparkle

Walking on through the sea mist, on a road lit only by lamp-light and the sound of crashing waves, I made my way towards the restaurant. I didn't want to drive as I was planning to have a couple of drinks, especially if there was champagne – I loved champagne. I loved restaurant openings too and over the years I'd overseen many, including all of Gianni's. He'd once said I was his lucky mascot and that I had to be there on opening night. I wondered now if that was one of the main reasons he'd invited me down here. He was so superstitious he probably thought the restaurant would fail if his 'mascot' wasn't there. Gianni was superstitious about cooking too and always added chopped parsley along with garlic and olive oil when he started a sauce for pasta. I couldn't taste the parsley, it just sizzled, curled up and lost its green colour, which had seemed pointless. I'd asked him why he'd continued to use it, and he'd said: 'It's the way my mama taught me, and I've never done it any other way, I think if I do it will all go wrong horribly.'

When we first married, his mother had bought us a broom, which wasn't on my wedding list of fancy china and designer kitchen gadgets, but apparently it was to 'sweep away evil'. I couldn't detect any in our little flat in Balham, but Gianni had sprinkled the corners with salt to purify the place so I guess we were safe. It seemed like madness to me, but it was a huge part of who Gianni was and I loved him for it, even when he threw salt over his left shoulder while cooking to keep the devil away as I passed and got a faceful.

During my life with Gianni I learned that in Italy it's bad luck to spill olive oil, to avoid eye contact when toasting, to bump glasses with non-alcoholic drinks, toast with plastic (God forbid) or cross your silverware on your plate. Any flouting of these rules and no amount of praying would halt the wars and pestilence it might bring to one's home – though again, I stress, we were in a flat in Balham, not known for its dances with the devil or rampant pestilence.

When, after a few years, Gianni started to irritate and upset me, as husbands sometimes do, I took great joy in defiling these superstitious quirks and started slowly by cooking with salt and never throwing it over my shoulder, then as our lives became more angry and resentful and he didn't come home from the restaurant, I would hurl olive oil across the kitchen, apparently inviting the devil over. I'd drink too much wine from plastic glasses while toasting myself, but my lowest point arrived one evening. When clutching my plastic glass I drunkenly shouted, 'Come on Lucifer, bring it on big boy' at the top of my voice. I couldn't look my neighbours in the face ever again.

I smiled to myself at the madness of it all as I crunched along on the snow; I was glad I'd worn the cottage's resident wellingtons as I carefully navigated through the crispy ground in the near blackness. I could laugh about it now, but by flouting his rules, laughing at his superstition, I was trying to get Gianni's attention, I wanted to be caught. But he never seemed to be aware of the slick of oil across the floor, the mounds of salt and the pile of plastic glasses in the sink – I guess we'd both given up by then.

The miscarriage had taken its toll, it had bitten into our lives, leaving scars and pain. The doctor was encouraging, and after an examination said she could find nothing wrong with me. 'It's just one of those things,' she said, gently, 'you and your husband should take a holiday, relax and try again.'

But after a second pregnancy, followed by another devastating miscarriage, it seemed no amount of salt sprinkling and sweeping could keep the devil from our door.

Marriage and a family had always been at the end of both our rainbows, and finding each other in our thirties had been a lovely surprise. But I was obsessing about becoming pregnant and it was driving us both apart, Gianni feeling the pressure to 'perform' and me like some kind of madwoman, waiting every month for a sign, sitting on toilet seats with tests, only to be disappointed. I was aware I needed something else to focus on, and when Gianni opened the second restaurant, I continued to work as part of the new team, despite my doubts about it being right for him.

Then just after we took over the new premises I started being sick in the mornings. I'd had a cold and my period was late, but I dared not hope again. It was only when Gianni made a passing comment about my 'fuller' breasts and my period was two weeks late that I took a pregnancy test. After the longest few minutes of my life, I sat in the familiar position on the toilet seat, and cried loud sobs when it was positive. I waited several hours before ringing Gianni at work, scared I might lose it. 'Can you come home now?' I'd asked, but he said no, he was too busy.

'It's just that… I have something to tell you,' I'd said, wanting to see his face. I lived in a bubble of eternal hope back then, this was our third pregnancy and it might be third time lucky – I had to believe that, even though I wasn't the superstitious one.

But throughout my phone call Gianni didn't pick up on the excitement in my voice and kept insisting he was far too busy because one of the investors was due in any minute. I was aware I'd become needy since the second miscarriage and many times he'd come home to me sobbing, or listless. So I blurted it out – knowing he'd be pleased – and within minutes he was home and I really felt this baby would make everything all right between us. I was once more restored to the pregnant glory of a Fabergé egg, and felt like the queen bee as Gianni rubbed my feet, mopped my brow, made me drinks and meals and wouldn't let me do anything around the house. It was bliss, and I was in heaven with just a little fretwork of worry around the edges.

Given our history, we waited a few weeks this time before he rang his mother and brothers in Tuscany, and when I was four months gone we felt it was almost safe to let everyone know. So we began to make plans and he told the staff he might need extra cover in a few months' time because he wanted to take a month off (he'd never taken longer than a week off, and even then he was on the phone to the restaurant every day). We were both beside ourselves, and allowed ourselves to consider turning the spare room into a nursery. We shopped for paint – pastel lemon because we didn't know whether we were having a boy or a girl – and I remember the lady in Homebase congratulating us as we bought it, along with matching curtains and a border. Gianni painted the room straight away, and though I was only five months pregnant by this time, it felt good. I felt healthy and happy, my only sadness being that my own parents who'd died several years earlier wouldn't meet their grandchild.

I thought about my children a lot – I still do. I like the phrase 'my children', I never say it aloud, and only in my head, but I haven't forgotten them.

Once or twice as the wind hit and the snow thickened on my walk to the restaurant I seriously considered going back. But I'd got this far and at least the restaurant would provide shelter. There was no denying I was curious to see the place and to learn what else Gianni planned to offer his customers; I hoped he'd taken on board my reservations but I wasn't holding my breath.

Towards the end of our time together, when we'd abandoned each other, I felt Gianni's food became less edgy and more bizarre. He seemed to be working out all of his emotions through food and it led to some crazy concoctions which said more about the state of his head than anything culinary. From behind a timbale of samphire and sea slugs I recall him saying that I wasn't giving our marriage a chance, but I didn't see the salvation of our relationship in working eighteen hours a day in a bloody restaurant. I'd felt slightly pushed out when the army of staff and advisors arrived at the restaurant with no name, so had been building my own career while Gianni was building his restaurant. Consequently, I now didn't feel like this was part of me – it was Gianni's restaurant, and Gianni's world.

I'd wanted something else, and though he tried to get me involved in the restaurant, seeing it as something that could bring us together, this wasn't a quick fix, this tear in our marriage wasn't about work it was about loss. I was unhappy and he couldn't bear it because he felt it was his job to make me happy, and when I cried not only did he feel a failure as a father, he felt like a failure as a husband.

Not long after we'd parted, I remember going back to the restaurant with Cherry for her birthday. I was missing Gianni and desperately wanted to see him, just to say hello, and hope there were no hard feelings – I wanted to say let's just move on but stay in touch, stay friends. But Gianni still couldn't accept that I'd left him and he was pretty unfriendly when I popped into the kitchen. At first he didn't even acknowledge me and continued to chop aggressively at raw meat with a large knife, which made me nervous.

'How's it going?' I said lamely.

He stopped and just looked at me. 'How do you think?' he said, and I saw tears in his eyes, which shocked me. Gianni always loved being the man, and he had an old-fashioned attitude about his role, which had been instilled in him by his mother. He had to protect his woman, hide his feelings and soldier on, and looking back I realised that was the biggest problem between us. When I needed him to cry with me and share our pain, he couldn't and I'd seen this as being detached, insensitive. But that night in the hot kitchen, I wondered if perhaps I'd misunderstood him after all.

'Gianni...' I said, touching the sleeve of his shirt.

'Onions,' was all he said, and gestured to his eyes. But I knew it wasn't the onions making him cry, Gianni was pulling away from me again, refusing to acknowledge his feelings.

I remember feeling so sad, but later that night, after almost crying in the kitchen, he appeared front of house and walked around like a bloody rock star. It was a theatre to Gianni. I realised that the real, caring Gianni that I'd married still existed but he had closed it off to me and all that was left behind was his arrogant façade.

I kept on walking through the snow, the sound of the sea beating against the wall and was relieved to see some lights swinging in the wind and realised this must be Il Bacio restaurant.

Arriving at the restaurant, I opened the door, went inside and was immediately sucked into an empty shell. There were a few people dotted here and there – some had wine, others seemed to be sitting at completely empty tables. There was no music, no sound of laughter, no atmosphere, and I couldn't help but think how different this was from his first restaurant with the cosy little tables and candles in Chianti bottles. A shiny white floor lay beneath white tables, and huge balloon lights hung on long silver cords above, their light shedding a stark exposure of the nothingness beneath. I felt like I'd walked into a very modern museum filled with thick, white, snowy silence, not unlike his second London restaurant, described by one critic as 'dental surgery chic'. The decor had moved on from 'dental chic' and was now full on 'operating theatre', all steel and clean lines. I fully expected Gianni to be in scrubs asking the sous chef to hand him a scalpel.

Some of the customers at the empty tables were looking hopefully at me, like I might know where their food was perhaps? So I tried to avoid eye contact with them and just took in the dining room as I walked through – no flowers, no pictures on the walls and not one single Christmas decoration. And this wasn't just an absence of festive warmth, it was a trip to the bloody Antarctic. Christmas was a week away and surely the customers would have enjoyed a little frisson of festivity? It didn't have to be the traditional kind of baubled tree, perhaps a sleek monochrome one, some space age tinsel? But it seemed Gianni wasn't celebrating this year.

I couldn't see any sign of the kitchens, where I presumed he'd be, and on looking around I noticed a camera on the wall. What the hell was he trying to create here, I felt like I was on *Big Brother*!

I looked into the camera, and jumped when I heard Gianni's voice say, 'Look to your left.' It was coming from a sound transmitter on the wall, but sounded like he was locked in a cupboard. CCTV, disembodied voices, I knew Gianni put up barriers, but this was literal! I gazed around, seeking an answer and finding only white, then heard a tinny Italian voice shout, 'The door is in the wall.' I felt like I was in a John le Carré novel and was tempted to go all MI5 and answer 'It's cold in Siberia this time of year.' I was also tempted to just set off back to the cottage and leave him to his own ridiculous devices. This was already shaping up to be a disaster and I didn't want to be a spectator at Gianni's funeral – because that's what it felt like. This was opening night – so where were the staff with smiles and canapés? Where were the champagne flutes and reassuring kitchen sounds of pans and steam and food being prepared? More immediately though, where was the bloody door? I ran the flat of my hand along the wall, trying to find the damn door, knowing everyone was staring at me and feeling like bloody Marcel Marceau. What was wrong with an actual door for God's sake?

I gesticulated at the camera, 'This is stupid Gianni, give me a clue, am I getting warmer?' I hissed.

I was about to shout, 'I give up,' and take a bow to the sparse audience, now waiting with baited breath at their tables, when I felt something move on the wall. I pushed it and it gave way easily, too easily. I almost fell in as it opened into the kitchen. It was like stepping into Narnia as I entered another sparse room, only this one was like a spaceship, all steel and minimalism, fine lines and shiny metal.

I was taking everything in, then spotted Gianni sitting in an old leather armchair. It seemed a little odd, seeing as he had customers waiting for food, but he wasn't employing me to criticise his work ethic and I didn't want to come in all guns blazing. One of the problems we'd had when we'd been married was that I could be a bit bossy and he'd resented it, so I had to remember that I was here to do a job, not change my husband. I was getting paid well to launch this restaurant; Gianni's temperament wasn't my problem any more.

'Looking good,' I said, gesturing towards the high-end white goods (which were silver).

'I know,' he said, quite seriously, 'I do look ass good in this chair.'

'Not you! This kitchen it's gorgeous, in a NASA kind of way... but why the Secret Service style door and CIA technology?'

'I need security, privacy, I don't want just anyone to wander into my kitchen.'

'Yes, but mightn't it be nice for the waiting and kitchen staff to be able to *wander* in?' I suggested sarcastically.

He shrugged.

'Are they still out there?' he suddenly asked, like he was referring to an alien invasion.

'The customers, you mean? Yes, there are a few couples, and a man on his own, it's not exactly buzzing.'

'Oh no! A man alone? He must be the critic, he hates me.'

'Why?'

'Because I hate him.'

'Well, start by liking him and he might like you.'

'It's so easy for you isn't it, Chloe, the smiley girl with the blonde curly hair, everyone smiles back.'

'No it isn't easy, Gianni,' I snapped, angry that he should say this about me. 'You might find this hard to believe, but sometimes I don't *like* people, in fact sometimes I really *dislike* them. But if they happen to be customers or clients, I smile through gritted teeth and say complimentary things to them until they bloody love me, because in business they are what matters, not me. It's easy to do, it's a scientific fact that if you smile at another human being they will invariably impulsively return that smile – you should try it sometime.' Despite wanting to keep things professional, the old dynamic had already clicked in. Me the nagging wife, Gianni the genius who never took my advice and if I tried to offer it I was usually labelled 'bossy'. His ego was impossible to crack and his comment about it being easy for me made me cross. I couldn't count the times I'd had to paint on a smile when my heart had been breaking – and he knew this. He knew what I'd been through. I was furious to think he could say something so bloody flippant and waft my pain away like it didn't matter. I may have looked like the smiley girl with blonde hair, but that's because I was clever enough to hide the wretched, childless wife from the world.

I pushed it all away, now wasn't the time to scream and yell and tell him what a self-obsessed tosser he was. I glared at him, alarmed and annoyed to see he had a glass of whisky in his hands, and he wasn't making any attempt to get up from his comfy seat. This wasn't the sign of a man about to face the public on restaurant launch night.

'Have they ordered?' I asked.

'No. I slave here alone and the pissing peasants say it is not enough. They want a sodding *menu!*'

He said menu like they'd each asked for an internal medical examination. Given the 'medical chic' setting, this wasn't completely out of the question.

'What are you going to do?'

'Drink.'

'I mean about the guests.'

'Drink.'

'No, that's not the answer, you have to face this. You need a menu,' I said. 'You have to give them a choice.'

'I give them a choice, I offer them my crisp sweetbreads… or to go home.'

'Really, Gianni?'

'They don't need a choice, I am choosing.'

'Why?'

'Because these holy mackerel don't appreciate the fine dining.'

'Were you rude to them when they complained?' I asked, not waiting for him to answer – of course he was. 'You can't shout at people here, you can't call them asses and mackerels or clowns, or whatever other messed-up stuff you say. It's rude and you aren't in London now, Gianni,' I said this gently because I'd never seen him so downcast. It was like this rejection of his food had really taken the wind out of him. 'And who is the critic, Gianni?'

'I don't know, the critics are all ass badders…'

'Bad-asses,' I heard myself correct him, something I did all the time when we were married, but he never listened. 'What's the newspaper called?' I asked, ignoring his rant.

'How do I know? Fiona, she has it in her phone… the Devon Donkey I think.'

I'd made a list of the local newspapers in the region, and this most certainly was *not* on my list. Gianni was just being annoying, unhelpful and doing what he always did – closing down a difficult conversation.

'Small-minded little people,' he was muttering to himself.

'No, it's the local people who will be your bread and butter, and you must be nice to them, and essentially give them what they want. Come on Gianni, this is your dream, don't lose it before you've even started.'

'It was a dream, it died.'

'No, don't give up, sometimes if you want something badly enough you have to fight for it,' I said. Is that what I'd wanted him to do for us? Had I hoped when I walked out of our home that night that he'd run after me and beg me to come back? I didn't think so at the time, but sometimes we don't know ourselves.

'I have to defend my art,' he was saying now.

'Oh get a grip, Gianni, you're serving up dinner, you're not installing in the bloody Tate Modern.'

'You have no soul.'

'And you have no business sense. Real people want real food… what did you offer them?'

'Crispy sweetbreads and chickens' feet – you will have to eat it all now because I have too much left.

'It's a "specialised" menu Gianni, not everyone likes offal – did you offer them anything else?'

'Yes, it was all on the plate – a tasting starter to share.'

'Okay, so what else was on the plate?'

'Snail semolina, lamb livers and squid ink shortbread on a bed of lentils.'

Christ this was worse than I thought, less fine dining, more Bushtucker Trial.

'And the main, was it something Christmassy?' I asked, hopefully.

'Of course. I give them Christmas on a sodding bloody plate!' I wondered for a moment if that was the title, and tried not to think of the organs he could harvest from that poor bird. I was going to become vegetarian in January. 'My turkey she is stuffed with tangerine sorbet, and mistletoe drizzle,' he snapped.

This wasn't a meal, it was a mid-life Christmas crisis. What had happened to the man I'd known and loved who served pasta made with pine nuts, basil and love? This amazing chef who once cooked organic chicken Italian for Sting and Trudie, pizza Rusticana for David and Victoria, was now reduced to this mouth-curling culinary madness. Yes turkey, tangerines and mistletoe all scream Christmas, but stuffed together with a huge price tag they were screaming something else.

'It's a very… *experimental* menu for a small seaside village in Devon,' I offered. 'I'm not saying these people wouldn't appreciate your fine dining, but what about local pork, lovely Devon cheeses and cream. The Gianni I know always made the most of local, seasonal ingredients, even if he added a surprising twist.'

'The delivery man is a clown ass, and never came with the order.'

'He just didn't turn up? Like the staff?' I recalled Sue's story of the abusive avocado/plum throwing and wasn't surprised the delivery man had been a no-show.

'The staff have walked out… the critics hate my food, I am too much of a bloody genius for them.'

'Is that true or is it because of the way you are with people sometimes?' It was a question, but I knew the answer. He could be really selfish and insensitive to customers and critics, his food always came first and if anyone dared to dislike it, then it was off with their heads. He was like the Henry the Eighth of the cookery world – in fact Gianni probably wouldn't have been out of place in Henry's court given they served up grilled beavers' tails and whole roasted peacock.

'You hurt people, Gianni,' I said.

'You talking about when I threw the Kobe beef sausage at the man?'

'I wasn't, because I don't know about that. And I'm not sure I want to.'

'Simple, he is a critic, from the local news, trashy paper fake news asses...' he said defensively. I had to back off slightly, he was beginning to sound like a beleaguered Donald Trump – he'd be denying any involvement with Russia next.

'Okay, okay, calm down. Tell me what happened with the critic and the sausage,' I asked – a sentence so surreal I couldn't imagine in what context it would ever make sense apart from this one. I was sounding more like his wife or mother than his new employee, and discovering that old habits are hard to break. At least I knew how to calm him down... I hoped.

'He hated my sauce, so I threw sausage at his dickhead.'

'Oh, that's strange, I don't recall reading that in the customer care solutions handbook,' I said, sarcastically.

'I don't have that book,' he sighed, seriously.

'Apparently not.' I was horrified (though the real crime here was that he had turned Kobe beef at £100 per pound into a bloody sausage, but that was Gianni Callidori). 'Gianni, you can't behave like that and hope to keep everything you've got,' I added, thinking about our marriage. But for now, this wasn't about me, or him, it was about his business and the fact that if this one failed he had nothing left. How the hell was I going to turn this turkey around?

'I just get so angry, I do the boiling and bloody hell, pfft, I go.'

'I know, but I'm still trying to work through how you came to assault someone with a sausage, I'm sure that's a criminal offence.'

'I do feel bad about that bloody sausage,' he said, nodding and taking another swig of whisky.

'Good.' I was vaguely comforted, at least he had some remorse.

'Yes, it was from the Tajima strain of Wagyu cattle, raised in Japan's Hyogo Prefecture – the best! Wasted on that disgusting pig-dog.'

Oh, so he wasn't sorry, he was as conceited and arrogant as he'd always been.

'I can't be tied down, I am creative. I call up the papers here and tell them I am an artist and not to send peasants to review my work.'

'Great, so you've already done some great PR?' I said, feeling cross that he'd made my job even harder and I hadn't even started yet. How the hell was I going to invite the good people of Appledore to spread the word if he was pulling tricks like this?

'I had to do it, Fiona stormed away.'

'I'm not surprised, you'll be lucky if I stay for the next two hours,' I hissed. 'Gianni, you've alienated the local and regional newspapers, and so when one of their critics comes along it's about damage limitation, you should have courted him like a lover, offered him everything. Instead, you attack him with a sausage – nice! This restaurant won't last five minutes if you carry on thinking you're God.' Gianni was about to object, to offer some explanation, but I held up my hand in a 'stop!' gesture.

'Listen. What you could get away with among the bored, indulgent, glitterati won't wash in a place like this. In London they think you're a crazed genius, here they think you're a psycho – see what I mean… it's all about interpretation?'

'I don't want just anyone eating here – have you seen my dining room? Directly from the hands of the masters of Italian workshops, it has a distinguished and unique aesthetic.'

'Oh get over yourself. A distinguished and unique aesthetic? What you need are customers with an appetite and a wallet.'

'Vulgar… just vulgar, but I rise above your words… I create art.'

'So you've said, many times – I'm very happy for you, but not everyone looks for art in their food.'

'If not art, then what is there?'

'Mmm let me see, quality and…' I screwed up my face to deliver this next word, 'quantity?'

'Quantity?' He looked at me like I'd just confessed to strangling a kitten.

'Yes, and don't look at me like that. Your portions are too small, they're doll's-house-sized titbits masquerading as dinner, at the risk of sounding vulgar,' I said repeating his earlier criticism. 'You are paying me for my advice and my expertise, I've done better restaurant launches and cleaned up bigger messes than this, but only when people listen to me. So, here are my "off the top of my head", initial thoughts. It's not rocket science – all you need is a good, basic menu and adult-sized portions that taste good and satisfy the customer… oh and lose the snail semolina.'

'I pay you to help, not to talk the rubbish.'

'Well, if that's how you feel then I don't think there's any point in me being here,' I said, and reached for my coat.

'No, you have to stay,' he said, rising from his seat.

'I don't have to do anything, Gianni. We're not together any more and I'm only working for you, I'm not living with you. If you continue to be rude I will just bill you for today and walk away.'

'No, Chloe, please stay…'

I looked at him closely and wondered why I was still standing there. I thought about leaving, but that feeling kicked in again, the one that made me feel protective towards him and made me want to help. Old habits die hard; I'd always seen through the act and knew how vulnerable he could be. I also knew instinctively that he needed me – and I simply couldn't walk away.

'Okay, but that's your final warning. Look, my other bit of advice – and I'm talking myself out of a nice pay cheque here – why don't you forget about this? Just put everything into your nameless London restaurant where people know you and love you – well, it's twisted, but it's a kind of love, I suppose.'

He looked crestfallen; 'Because my London restaurant with no name has closed, it has been bloody failing to make the money, people don't want my art any more. They say I go crazy now and take their money back. This is why I move here, to be near the sea.'

I was surprised; I had no idea Gianni was in financial trouble. I suddenly felt very guilty; I hadn't been aware of this, and our marriage woes can't have helped.

'I'm sorry, is it because of Brexit?' I said, almost hopefully, Brexit seemed to be the cause of most people's problems at the moment and I'd rather blame that than me. I didn't want to acknowledge that I may have played a part in this by leaving him.

'Yes, and I have the big bills of life.'

He'd always overspent, but in our first restaurant I was able to rein him in. By restaurant number two he was buying crates of champagne to make into droplets or foam, then there were the hand-made German kitchens manufactured in steel and expensive oak. In my view, his lack of financial nous was one of the main reasons for the failure of his second business, along with an unhappy marriage. There was also his rather fickle brand of customer, who wanted the latest thing and were now chasing it.

'Chloe, will you ask everyone to leave?' he suddenly said. 'I can't do this.'

'I'm sorry Gianni, that's not my job.'

'Please?' Again, the vulnerability, the big brown eyes and despite my anger towards him, I pitied him. He was a broken man and there was no way he was going to be able to open successfully tonight. I wasn't sure how long the few customers had all been sitting waiting, but surely it was just a matter of time before they found the invisible door and rushed in like zombies after our blood. I'd always believed in dealing with a problem before it arose and I have to say the thought of hungry people out there – including the only critic left in the area that Gianni hadn't yet hurt or offended – was stressing me out. So I took off the wellingtons and put on the high heels I'd brought with me for the evening and after finding the invisible door went into the dining room. Everyone looked up as I entered and I noticed one of the couples had left, so there were only five people in all. I wasn't sure if I should be grateful there were only five people here to face, or whether to be worried that only five people had turned up for the 'grand opening'.

'I am so very sorry,' I started, 'but our chef is sick…'

'You can say that again,' one of the men remarked.

'He offered us a plate with nasty semolina, some weird short-bread and a lump of fish and feet – feet! And for the price...'

'Oh, I must apologise, it obviously wasn't explained to you, but the delicious morsels you were offered were actually amuse-bouches,' I lied. 'They were merely titbits to tantalise your taste buds and optional, the delicious main meal was being prepared for you when the chef suddenly took ill. Can I please offer my sincerest apologies and propose a complimentary dinner on a future evening of your choice?'

They all looked at me blankly, they weren't buying this. They'd booked this restaurant for tonight and had been looking forward to a special evening; they didn't want dinner another night. The critic was now making copious notes and I felt like getting my coat and walking out – but people kept doing this to Gianni and he needed my help. I looked around wildly for inspiration, and spotted a crate of champagne behind the bar. I swooped behind and brought up two bottles, one in each hand.

'And, of course, Gianni Callidori would like to offer these from his personal cellar as an apology.' I held my breath waiting for a reaction – if this didn't work I had nothing else up my sleeve and they would all be straight on TripAdvisor bitching about those sweetbreads within the hour.

'I don't mind coming back another night,' one of the women said, and I wanted to go over and kiss her.

'Would dinner include wine?' She asked.

Knowing this would cost a fortune, I couldn't bring myself to say the word 'yes', so I nodded vigorously while handing out the champagne. I wandered around with the bottles and did lots of full on smiling, making a point of chatting with the critic about the weather and how excited the chef was to cook for him on his return. Eventually, they all left – apparently to go to a Chinese restaurant in Westward Ho! – chatting away happily and thanking me in advance for the meal they would enjoy later in the week. I waved at the door as they clambered into a taxi, and with my fingers firmly crossed that there would be no negative repercussions, I headed back into the kitchen. I may have saved tonight, but I wasn't sure I could save the restaurant.

'So your guests have gone,' I said.

'You were a long time. Were they bloody devastating not to have the full Gianni experience?'

'Devastated? Not really, they said your food was too small and too weird and they didn't want to eat feet. So if you'd like to think about that, they are all going to call over the next few days and book for another evening.'

'They can't resist, they have to come back – it ees an experience.'

'You can say that again.'

'These peasants know the talent when they see it.'

'Erm… yes, they also know a free meal when they see it.'

'Free meal… I'm giving it away?'

'Yes,' I said, 'you're welcome.'

But he just shrugged and poured himself another whisky.

'You're welcome,' I repeated.

'What is this thing you are saying now?'

'I just pulled you out of a hole. The guests in that dining room were revolting.'

'I bloody know.'

'No, Gianni, I mean they were upset, they were about to cause a scene, write terrible reviews, tell all their friends what an awful place this is. Do you want that?'

'Of course not, you holy cow.'

'Gianni please don't call me a holy cow,' I said, worried he might use this on a customer at some point in the future when I wasn't around to rescue the situation. His cursing became more outlandish and out of context the more stressed he became.

'By the time I'd arrived at this restaurant you'd caused so much chaos the only thing for it was to offer your customers complimentary food and drink.'

'How could you do this, you have not the right to offer everyone my food for nothing,' he was becoming angry now, but so was I.

'Don't you dare say that to me, you sent me out there because you were too much of a coward to face them yourself,' I spat. This really wound him up as I knew it would, no one tested Gianni's macho pride, not even me.

'You are so bloody stupid, you will ruin me.'

'How dare you,' I yelled. I wasn't being spoken to like this, I was hurt by his anger towards me and his complete lack of real appreciation for what I'd done that night. I wasn't going to start screaming back at him, those days were gone and I didn't have the energy, so I picked up my coat from the back of the chair, and moved away from the war zone.

He continued to shout at me as he banged crockery and pans, threw cutlery into a basket, all noise and Italian bluster.

'Gianni Callidori doesn't give it away,' he yelled.

'Tonight he does. And he gave something else away too,' I said, walking towards the door. 'He gave *me* away, and I doubt anyone else will care enough to step in and help. Goodbye again, Gianni,' I said, and just like I had before, I went to leave him.

'NO, NO,' he shouted and ran towards me, shutting the invisible door behind me and trying to usher me back into the kitchen, but I stood my ground and stayed by the door. This wasn't an empty threat, I wanted out, he'd made me so angry. After all I'd done, he hadn't even said thank you, he'd just complained about it.

He was looking at me now with genuine fear in his eyes; he knew I was his last chance, and yet he'd still been unpleasant. He hadn't grown at all; this man was impossible.

'Gianni, I can't do *this!*' I gestured towards him. 'I went out there tonight and faced an angry, jeering crowd' (okay five people, I exaggerated slightly) 'for you. And when they left, they were calm, happy even – and that was because of me, I showed them some respect. You, unfortunately, don't know the meaning of respect, and I refuse to walk on eggshells around you as others have over the years. I'm not your bitch, Gianni, I'm used to working in an environment where people are appreciated, where they say "thank you" to each other, and believe it or not, they sometimes even smile.'

He stood in front of me, his face a picture of confusion, and in the middle of all this his mouth started to twist slightly.

'What's the matter, do you feel ill?' I asked. He was a man in his late forties under considerable stress, he might be about to have some kind of medical event. An untimely death was all I needed tonight.

'No, I'm not ill, I'm smiling.' He looked awkward; his face wasn't used to smiling and it showed. I wanted to laugh at this, but I resisted, I had to show him I meant business.

'That's not a smile,' I sighed, 'it's an evil grimace and it's not nice.'

He looked a little put out. 'Chloe, I'm… sorry. I am filled with myself all the time. Fiona before she leaves she say, "Gianni, you are going up yourself all the time, you are right up."'

I wasn't quite sure what he meant, but I got the gist (I think). 'Yes, and Fiona is just one of many people you've upset for no good reason over the years. You're no different with me, in fact I don't even know why I came here.' Was it guilt at leaving him? Was it because of a shared history, for the good times? Or was it some kind of leftover love? It certainly wasn't money – I doubted I'd even get paid now on learning about his tragic financial situation.

'I am a wasting of space, everyone hates me… except you. Please, please Chloe, I will change. I do respect all of you and I am appreciating everything you did tonight – you know me, you know I find it hard to say bloody thank you sometimes.'

I was amazed at this response, Gianni rarely if ever admitted to something that might be perceived as a weakness.

'Finding something difficult is no excuse; I didn't find this evening easy, but I did it!'

I waited for the string of swear words, the burst of anger in response to what I'd just said, but what he did next took me by complete surprise.

Slowly, he lifted his hand to my face, where his fingertips brushed it, just as he had all those years before, and the echo reverberated in my heart.

'Thank you,' he said quietly, slowly pulling his hand away, but his eyes remained on mine.

And outside the snow continued to dance and swirl and the sea kept pounding onto the shore, while inside, it felt like time had stopped.

Chapter Seven

Sausage-Slapped for Slating Slug Semolina

His hand on my cheek was just like the first time, and though it was a matter of seconds, it seemed to last for ever. It was enough to remind me of the man I'd fallen in love with and I knew I couldn't turn my back on him, whatever he said or did – the crazy, holy mackerel. 'I am at the very end of my wits,' he admitted. 'I can't go back to London, everyone hates me there, so many nasty ass monkeys.'

'Gianni, they don't hate you,' I said, ignoring his colourful and rather surreal insult. They've just found another trendy restaurant to talk about. Now it's time for *you* to find something fresh and new,' I said, thinking how the same applied to me too. I loved my job but ending my marriage had made me realise that I needed more than work and a flat to come home to every now and then that felt like just another hotel room. I stopped thinking about me and continued to give Gianni a motivational speech. 'This is your time,' I repeated, 'don't keep looking back and wondering where it all went wrong. Your London customers just wanted somewhere to be seen, and for a few years you filled the brief,' I explained.

'What are you meaning, I fill their briefs?'

'That doesn't matter,' I said before this got completely lost in translation. 'I just think you should see this as your second chance, so let's try and get it right, I want to help you.'

'Thank you,' he said, for probably the second time in his life, but it still sent a warm buzz through me and I wondered if perhaps Gianni had changed, after all.

'I was also thinking that perhaps you should send the critic a crate of your finest vintage champagne with an official invite to return?'

'Vintage champagne for an ass pig?'

Okay, so he hadn't changed that much.

'No, he's not an... ass... pig, whatever that is. He's a well-respected food critic,' I said, completely unaware of who he was. On local papers the 'food critic' was often the same guy who wrote the traffic reports and obituaries, but I wasn't telling Gianni that. 'You have to stop being rude and start working out how to make the best of things. Firstly, there's been no local publicity, oh except apparently a piece in the local paper tomorrow about the chef hitting someone with a sausage made from ridiculously priced Japanese beef, probably under the headline "*Critic Sausage-Slapped for Slating Slug Semolina.*"'

He leaned forward and put his head in his hands. As a wife I would have comforted him, but in my capacity as PR and events manager I simply continued to list the problems. It wasn't easy but it was quite liberating.

'On another note, the decor is very Gianni Callidori, but walking in here on a wintry evening a week before Christmas, I felt like I'd arrived in A and E. The bright lights, the cold whiteness… no Christmas decorations. This is a restaurant by the sea… I want open fires and cosy.'

'Cosy? Cosy? Gianni Callidori doesn't do the bloody "cosy".'

'You did once, Gianni,' I said, leaning towards him. 'Our first restaurant in London was warm and cosy, red and white checked cloths on the table, candles, wonderful Italian food, it had… heart, something I think you lost along the way,' I added.

He scowled slightly, but then remembered that I wanted smiles and if I didn't get them I might abandon him to sort his own mess out, so he made a hilarious attempt to turn his frown upside down.

'You look like you're about to vomit,' I said, watching the twisting mouth, the slightly craggy features moving against their instinct.

I'd never been intimidated by his loudness or his arrogance, and now I could be more objective. I found him quite amusing, sitting there like some landed gentry surrounded by a magnificent kitchen empty of food and staff. He had everything, yet nothing. I knew this because my life was the same, I had this big, glamorous working life, but I came home to an empty flat – everything yet nothing. Funny how our lives were running at a strange parallel, even though we were apart.

'You can still be sleek and modern, but still romantic… cosy even,' I continued.

'Cosiness is a cliché, and romance a concept,' he spat.

'Ooh, steady on tiger,' I smiled, knowing this was just Gianni sounding off. I remembered how romantic he used to be with me, a dozen roses, walks on the beach waiting for the sunset… and the Christmas bauble with the engagement ring inside. Gianni knew romance, he'd just forgotten it.

He got up and started walking back into the restaurant. He was now standing in the secret doorway, holding it open for me. I assumed he was showing me out, but instead he surprised me by gesturing towards the table in the window.

'I have the table,' he said. 'No fussy decorations, no bloody science rockets or menus, just beautiful seaside. It is the best table in the house.'

I followed him through the dining room and towards the front of the restaurant where huge landscaped windows looked out onto the seafront. I hadn't really noticed this when I'd first arrived, I'd been too busy being blinded by the whiteness, and I don't mean the snow.

'This will be a lovely view on a summer's evening,' I said, feeling like we were finally communicating, but refusing to say 'wow' because this would only feed his ego.

'It is bloody lovely tonight,' he said, slightly affronted.

He pulled out a chair for me at the table. He was always the gentleman, even when he was annoying and stroppy – and despite it being old-fashioned machismo, it always made me melt, ever so slightly.

'It is lovely,' I said, taking the seat. 'But I still think you can improve. The view on a summer evening will be amazing, but at the moment it's just blackness. And as I said, right now this restaurant needs Christmas cosiness – soft candlelight, a few classy snowflake decorations… a bit of sparkle.'

'Kitsch… she's here with the dirty kitsch again. You always did like the nasty sparkle.'

I looked at him and saw the familiar twinkle in his eye. He was teasing me, something he hadn't done for so long now that I'd almost missed it. Until this moment, I'd had the public face of Gianni Callidori, defensive, cool, impenetrable. But here, in the window, looking out onto a snowy winter evening I detected a definite thawing.

Like a naughty child, he was playing with me, and I knew how to play back. 'So, I bet you're glad we're apart, at least you don't have to put up with my awful Christmas decorations… my nasty sparkle.'

He shrugged, but I saw a glimmer of something in his eyes. And realised to my surprise that I'd missed his faux strops and shrugs. There was a time, way back, when I'd actually enjoyed the combat and even now I could still handle him in one of those moods where every other word started or ended with 'ass'. And he still made me smile.

'So, here's an idea – and more nasty kitsch for you,' I said. 'What about adding one accent colour to some tasteful decorations – in a pale blue to echo the sea?' I said, warming to the theme.

'Why not?' he shrugged, 'I could also cover everything in the sodding Christmas gold to echo the bitch.'

'Gianni, I am offering you my professional advice.' In fact, I was going above and beyond, an events and PR person wouldn't normally get involved in decor to this extent. 'I get that you might not want to hear what I'm saying. And you might not be bothered about "sodding Christmas" decorations this year – but your customers are.'

'Sod off with the sodding Christmas, I don't want it and my customers will have to do what I say.'

'Yes but you don't have any customers, that's the problem.'

'It's their bloody problem… they are stupid asses and you have no idea what you are talking about.'

'Thank you, your charm and sensitivity always wins me over in the end,' I sighed. 'Gianni stop being a stubborn ass,' I said, aware his cursing were beginning to rub off on me. 'You're in trouble and you have to make this place work, you've given everything up to come here, you *can't* let it fail.'

'It already fails, I have five customers and you give them free meals and send them away for another night – you have ruined me, Chloe.'

I glared at him, oh he still had that talent to make me want to kill. I was furious, he just made these outrageous accusations and detonated these little bombs into the conversation. Did he mean what he said or was it just for a reaction? I didn't care, I was too blinded by rage to even try to work it out.

'How dare you,' I hissed, for the second time that evening. 'You've ruined yourself, don't blame me. I think it's time for me to go. I told you before I'm not your wife any more, and you're not my problem. I'm working for you, and I won't allow any employer to speak to me like that.'

I know I was being dramatic, sweeping out like that, but I hadn't signed up for a holiday at Gianni's irritation villa. I was here to work, and stay professional, and the novelty of trying to piece together his mess had definitely worn off. No one can say I hadn't tried, I wanted to give Gianni the benefit of the doubt after his first outburst but I couldn't keep going back and forth like this. No – it wasn't going to work

I grabbed my coat, and putting my clutch bag under my arm, I slammed the door and headed out into the snow, setting off down the road in the darkness, powered by anger and still wearing my bloody stilettoes. Damn that man, he made me forget my wellies and I would now have to hobble back to the cottage, because I certainly wasn't going back for them. I staggered around like Bambi on ice, hoping he wouldn't chase after me and laugh at the spectacle – then again, I wished he would. I was reminded of the previous year, when I'd walked out of our home after another row where we blamed each other for everything, and nothing. I'd told him I was leaving and he let me go just like he had now. If he'd tried to stop me the first time, if he'd chased me and told me he loved me and asked to try again, things might be different, but he was as stubborn as I was and when we reached a stalemate neither of us would budge. Was this the final stalemate for us? Could we ever work together again, or even be friends? The way I felt tonight I found it hard to understand how I'd even loved him for so long – and most of all, after everything, it hurt like hell that he could still just let me go.

Chapter Eight

Tweets, Tinsel and Fire

The following morning I woke still feeling upset about how things had ended with Gianni. He was like toothache; I wanted to make it feel better, but I kept poking it and was surprised to find it still had some feeling. My own emotions were a cocktail of blame, guilt and pain. I'd thought coming here and revisiting our relationship in a different capacity would exorcise the ghosts, but seeing him had only confused me more and brought fresh pain, perhaps I would be better just leaving now before we unearthed any more hurt?

I looked out of the window onto a thick white blanket of snow everywhere and when I turned on the radio 'Silent Night' was being sung by a choir. It wasn't easy to escape Christmas even here in a quiet seaside town that only really came to life in the summer. I turned off the radio but Christmas wouldn't go away, and I thought about those first Christmases we'd spent together and how happy we'd been.

The business had been new and though I worked away a lot and Gianni worked long hours, our times together had been special.

Sometimes I'd go and help in the restaurant after I'd finished my own day job just so I could be near him. It was intoxicating to be around him then, the way he commanded the kitchen, demanding the best, and always getting it. He wasn't an easy man to work for, but the staff respected him, and many of them told me he'd softened since he'd married me.

'It used to be like walking on eggshells around here and we were all a bit jumpy,' a young commis chef said. 'But now he has you there's a permanent smile under the frown.'

I knew how difficult he could be, but at home, with just me, he was quite different. He would run me baths filled with fresh lavender to help me sleep, rub my feet when I was tired. And sometimes, even after a long day in the kitchens at work, he'd come home and make me pasta with his mama's special sauce. 'It is made with love, olive oil, tomatoes and sunshine,' he'd say, as I curled up on the sofa with a steaming bowl of comforting pasta smothered in rich, sweet tomato sauce.

Looking back, those days had probably been the happiest time of my life. But then slowly, things began to fall apart. The press began to do articles about the genius Italian chef who produced brilliant dishes from his mama's recipes and gave them a cutting-edge twist. This attention brought more customers, and even more press attention, which ultimately turned Gianni's head. He was a boy from the Tuscan Hills, his family had lived off the land for centuries and this was beyond anything he'd ever imagined when at nineteen he'd packed his bag and left his little village for London. He always thought a small Italian restaurant was his dream, but when people came along offering him bigger ideas and huge amounts of money, he was seduced by it. I think for a while I was too and we talked about a bigger restaurant, a better future for our family, and as I was five months pregnant and further than I'd ever been, we were cautiously confident of a Callidori dynasty.

I felt so well and happy and confident. This time everything felt different, the sickness had stopped earlier, I didn't feel ill all the time and everyone told me I was blooming. I cut down completely on work and spent my days reading baby magazines and obsessing about names, delivery, trimesters and whether to buy disposable or 'real' nappies. It was a whole new world, and I loved it, but with almost four months still to go before we met our baby I was impatient, so when Gianni had to go away for a few days to Italy for truffles, I stepped into the breach at the restaurant with no name.

The new restaurant didn't feel as homely as the first one, which I missed dearly, especially at Christmas, which was now fast approaching. My pregnancy had renewed my interest in the business as this was to be our 'family' restaurant and I wanted to be involved again for our kids. While Gianni was away, I called a meeting to discuss the Christmas menu and though I knew the staff humoured me because I was married to the boss, I hoped that I could prove myself to them and change things around. I was sitting at the big round table in the offices, excited about the festive food, people pitching in ideas, and delighted that everyone seemed so receptive to me, when I suddenly felt a familiar, dull, throbbing ache in my stomach. I drank a glass of water, telling myself it was nothing, and continued on with the meeting, refusing to even acknowledge what was happening. Life couldn't be this cruel, it was just indigestion, a mild tummy bug and if I ignored it, then it would go away. But when the throb became a deep, unmistakable cramp, I just knew.

I remember sitting in the plush toilets in the new restaurant's towering white block. The floor was white, the walls were white and all I could see was the ribbon of red blood, trickling along the white tiles. I was filled with pain and self-loathing, it was all my fault. I'd lost another baby, I hadn't kept our baby safe, I was a terrible mother and Gianni would have to find someone else to have his babies, someone he could trust. It sounds irrational now, but after three miscarriages I was completely irrational and unable to cope with anything.

Of course Gianni came straight back from Italy and was with me for the few days after, but he didn't know what to say or do. Everything he said I snapped at and if he tried to help me I rejected him. He made tea and it was too strong; he made his special pasta and it was too salty; he tried to tell me it didn't matter and I told him he was wrong, that it was the *only* thing that mattered and my life was over.

In the end I just said, 'Go back to the restaurant, I'm fine.' I hated myself for being like this and knew it wasn't his fault. The restaurant was his solace and it wasn't long before he was back in the middle of all the stress of running a big restaurant and I worried I was losing him. I knew it had hurt him every time we lost a baby and in my darkest times I begged him to find someone younger, healthier who might carry his longed-for child.

'I can't even think of it,' he said. 'You are the love of my life and I only want to have children with you. We will try again and

I promise you we will have our precious baby.' But even Gianni's promise couldn't make it happen, and still he threw salt over his shoulder and I heard that his mother had spoken to her priest in Italy where prayers were said and candles were lit. Even now I find it comforting to think someone prayed for my lost babies, that they had their own little candles, and their wider family acknowledged their brief existence. It's always been a great comfort to me to know our babies were loved.

The grieving was worse each time, but I never wanted to give up, and once I was back to health and feeling better in myself, we tried again. Filled once more with renewed hope, a clean slate, we knew just one hit would eradicate and even justify all the hurt that had gone before, and make it more bearable. It was impossible to believe that all that pain and loss would lead, ultimately, to nothing. But after two more years of sitting on the toilet in tears holding another negative test and visits to doctors for examinations, it felt like I'd lost myself. I'd always found it hard to get pregnant, and even then I couldn't keep them, but now the months had turned into years and the prospect of a family was quickly slipping away. We sought medical advice from different specialists but test after test revealed nothing, except now I was older and the chance of becoming pregnant and carrying a baby to term was even less. I was now almost forty and I knew time was running out. With Gianni working long hours and becoming unreachable, I turned to Cherry during those dark days. She suggested that the strain of trying for a baby was becoming too much for me. That I'd changed and that she was worried I was slipping into a depression.

'But Gianni and I desperately want a family,' I'd said. 'It's what we've always planned, always talked about.'

'It's not everything. Why don't you do something that's just for you and not about getting pregnant,' she'd said gently. 'I think it's making you ill and you need to face the fact that this might not happen, after all.'

It took my friend to show me how crazy my life had become and how this desperate need for a baby was destroying me. I'd been living with Gianni through all this, but he was so busy building a restaurant empire he hadn't noticed what was going on at home. I wonder now if perhaps he knew exactly what was going on, but couldn't face it.

The restaurant was up and running and there wasn't really a role for me any more, so I took a freelance job as an events planner with a small company. Over the next couple of years this led to bigger and better things and, like Gianni, I threw myself into work. I still longed for a baby and tested regularly with a fluttering heart and a dry mouth, but it wasn't to be, and now time had run out.

For Gianni, I think my pregnancies and the fleeting taste of fatherhood had made him want it more. Sometimes I'd catch him looking at a baby on the TV and an expression would come over his face and I knew he was thinking 'why can't that be us?' I couldn't bear to be the one to stop him being a father, and told him to leave me and find someone who could give him what he wanted. But again and again he told me not to be stupid, there was only me for him. I was still a little crazy, even at forty-three I kidded myself that it might happen again, people had miracle pregnancies in their forties, didn't they? But by my forty-fourth birthday when

I still hadn't conceived I knew my chances of holding that baby had slipped through my fingers. And as much as Gianni kept his feelings to himself, I realise now, I did the same. If I found things difficult to deal with I often pretended they weren't happening, or didn't face the problem, hoping it would right itself. I hadn't dealt with my grief or loss, not just for the babies themselves, but for the life we'd planned, the future we'd been excited for. Instead of talking it through, reliving the trauma and facing up to the cards life had dealt, I worked harder, took on bigger, more successful clients and travelled all over the world. And as much as Gianni was hiding away in his kitchen, I was running away every time I stepped on a plane. Now I know that you can't leave the grief behind, because it stays with you, the scars nestle inside your heart and become part of you. And somehow, we both had to accept the past, and move on, without forgetting what we'd lost.

I had taken this job in Appledore hoping that Gianni and I could work together as two individuals but coming here had crystallised everything, the pain and the memories. And however much I tried to convince myself we could do this in a business-like way, now I wasn't so sure.

The 'opening night,' at Il Bacio had been difficult, and the following day I couldn't face Gianni and decided it best to work from home. I wasn't even sure I was going to continue, but I'd spent the night tossing and turning, going over the past and everything we'd been through. By morning I had decided to give Gianni one more chance.

I took my laptop and went back to bed with hot coffee and warm, buttery croissants, thinking how much better this was than my usual jobs involving offices and people. The solitude was nice, and it occurred to me that I'd worked all my adult life and rarely found time in the day to do what felt good to me. I was always doing something I had to, something that needed doing. Perhaps it was time to take my foot off the gas a little?

The coffee was good, the croissants flaky and sweet and I sent a few emails, made some plans and then did something outrageous – I read a book about summertime in Paris. It felt deliciously naughty reading about blossom and sunshine and romantic walks along the glittering Seine, but who said I wasn't allowed to do this in the middle of the day? Perhaps I needed to break the rules a little and let go sometimes? Work had eaten me up over the years, I'd allowed it to swallow me whole rather than face reality, and now I had to look at who I was, where I was, and where I was heading.

Eventually, I finished reading, got dressed and, peeping outside at the white seascape, decided to explore. Before I headed out, I chopped lots of root vegetables and along with some chunks of beef put everything in the slow cooker for a wintry beef casserole later.

I was soon making my way to the windswept, snow-covered beach, the wind whipping my face, my scarf flying in the air and my heart fluttering happily. I was still annoyed about Gianni's stubbornness, but I realised now this job could be a piece of cake if I just relaxed a little. I had to stop trying to organise him and just make sure my own end of the deal was carried out and this restaurant was the success I knew it could be.

I'd never seen snow and sea in one place before and was excited to walk through it and breathe in that fresh, minty air. Having left the warmth of the cottage, the cold was now seeping into me, but I ploughed on, head down as I set off for the front, where the waves were several feet high. I stood in awe, across the road, just watching the waves batter the promenade, the carnival lights strung along the front swishing in the wind – it was hard to imagine people walking along here in shorts under an August sky.

I trod carefully along the road to avoid the icy patches. It seemed the shopkeepers had shovelled snow from the pavement so customers could enter with ease. It made me think about Gianni, and I doubted very much he'd be shovelling snow that morning – he probably still had his head in his hands. And again it crossed my mind that he would be finding all this perceived 'failure' difficult to handle. Being Gianni he would probably become more defensive and more difficult and only make things worse. He always reacted like this when he was under pressure, I always put it down to his Latin temperament, and though I didn't know his mother well, he was the only son, and clearly her prince. I reckoned he was rarely told off and nothing was too good for him as far as Mama Callidori was concerned.

I was thinking about Gianni as I wandered in and out of the few shops that had remained open in this wintry weather. The deli smelled delicious, smoked meat and sawdust laced with spices and a wonderful undercurrent of warm bread baking. I bought some tasty ham and couldn't help but be seduced by the home-made Christmas chutney. I thought the fig jam would also make a good Christmas version of scones with cream and added that to my basket. I'd just welcomed Christmas into my kitchen, and it felt good.

After my little shopping spree, I walked along the front to the Ice Cream Cafe, and went in, to be greeted by the sound of Michael Bublé singing 'It's Beginning to Look a Lot Like Christmas', and as I closed the door and turned around, I saw that the whole cafe had been decorated. It was now a Christmas confection of pink, peppermint and silver sugar canes, tinsel and a huge silver tree in the corner covered in bright pink and green baubles shaped like luscious ice cream cones. This was how a seaside Christmas should be, somersaulting waves, snowy beaches and trees with cone baubles.

Roberta was behind the counter, with a woman she introduced as her daughter, Ella – she was about my age, attractive with short blonde hair. Just like her mum, she was smiley and friendly and when I asked if it would be mad to ask for an ice cream sundae a few days before Christmas, she laughed.

'Not at all,' she said. 'We do special Winter Sundaes – and this week we're doing Christmas Sundaes.' My mouth soon began to water when she described the seasonal ice creams on offer.

'Christmas pudding, spiced fig, eggnog, Baileys, Victoria plum, damson gin,' she started. 'Those are my favourites, but there's also mincemeat, tiramisu, Christmas cake, Christmas trifle flavour with sherry and nuts and winter fruits.'

'Stop!' I said. 'I want them all.'

'Well how about a "Christmas Orgy"?' Roberta, the older lady suggested.

I smiled uncertainly, not quite sure what she was suggesting.

'That's Mum's name for it,' Ella giggled, 'but the official name is "Tweets, Tinsel and Fire". Mum's our marketing manager and she wants everyone who has this sundae to tweet a photo of it and the person who gets the most retweets will win a week's supply of sundaes. But we've had a few teething problems haven't we, Mum?'

Roberta sighed and rested her face on her hands on the counter. 'Oh Chloe, it's been a bit of a cock-up if I'm honest. I got my personal account confused with the cafe one and invited Fred from the chip shop to come over and have a Christmas orgy... and photograph it. I can't tell you what his response was, but I'm considering taking out an injunction, the man's a beast.'

Ella was laughing, 'What do you expect, Mum, you invite a red-blooded male to have an orgy, you're going to get a response!'

'Oh I know, love, but he's an old man, I'm looking for someone younger.'

'Yeah I reckon Fred's Zimmer frame and oxygen tent might get in the way of any bedroom action,' Ella laughed and went on to describe the orgiastic sundae. 'So, imagine this,' she started, 'three scoops Christmassy ice cream, on a bed of cinnamon spiced figs, with a drop of sherry, a Father Christmas beard of whipped cream, a sparkler and three wise chocolate monkeys. Sorry it has to be monkeys, we couldn't get a mould for wise men,' she added.

'That's because there's no such thing as a wise man,' Roberta quipped with a smile.

'You can say that again,' I laughed, 'and in the absence of wise men, chocolate or otherwise, I'll have a sundae with wise monkeys instead.'

As Ella made the ice cream in a fish bowl glass, I took a stool at the counter, and let myself be seduced by Michael Bublé and the decorations. I remembered that first Christmas Gianni and

I had shared here, and thought of all the other Christmases we'd spent together. Being with someone for fifteen years you become part of them, and they of you, and it's hard to lose a part of yourself. I cared about Gianni and his future and that's why I had to see this through and end it well. Even if it meant more tears and tantrums along the way, here in this cafe I could always ease the pain.

'So you're working with your ex at the restaurant?' Ella said, putting the huge sundae on the counter. It looked magnificent and I was relieved to be lifted away from the past with the sheer loveliness of the ice cream.

'Yes, I'm working for him.'

'God, you're brave, I couldn't work with my ex, he's lived in Spain for years and I still have dreams about drowning him and his new wife in their infinity pool.'

'We have our moments,' I smiled, digging into the creamy topping. 'I think we always will, but there's a bond between us and it's sometimes hard to break free. It was his dream to live and work by the sea, and when we bought Seagull Cottage a few years back I thought we might move here together one day. Then we broke up, and he's doing it alone – but I'm happy for him, I'm glad he's following his dream, and I want to help him.'

'That's great, but while you're working towards his dream, don't forget your own,' Ella said.

'I won't,' I said, shaking my head, and wondering what my dream was, and if I even had one any more? Once I'd faced the fact that babies weren't going to figure in my life, I kind of gave up on dreams, it was all I could do to get up in the morning. Then

I threw myself into work and I didn't have to think about what I really wanted, and now?

'So what's your dream?' Ella was asking, as if reading my mind.

'I'm not sure, I've spent so many years hoping for things that never happened I think I'm scared to make plans.'

'Then don't,' she said. 'Just go with the flow, take each day as it comes and live it, who said anyone had to make plans?'

'You're so right,' I said, savouring all the Christmassy flavours with a musical backdrop of Johnny Mathis now on the jukebox singing about chestnuts roasting on an open fire. I gazed around at the lovely decorations, lots of sparkles and snowflakes and the big Christmas tree.

'Lovely aren't they?' Ella said. 'Dani our assistant manager put them up.'

'Must have taken her all night,' I said, 'there was nothing here yesterday.'

'Yes, she's more energetic than any of us,' Ella laughed. 'I haven't even had time to put decorations up at home, just hoping my kids will be able to get off their phones long enough to decorate the tree at least. We've all been so busy with our new retail side of things there's been no space to breathe, let alone prepare for Christmas. I can't believe it's less than a week and I haven't shopped or anything.'

Roberta was now wiping tables and dancing to Johnny Mathis as my ears pricked up at the word retail, and Ella explained that their home-made ice creams were being sold to local restaurants.

'I think Gianni might be interested in your ice cream,' I said, though really it was me who was interested. Gianni would no doubt roll his eyes at something so simple as Baileys ice cream or as festive as Christmas pudding ice cream, but if he wanted to make this work he'd have to be more open and there's one thing I knew his restaurant customers would love – authentic Italian ice cream with a twist.

'I passed the restaurant the other day, it's very… white?' Ella said.

'Yes, it looks like an operating theatre,' I nodded.

'Well if it is, no one's going to get operated on,' Roberta said, walking towards the counter. 'I saw on the Twitter that the chef choked a food critic from Exeter with a foot-long sausage, and then he tried to stab him,' her eyes were wide with wonder and she was nodding as if to confirm this.

This was exactly the kind of thing I had tried to warn Gianni about, rumours on social media soon became fact, and this wasn't London where drama was absorbed into the atmosphere and labelled 'colour' or 'genius'. Here it was seen for what it was – an assault with a dangerous (and expensive) weapon, though where the stabbing came in I couldn't imagine.

I tried to play down the sausage incident (though worried it could be a test case – I doubted the crime had been committed before) and pushed the more positive aspect, that Gianni was open for business.

'In fact, the restaurant opened last night. I can recommend it,' I added, not mentioning the fact that all the customers complained and had to be bribed before I stormed out because he was so arsey.

'That's not a bad idea for our works' outing,' Ella said. 'I haven't had a chance to book anything yet, there'd be loads of us though – me, Mum, Sue, Dani, probably my two kids, and then their plus-ones, might be about ten of us at least.'

A booking for ten would be wonderful for Gianni, and they all seemed so lovely I knew they'd be gentle with him.

'Well, this could be the answer to your prayers, I'll book you in if you like?' I said, then wondered why I was even bothering to do this for that ungrateful git. Most new restaurant owners would be thrilled if I told them I had a ten-strong booking for Christmas week, but who knew what Gianni would say? I didn't even know if we were still speaking to each other after my dramatic exit into the snow the previous evening. Also, it was probably a little mad for me to be going around Appledore recruiting customers when Gianni didn't have any staff to help him cook or serve them. 'Actually, I was wondering do you know of anyone interested in kitchen and restaurant work? Gianni could do with taking on a few more people over the Christmas season,' I fibbed.

Ella thought a moment, then said that one of their staff members, Marco, was looking for extra work and might be interested. 'He's only young, not very chatty, but he's a brilliant baker, makes the most delicious breads and cakes, and I think a restaurant would be good for him, might give him that next leg-up.'

'Yeah, it's just that Gianni isn't easy to work with, and I'd hate for him to scare any young, vulnerable staff.' I thought it only fair to warn her if she was going to send this young man into the flames of Gianni's evil genius.

'Mum, would you describe Marco as vulnerable, or scared?'

Roberta roared laughing, '*Scary*, more like,' and Ella agreed.

'He'll be here in ten minutes to start his shift,' she said, 'see what you think,' and she and Roberta looked at each other. I couldn't quite make out what the look meant, but they were smiling, probably glad to find some proper restaurant work for this keen young lad.

A few minutes later I was still ploughing through the ice-cold deliciousness of 'Tweets, Tinsel and Fire', when 'the keen young lad' turned up for his shift.

'Hey Marco, Chloe here says a new restaurant has opened down the road and they need staff,' Ella said as he walked in behind the counter, unsmiling.

'Whoopee do,' he monotoned, his facial expression unchanging as he leaned on the counter.

'I thought you wanted extra work?'

'What I *want* is extra money,' he shrugged, and for a moment I wondered if Gianni might have fathered a long-lost child.

'Oh… I don't know how much he's paying,' I said, shocked that there was another person on earth as rude as Gianni.

'I don't work for nothing,' he said, and turned to put sundae glasses in the dishwasher.

'Then you need to tell Gianni what your fee is,' Ella said. 'You need to tell him what you want. So what do you want, Marco?'

'To be left alone,' he answered under his breath.

Ella smiled and rolled her eyes. 'Told you,' she mouthed.

'He's perfect,' I mouthed back. I was worried Gianni might upset new staff – but with Marco that would be impossible.

Ella nodded and I texted Gianni and told him I had a brilliant person for his kitchen staff, which of course Gianni didn't bother to reply to. And when I'd finished my delicious, spicy, fruity, creamy sundae laced with sherry, I said my goodbyes and promised to call Marco with details.

'Could I have your number?' I asked him.

'No, I'm here all day, call me on the landline,' he said, without a thank you or a goodbye. He clearly hated everyone. God he was perfect.

Chapter Nine

A Japanese Sausage and God's Gift to Cauliflower

The ornate iron seats where holidaymakers would sit and watch the sun set over the sea were covered in white. As I left the cafe I stood a while looking out on this beautiful but bleak snow-sea-scape and it was good to have the time and space to do this – my life was so busy away from here. Appledore was bringing me much more than I'd expected, and I'd just had a fun half-hour conversation with two lovely women, I'd eaten a fabulous ice cream and found someone to help Gianni in the restaurant. And if he could abandon his ridiculous non-menu, and accept the fact that people round here wanted good, unadulterated food, I knew in my heart we might just be able to make a success of his restaurant.

And as for me, Ella was right, I had to live for today, but recently I had begun to wonder where I fit in the world. If you'd asked me ten years ago, I'd have said I'll be a wife and mother, with two cars in the drive, a mortgage, a restaurant, holiday home in Devon and a few quid in the bank. But now I had none of those things because life always seems to have different plans for us, regardless of what we want – or think we do. I had to concentrate on the positive though, no anxiety, no loneliness, and today no Gianni. If I avoided him, I avoided stress. I'd sent him some emails, made a plan of action and until he responded, I'd done all I could do. So now I would go back to the lovely cottage and enjoy a delicious supper alone by the fire.

This past year I'd worked such long hours I'd existed on ready meals at midnight most of the time. Here I felt a sense of liberation, like I was clearing my head and starting afresh and I walked carefully up the little streets with my bags, looking forward to a quiet evening alone with my food and my books. This was such a change for me, I usually spent my evenings at events, and if I was home I would be poring over plans and accounts, making last-minute calls and sending emails. This job was an opportunity to take stock and take some time for myself for once.

Arriving at the cottage, I opened the door to be greeted by the comforting smell of casserole, and before even taking off my coat I rushed into the kitchen and lifted the lid. The warm, aromatic whack was like a drug, instantly soothing me as I stirred the rich gravy. I added roughly torn handfuls of thyme and parsley, and as I stirred through the savoury steam, my mouth watered. I may not have had Gianni's flair in the kitchen but I enjoyed hearty, homely food and having the time to cook it. Gianni and I used to eat like this back in the early years, before he decided it was too mundane and everything had to include sea slugs and chickens' feet. But give me a casserole any day. After much nurturing, I left the casserole and went to light the fire. Choosing a ghost story from the cottage book shelf, I glanced out of the window, watching the wintry afternoon turn to early evening over the seascape in all its shades of pale greys and whites. There was something in the air here that I found soothing, I felt calm, almost happy, in spite of everything.

For someone who worked on big, global events all over the world this should be an easy task. A small restaurant launch in a little fishing village in Devon should be a doddle – and it would be if it wasn't for the fact I was working with my awkward ex. But I loved Appledore, and despite the end of our relationship, it still held happy memories, scattered around the cottage like the sprinkles of good luck salt Gianni had placed in the corners all those years before.

We'd bought our first real Christmas tree together here, from the nearby garden centre. We'd hauled it from the car, and carried it into the cottage. Gianni had the front and I held the back, and as I struggled and giggled, I joked that I felt like the back end of a pantomime horse. He neighed all the way down the hall and we ended up collapsing in a hysterical heap. He'd been fun in those days, we were always laughing, when had it stopped?

I was suddenly ripped from my memories by my phone ringing and, looking at the name, saw Gianni had actually bothered to respond to my texts. That was a first.

'Hi,' I said, sitting down in front of the fire. 'Did you get my text about Marco? He wants some more information on pay and hours and stuff?' I was looking into the dancing flames, making shapes in my mind and thinking about decor for the restaurant – oranges and reds and sparkles, a Christmas tree by an open fire, a winter seascape… I was so inspired here.

'I text Marco,' he answered. 'I say to come here tomorrow and that he have to be excellent to work for me.'

'Oh that'll go down well I'm sure,' I said, looking forward to watching these two hit it off.

'This is the truth I tell him, I won't have the rubbish.'

Oh God, was I banging my head against a wall with this man after all? 'I also texted you earlier about a possible booking for ten but you didn't respond to that either.'

'I was busy.'

'Busy? By *busy*, do you mean hitting people with sausages or locking yourself in a back room while customers wait to be served Gianni?' I said, hearing myself sound like Sybil Fawlty ranting at Basil. It was definitely beginning to feel like I worked at Fawlty Towers.

He didn't respond.

'You mean you just couldn't be bothered. But you've never had to bother have you, Gianni? You're good-looking, talented, confident – and everything you've ever touched has turned to gold. But now you're going to have to pull your finger out and be nice to people – and I don't think you can do it. Hell, you can't even employ your own staff! And you've probably just lost your first one by telling him you "won't have the rubbish" before he even came for the interview, which has to be a record – even for you.'

'Why you say these things, Chloe? I am having the hard time and my finger is being pulled out. I am gritting my teeth and smiling as you tell me to do, but still they are the rubbish. I am the best and I need the best.'

'Well, all you've got right now is me, so either take it or leave it, but right now Gianni I've got better things to be doing than listening to you moan,' and I put down the phone without waiting for his response.

It was out of work time and I was quite justified in refusing to have a conversation with a stupid chef who thought he was God's gift to bloody cauliflower. Even if he was my estranged husband.

I went back into the kitchen, still cross as I sprinkled brown sugar, cinnamon and honey on the plums I'd bought earlier and popped them in the oven for roasting. I plunged my hands into flour, sugar, oats and butter, rubbing it through my fingers. The grit of the sugar and the squelch of butter was satisfying and along with the sweet, cinnamony smell now coming from the stewing fruit, I was feeling a little softer around the edges. Eventually, I placed the hot, sweet plums into an oven-proof dish, covered them in the duvet of crunchy, tasty crumble and closed the oven door. I would eat supper while my crumble cooked to crunchy perfection and the winter fruit bubbled excitedly underneath. And I would forget all about Gianni Callidori.

My mum had taught me to make crumble, and I hadn't made it for years. 'It's a family pudding,' she used to say. 'One day you'll bake it for your kids and all sit around the table arguing and laughing and eating.'

It was an image that had stayed with me, and one I clung on to even when I knew that I probably wouldn't have a family. Even now, I made the crumble knowing only I would eat it and wondering deep down what was the point? Then I reminded myself how lucky I was to even have this lovely food, when some people were starving, and was just about to serve up my delicious stew when my phone rang again.

I could see it was bloody Gianni and I wasn't in the mood but decided to answer anyway, to tell him to bugger off.

'Gianni…' I started. 'You opened last night, surely you are getting ready for this evening?' Had he forgotten?

'There are no bookings and I need to stock take for a couple of nights.'

'You mean take stock, you want to plan ahead?'

'Exactly, I was rushing, rushing, rushing… and now you say slow down and I do.'

That made sense, the previous evening had been complete chaos and I was pleased he had actually listened to my advice.

'Great, I think it's wonderful that we have a couple of days free to work on everything before you open for good,' I smiled.

'Chloe… I'm sorry,' he suddenly said.

'Gianni Callidori sorry?' I was amazed.

'Yes, because you are kind and you care about my restaurant like I do. You are the only friend I have in the world,' he replied.

I was shocked at the vulnerability in his voice. Was I really his only friend? If so, it made me want to cry.

Gianni had been popular when he was at the height of his fame, with lots of so-called friends, but he'd just been a dancing bear for others who wanted to make money out of his talent and success. It seemed no one had stuck around for him when it all crashed and burned and the money was spent. And I suddenly felt the weight of responsibility upon me, I owed it to him to be there.

'So let me help,' I said. 'I know I'm not an amazing restaurant manager or millionaire investor like you've been used to. But I've learned over the years what works, what people like. I think I know what sells, but I'll need you to listen and be co-operative. We need you to be sensitive to your customers and your staff, okay? Round here they want real food for real people,' I said, pleased with the simple but effective soundbite – I made a mental note to put that in the press release.

'Okay I will,' he said, sounding like a small child who'd just been chastised by his teacher.

'And I'll do what I can Gianni, but you need to know, if you are rude to me or to the customers, I will walk.'

'I am sensitive and I am sorry.'

'No, you're not, that's the point,' I sighed...

'Chloe. You can help me.'

I softened at this, a little chink in his armour.

'I just hope it's not too late.'

'No, I will pull out all of the fingers.'

'I suggested you pull your finger out, which means do something, get a move on, make a difference,' I explained.

'But how can I?'

I knew he didn't really get it and was most likely just agreeing with everything I said so I wouldn't leave. The only thing that really talked to him was food. 'Gianni, why don't you come round for supper tonight?'

'I remember you cooking for me when we were first married...' he started, with a smile.

'Yes, I do too,' I sighed, remembering the way he'd gently chastise me for not using enough salt, or overcooking the pasta.

I was never going to be a brilliant cook like him, it wasn't my talent, but sometimes I'd wished he'd just enjoy the food I'd cooked because I'd cooked it for him, with love.

'So supper will be nothing special so try not to turn it into an episode of *Masterchef*,' I warned, with a smile.

'I look forward to it,' he said, 'I will be giving the marks out of ten.'

I laughed, hoping he was joking. 'Great, we can talk through some ideas over supper and who knows, I might even convince you that not everyone wants snail semolina – or for their meat to be flown halfway across the world in first class.'

'It isn't,' he snapped.

'But the prices you charge would suggest that,' I said gently. 'Look, all I'm saying is if tonight you would like to share a meal and talk, I'm here.'

He mumbled something then put down the phone. I wasn't sure whether he was horrified or touched at the prospect of my simple supper, but I set the table for two just in case.

Despite the fact I wasn't absolutely sure if he would even turn up, I waited to eat supper, and while I did I put some make-up on. Having been out in the snow earlier, my hair was frizzy so I tied it up and I put a wool dress on that I'd bought for this trip. I think, subconsciously, I'd bought it with Gianni in mind, it was navy blue and Gianni always said the colour suited me. 'It brings out your beautiful eyes,' he would say in his lovely, lyrical voice. That was the Gianni I fell in love with, the one who looked into my eyes and touched my cheek, not the one who later ignored me and couldn't even bring himself to talk to me.

We'd ended up in separate bedrooms with separate lives towards the end. Neither of us could deal with the disappointment of our life, the journey hadn't been the one we'd expected. And we'd both been too stubborn to take a different route, but this was a second chance to be in each other's lives and I didn't want to lose him, even as a friend.

I put my high heels on, thinking how much Gianni used to like me in heels, and the way he used to take them off slowly and caress my feet at the end of a long day. Then I reminded myself this might be a supper shared by ex-lovers, but it was essentially a business meeting and I had to remember that. Then again, the previous evening kept drifting back, the way he'd held out my chair, the way he'd said my name.

I checked the crumble, which was now ready, and I took it out of the oven, bubbling, to stand for a while. I was compelled to make the table look warm and welcoming with a red cloth I found in the cupboard. Then I opened the back door and, in only my dress and high heels, I went out into the snow and harvested what winter foliage I could find and returned with a handful of evergreens, tied them with some ribbon I found in a drawer and put them in a glass jug on the table. I opened the wine so it could breathe and put that on there too, then found a candle and pushed it into an empty wine bottle and lit it. The table looked lovely, but I couldn't help but think it looked like a romantic meal for two. This wasn't appropriate, we were working together, so I blew the candle out. But the table didn't look the same without it, so I lit it again and was just wondering if I should blow it out again when I remembered the casserole. It would be ruined if it stayed in the slow cooker any longer, so I turned that off, and twenty minutes later I looked at my watch. An hour had passed since his call. He wasn't coming.

Chapter Ten

Chloe's Christmas Crumble

I opened up the lid of the casserole and waited for the steamy hit, but this time it was laced with sadness and disappointment. I didn't understand why, it wasn't like I wanted this to go anywhere, we were over. I was just pondering this, when the doorbell rang. I put the lid back on and ran to answer the door and opening it, I almost gasped like I was seeing him for the first time. There he was, tall and imposing on the little cottage doorstep, his hair tousled with snow, his breath steamy, how handsome he was. I had this urge to hug him, but I stopped myself, I felt slightly out of control. I'd thought I was okay, that I could have my almost ex-husband over for supper to talk business, but clearly it wasn't going to be that easy. Ever since seeing him yesterday, I'd been vaguely aware that when I came into close proximity with him my instinct was to hug him, climb into his lap, snuggle on the sofa. It was probably the smell of aftershave and garlic that reminded me of the good times we'd once had, and I had to admit I missed it all, but I had to keep myself in check because to suddenly lunge at him after all this time would be inappropriate and probably alarm him. Anyway, this was about us moving on, not recreating the past, and the best we could hope for now was to be friends.

'Come in, I thought you'd changed your mind.'

'The idiots in the wine shop don't know what they are doing…' he started and handed me a bottle of red.

'You didn't say that to them, did you?' This, I'd decided, would always be an echo of my constant refrain in our marriage. I was always worried he'd shared his feelings with whomever he was venting about. Unfortunately, he often had.

'I tell them they don't know Italian from the Chilean, and trusting in me there is the world of difference. The Chileans, they don't know how to make the wine.'

'Oh, okay,' I said, not wanting a bloody lecture on New World vs Old World wines and worrying my bottle of Australian Merlot from the deli may not cut it. I took his wine through into the living room and beckoned him to follow me.

'Chileans are one-pot cooks who drink the grape brandy…' He was still talking. There were times when you couldn't get him to say hello, but annoy him or excite him about food or wine and he didn't shut up. 'What in jeepers creepers name do they ever know about wine?' It was a rhetorical question and demanded no input from me, and I consoled myself that at least his condemnation of whole countries meant he wasn't actually offending anyone personally.

'This place she hasn't changed,' he said, opening the cloakroom door and peering in, like he was looking for the answer, a way of finding his way back. My heart dived as I saw his eyes taking in the children's wellingtons, it was a moment, no one else would have even spotted it, but I knew. 'No... this place hasn't changed,' I smiled, trying to brush away our hurt. 'It's just you and I who've changed.'

I took his coat and he sat on one of the sofas, rubbing his hands in front of the fire and I poured him a glass of wine and sat down on a nearby easy chair. To join him on the sofa felt too intimate now, that was all in the past, we were different people with a different relationship now.

'I thought you might have been staying here in the cottage,' I said as we sipped our drinks.

'No, no... too sad.' I heard the catch in his voice, the vulnerability I'd seen yesterday in the restaurant was back again.

'It's not easy coming up against the past, is it?' I said, into the aching silence. It was as if we'd been transported back to the space we used to inhabit, but we were strangers now, and in this little room there was an ocean between us.

He shook his head and sat gazing into the fire, he obviously didn't want to go down memory lane with me, so I just stared into the fire too, until I couldn't bear the silence any longer.

'So I made a casserole,' I said brightly. 'It's only simple,' I added, unnecessarily, still trying to fill the silence. This was a strange situation, me and Gianni together in this living room, drinking wine like we used to. I could handle him in the restaurant where it felt like work, but this was too intimate, old feelings were being awoken and I was beginning to wonder if my subconscious had brought me back to Appledore for something more than work.

After a few hasty sips, I suggested he take a seat at the table and I went into the kitchen, as much to get a grip on myself as to get the food ready. I took the two plates I'd left to warm in the oven and lifted the lid of the slow cooker – the aromatic smell of meat and vegetables with herbs was delicious. I was hungry and yet I wasn't sure if I could eat it, because for some reason I felt really nervous, there was something about his presence in the cottage that had overwhelmed me. He was so big, so commanding in his own quiet way, I felt like I'd never seen him before, like he was a familiar stranger. But as I walked into the living room and saw him sitting at the table – I felt a rush of warmth for him, it was lovely and so civilised to be able to break bread with someone I used to love.

As I put the plate down in front of him, he looked closely at it, sniffing like an animal discovering something in the woods. And I remembered why I rarely cooked for him, he was a perfectionist and I was scared he'd judge.

'Casserole,' I said.

'Casserole,' he said, looking at the plate of food.

He'd probably never had anything so boring in his life and I waited for him to put his fork in the steaming vegetables and meat and give his verdict. I poured more wine as he began to tackle the dish, and I was pleasantly surprised to see him actually eating it.

'Okay?' I asked, my own fork in mid-air, finally ready to take a bite myself.

'Bellissimo!' he said and went right back to it.

I almost wanted to cry with relief. Gianni wasn't criticising my food or making suggestions for change as he often had when I'd cooked for him before. Dare I say it – Gianni was either enjoying the meal or being sensitive to my feelings, and either way it felt like a gift.

We chatted during the meal and when we'd finished I offered him dessert, and he surprised me once more by saying: 'Yes I will try the Chloe dessert.'

I liked the idea of 'the Chloe dessert' and when I returned with a tray with two bowls of hot crumble and a pot of clotted cream he actually smiled. 'It's Chloe's Christmas Crumble,' I said, laughingly. 'Plums with cinnamon and cloves in mulled wine with some orange zest to give it a little citrus kick.'

He didn't respond, he just tasted, and I watched him, and despite asking him not to, he still made me feel like I was a bloody contestant on *Masterchef*, waiting for the judge to let me know what he thought.

It doesn't matter what he thinks, I told myself as I started to eat mine and the fact that his dish was empty only moments later spoke volumes.

'Let's take a comfy seat,' I said after a little while sitting at the table. I found the candlelight had an effect on his eyes and I kept looking at them, and he kept looking at mine. After a slightly awkward start I'd been surprised how easily we'd slipped back into the people we once were. Despite all our marriage woes, I think we both actually enjoyed each other's company, especially without all the baggage we'd been carrying around before we split.

The firelight was so pretty, and the crackling logs and the flickering flames were almost too romantic, like they were encouraging us to snuggle up closer. Outside the snow was falling and I just kept thinking how Christmassy it felt – even without decorations or cheesy Christmas music. We sat in silence for a while, the food now gone, we had nothing to focus on, but I kept thinking how handsome he was. Looking at him now, I could see why I had fallen for him all those years ago – and he still looked good. I wondered again about the redhead, it was none of my business but the idea of her was making me feel unhappy, very unhappy.

So in an effort not to dwell on the beautiful woman draped over his arm in the photo on Facebook, I made some small talk about his menu, then gave him another lecture on how to behave. But it was warm, the wine was flowing and I began to feel relaxed sitting there on the sofa in my navy woollen dress.

If I hadn't felt quite so relaxed I wouldn't have asked: 'Do you have a girlfriend, Gianni?' I tried to be matter-of-fact, like it didn't matter either way, but I did lean into him as I said it. That red wine had a lot to answer for.

'No,' he said, and looked away from me and into the fire.

I couldn't leave it at that, I wanted to know and if he wasn't prepared to tell me now, on a relaxed evening like this, he wouldn't tell me at all. 'I bet you've had lots of women chasing you since we split,' I heard myself say. I was intrigued, but at the same time I wasn't sure at this point if I could stand the pain to know the truth. If he said yes, I might cry and my instincts would be all over the place. Hell, I might crawl into his lap and curl up like a big cat – and this was supposed to be a business supper.

'There has been no one,' he said, like he could read my mind.

After more than half a bottle of wine, the joy that suffused me was overwhelming and my mind began to whir. Did he still have feelings for me? I had no idea. Until recently I didn't think I had feelings for him, but my instincts were saying something quite different. Clearly the wine wasn't having the same effect on him, because he seemed uncomfortable.

'I hear *you* have a boyfriend,' he suddenly said. He was staring into the flames, not looking at me.

'No, I don't.'

'You have been out with a man, I see the Facebook.'

'Oh he was nice, nothing special.' I wasn't going to let on that my Facebook photos were mostly elaborate lies made up to let him think I'd moved on and was having a fabulous time. It wouldn't do any harm for him to know he wasn't the only man who'd ever found me attractive. He didn't need to know that the handsome man cuddling up to me in those photos was more interested in *Star Trek* than me.

'Is he why you left me?'

'Gianni, we've been over this a million times,' I sighed. 'The guy in the photos was just… a guy. We went out a few times long after you and I had split up. I left because I was unhappy, because *we* were unhappy.'

'But I always think there must be someone else.'

'No that's not true, I had to get away, I felt like we were suffocating each other. I was still struggling, still coming to terms with how our lives had moved in different directions… and I needed to face my own future. I'd spent most of my adult life planning for motherhood, Gianni, and when it didn't happen I had to take some time out to think about it. I've spent years avoiding pregnant friends, toy shops, baby linens, Christ there was a time when I couldn't even watch a commercial for nappies without wanting to slash my wrists. Even now, when I think I'm okay, I sometimes find it hard to look in a pushchair, to congratulate someone on their "special news", to walk through a park in case I see a little one and start to wonder, would our baby have looked like that?'

'Oh Chloe, I know this… and I feel your pain like a knife in my own chest. I saw how you walk away with the tears in your eyes when you see a baby in the restaurant. I hurt too.'

'I know you do, but I was the one with the problem, the one who couldn't keep hold of our babies. I couldn't do the most basic human thing and keep them safe until they were ready for the world. I failed. I always said you should find someone else and have the family you always wanted, it's not too late for you.'

'But this was *our* problem, not yours, but you always making it your problem and you shut me out. You wouldn't listen to me, you keep saying "go get yourself another woman, Gianni", like I am a cat or a dog. Don't you understand? I didn't want *anybody's* family – I wanted *ours*.'

And in that moment I realised we'd both turned away from each other, it wasn't Gianni closing in, it was me shutting him out, or so he thought. I'd never meant for him to feel like that, but I could see how me constantly telling him to find someone new and have children with them could be perceived as cruel. When you decide to have a child it's not just because you want that child, it's because you love someone enough to want *their* child. Gianni was right, it hadn't been just my problem, it was his too. Gianni may as well have been impotent, because despite desperately wanting children, he only wanted them with me so couldn't have them.

'I'm sorry…' I said. 'I've been selfish and only really looked at this from my perspective. I knew you wanted children, but I'd been so wrapped up in my "flawed body", I didn't see what you were going through.'

And we both looked into the flames together, but apart, locked into our own thoughts. It was still difficult for us to share our feelings about what happened, both still afraid to open up the wound and allow what happened to hurt us all over again.

'I really must be going,' he suddenly said, and I saw the tears in his eyes as he stood up.

I understood, and followed him into the hall, taking his coat off the hook and handing it to him, our hands brushing, neither of us reacting. He put the coat on.

'I wish we could talk more…' I said, opened the front door and allowed Gianni to walk past me.

As he turned to look at me, he touched my arm, then reached round with both arms and hugged me.

'I can't talk, Chloe. I am supposed to be the strong one,' he said, and tears immediately sprung to my eyes. I felt a sting in my heart knowing how much this had hurt him too, but before I could say anything he mumbled something like thank you and set off down the little path. I stood in the doorway alone, shivering with cold and aching for the past, as he opened the gate and was gone.

Chapter Eleven

Chocolate Hearts and Sour Cherries

The evening had not gone the way I'd intended; what I'd intended to be a friendly reunion with business thrown in had turned into something very different. Now, the morning after, as I contemplated what was said, I wondered if I should have played things differently. I felt like Gianni and I had finally, if briefly, shared our real feelings and I'd seen everything in a different light. 'I am supposed to be the strong one,' he'd said, and that had been true throughout our marriage. I'd thought he didn't feel the same pain as I did, but maybe he'd just been fighting it? I knew he'd wanted to be a father, but was so locked into my own agony I'd never realised it had hurt him as much as it had hurt me. It had been tough for me to go through all that alone and I'd resented the fact that I felt he hadn't been there for me. But the truth was, I wouldn't allow him to grieve with me, I kept it all to myself and I wouldn't let him in.

I was worried about Gianni so I called him, left a message to say I hoped he was okay then tried to throw myself into work, sending emails, writing a restaurant press release and trying to put the pain behind me.

A little while later, I set off into the snow and after a long walk on the beach among the white drifts and the icy water, I gazed in a few of the little shop windows on the front. Many of them were adorned with Christmas decorations: simple snowflakes, lovely pieces of driftwood, glass fishermen's floats in turquoise and white sparkly starfish. I went in and bought a bag full of the ornaments, all white and silver with sparkles and accents of turquoise – I'd never done a seaside Christmas window, and I hoped Gianni would let me loose on the restaurant. I could really bring that white space to life and make it feel Christmassy without ignoring the fact that we were by the beach. I was salivating as I paid the shop owner.

Once home I left the bag of fabulous decorations in the hall, got out of all my snow-soaked clothes and ran a lovely warm bath.

It was ironic really, after my third miscarriage, I believed I could never be happy again, and the only way to move forward was to leave my marriage. I hoped in doing that I could leave the pain behind, but you don't, you carry it with you because it's part of who you are, and it changes you, it leaves a permanent mark on your heart. The daily, sometimes hourly little stabs of pain had eased slightly, but they would never go away, nor would I want them to because they were reminders of the little lives I'd carried for a short time. I had no little hands to hold, no shoelaces to tie, no baby knees to plaster – I just had my pain, and now and again it tugged at me like a child's hand and for that I was grateful.

I lit a few candles, took a glass of wine into the bathroom with me and was just wondering why anyone bothered to have a relationship when being alone was such bliss when my phone rang. It was in the living room, and I was determined not to answer it and have this lovely 'me' time ruined, but then it rang again and I had to forfeit my Jo Malone bubbles just in case there was some kind of emergency. Gianni had been at the restaurant alone all day, anything could have happened.

Eventually, I found the phone and picked it up to see it was Gianni.

'Hi, are you okay?' I said gently, still moved by his emotion the previous evening, and aware things were still raw.

'I'm okay. Where are you?'

'I'm at the cottage.' It's my turn to cook for you,' he said.

I softened at this, 'That's kind, Gianni, but really you don't have to do that, you've got enough on with the restaurant. I've been worried about you.'

'No worry about me, I am strong.'

'I know you are, but even strong men have to let go sometime.'

'I cook and that is my escape.'

That was the problem, he'd escaped into sizzling sauces and sweetbreads and driven himself mad.

'I will create a sublime meal for you from my new Christmas menu – yes, I have the menu!'

I had to smile at that; he was beginning to make some changes then, after all.

'So, you come to the restaurant, let me cook for you?'

'Snail semolina?' I asked suspiciously.

'No.'

'Sweetbread semolina?' I enquired. 'Surely there are a few chickens' feet knocking around?'

'No.'

'Okay then, I'm there,' I said, with a giggle. I was relieved that he seemed happy, mischievous even. I'd been so worried he'd allow the sadness from the past to pull him back, but if anything, he seemed to have recaptured the old Callidori Christmas energy.

'How long will you be?' he asked.

'I'm standing here in a towel, I may be half an hour or so,' I said.

'But I am freezing the piss off down here.'

'What? Down where?'

He answered by knocking on the cottage door. 'I am here, I collect you in the snow to take you to Christmas menu.'

'Oh God, Gianni,' I said giggling into the phone as I stomped down the stairs and opened the door.

'You mustn't drop the towel at least,' he said, walking inside as I stepped back to let him through and shut the door to keep the heat in.

I got dressed, threw on my coat and grabbed the bag of decorations as I left the cottage and climbed into his car.

Arriving back at the restaurant, we walked into complete emptiness.

'Tonight you are the customer,' he said.

'Oh good, am I doing a test-drive?'

'No you're tasting the food.'

I didn't tell him that was the same thing, but instead decided to make the most of the empty restaurant by waving my bag of decorations at him. 'Gianni, I thought these would look lovely in here,' I said, looking around the dining room.

'What are they?'

'Christmas decorations.'

'Chloe, you think this looks like a bloody Nando's?' he said.

'No, I think it looks like a bloody hospital.'

He didn't answer, just nodded reluctantly, but I saw a smile creep onto his face as he headed for the kitchen, holding open the weird hole in the wall for me. No one else would ever dream of being so critical of 'the great Gianni's' restaurant, but here I was again affectionately reminding him he wasn't the most brilliant restaurateur that ever walked the earth. Because this was a man who needed his bubble bursting every now and then, it was good for him, and I only had his best interests at heart.

Once in the kitchen he seemed like a lost child standing in this huge space alone. Here was everything he needed, except he couldn't do a thing because he had no staff, and no customers.

'Sit and I will show you my plans,' he said, handing me a typed list of dishes. I was impressed, he'd listened to my advice and given this some thought.

Gianni began to take huge sacks of vegetables from the cool storage, and I ran my finger along the list looking for anything difficult or weird, but was pleasantly surprised and excited to see 'Mary's Winter Casserole'.

'Ahh you named it after my mum,' I said, feeling almost tearful.

He smiled, as he carried a sack of sweet potatoes into the kitchen his sleeves were rolled back and his muscles were flexed and I had to look away. I'd always found him attractive, but I didn't want to confuse lust with anything else, I was conflicted and confused about my feelings and felt very vulnerable. Now in this kitchen with those muscles was not the time to be making any life decisions about what happened next.

'I never met your mama, but I know she taught you how to make the casserole, and so she taught me too,' he smiled.

I was touched, and felt my eyes prick with tears, Mum would have loved to see her casserole on a menu. And watching him rushing round the kitchen smiling, excited about the food and his restaurant, I think she would have loved Gianni too.

'You're cooking simple, Italian dishes – you're starting again, you're Gianni the brilliant young chef I knew way back,' I said, feeling hopeful and just a little bit proud of him.

'You think I change?' he asked, he seemed surprised, but sometimes we don't see changes in ourselves.

'Yes, the real Gianni got lost in 2008 somewhere between rustic cuisine and molecular gastronomy. You made real food in our restaurant in the back streets of Islington and then you bought a bloody spaceship in Hockney, invited all the terminal trendies and artists – then up you went in a puff of culinary smoke. You became impossible, and quite frankly so did your food. Now I feel like you could find yourself again here with this good Italian home cooking.'

'Yes but this time we make the English and Italian food, your mama's casserole with the English root vegetables, my mama's pasta with the fresh tomatoes and garlic, real Italian olive oil… delizioso.'

I was delighted to be part of this, and at the same time wondered if he was suggesting more, was this his subtle way of introducing the idea of me sticking around a little longer? If so, I wasn't sure how I felt about it. I had to admit my role here was beginning to feel blurred; was I the estranged wife, the Restaurant Events Planner, just a friend or all three? Had I been naïve to think I could just come back here and be friends or colleagues and nothing else, because however much I tried to keep this business-like, Gianni and I had once been in love, and had a shared history that couldn't be ignored. I hadn't seen him so happy for a long time, he was returning to his roots and this was where his heart lay, but I was beginning to question my own heart. The things I thought made me happy, like my career and a future travelling the world didn't excite me any more, I'm not even sure they ever did, they were an escape. But now my heart was tired and ready to lie down, but where?

As I watched him chopping sweet potato, I could see the rush of blood in his cheeks, he seemed enthusiastic, excited even, which wasn't an emotion I'd associated with him for a long time. One of us had definitely found what he was looking for.

'You're ready for this change, aren't you?' I said.

'Yes, this has to work and I'm trusting your advice,' he smiled. 'I'm trusting my Nonna's exquisite garlic bread with the secret ingredients too,' he added.

'So many family members involved in your menu, Gianni,' I laughed. And then, spotting another of my dishes on his list, 'Chloe's Christmas Crumble', I sighed, 'Ah you're including my pudding too?'

'With a couple of leeetle changes,' he said, opening a cupboard and taking out jars of cloves and spices. 'I cook my plums in the mulled wine too, and I add the ginger to the crumble – spicy,' he winked and then he opened the fridge, taking out handfuls of fresh vegetables, meat and fish and started chopping and frying.

Sitting here watching him cook, helping with menus, took me back to that first restaurant, when we were poor and happy and the air was hot with garlic. And from here the past didn't look as painful and hopeless as I'd thought it had been.

'So what can I do?' I asked. 'Let me help.'

He suggested I peel vegetables, 'But first the most important ingredient is the red wine,' he said, pointing to a bottle on the side. 'I bring it from the cellar, it's the Chianti from Gianni's… there were a few bottles left when we moved.'

'I never realised you'd saved them,' I said, recalling the gallons of Chianti we'd drunk together in the restaurant during those first few years. I'd forgotten how sentimental he could be. Perhaps he'd missed it more than I'd realised?

'It is shit wine, Chianti is made from the rubbish… but it takes me back eh?' he said, and I smiled as his words popped my rose-tinted romantic bubble. I opened the bottle and poured a couple of glasses And put his near where he was working and settled on a stool near the counter to sip mine. 'Remember that first Christmas at the restaurant? We opened on Christmas Eve and were both so nervous so we decided to have a glass of this first?' I said.

He smiled, and stopped chopping for a moment, the memory softened his face as he lifted his glass and took another sip. 'And then we decided to have another…'

'And another…' I laughed.

'I feel so happy, I was dancing with customers and everyone thinking I was the lovely guy,' he laughed at the memory.

'Yeah, it was a great night,' I smiled, 'and you *were* the lovely guy,' I looked at him as I said this, and he smiled back, appreciatively. 'And when everyone had gone home, we closed the restaurant and drank and danced some more,' I sighed, remembering the quiet aftermath of a busy night, flickering candlelight, wax running down the bottles. And despite our feet hurting so much from a twelve-hour shift, we both wanted to slow-dance around the empty tables. 'We were both young and invincible back then,' I smiled, and we looked at each other for a long moment, both remembering how we used to be. 'To the hungry years,' I said, and we smiled at the same time, our eyes meeting, my heart catching a little as our glasses clinked.

I continued to peel carrots in between sips and thought about the madness of the situation. Looking at that menu, my own food had certainly inspired him, and he'd listened to me like he'd used to when we'd opened Gianni's. How ironic that, on the brink of divorce, we were finally a team again.

Gianni continued to cook, while I drank, and I was feeling good, relaxing and beginning to thaw when there was a slight rumpus in the dining room.

'Who is that?' he said, grumpy at being disturbed.

'I'll get it – could be guests or burglars?' I said as I left the kitchen, and I swear I heard him laugh.

I dared hope it might be guests and rushed through to see because Gianni was lost in his mists of garlic and thyme, and being used to having 'people' to answer doors for him clearly had no intention of leaving his stove.

Running into the dining room, I was shocked to see Marco, standing there in all his dark, glowering glory, covered in snow. I'd completely forgotten that today was Marco's interview, but given that he had turned up tonight, I guessed that things couldn't have gone too badly; though you couldn't tell by looking at Marco.

He was as grumpy and uncommunicative as he had been when I'd met him at the cafe, and didn't flicker a smile, or even a moment of recognition.

'So you got the job?' I said, following him through into the kitchen. He gave a sort of grunt, okay he wasn't jumping for joy, but I doubted Marco ever jumped for anything. I was beaming, so pleased they'd found each other, and I looked from Gianni to Marco with a big smile on my face. Neither of them looked at me or each other and as Marco wordlessly took off his coat and put on his apron I just knew I'd been right, this was a match made in hell. It couldn't have been a better fit. 'So what are you cooking for me?' I asked Gianni, who to be fair, did smile vaguely in my direction. It was a half-smile and could have been a mild stroke, but I took it and smiled back encouragingly.

'I make the peasant food you like,' he said, with a wink.

'Oh you spoil me with your charm and flattery,' I laughed, answering him back like I used to when we were together.

Both Marco and Gianni were now busy at the stove, not speaking, not apparently communicating on any level, and yet, they were working together. Marco had fit right in.

Pleased with my industrial matchmaking, I wandered the kitchen admiring the finish. 'This really is beautiful,' I ran my hands along thick, Italian marble, was almost blinded by the brilliant white of the wall tiles, everything shone. It was warm now the ovens were on and the smell of spice and garlic coming from his cooking was heady, I hadn't eaten for several hours and was hungry. 'I hope that minuscule handful of pasta isn't for me,' I said.

Gianni looked up just as he was about to drop it into the boiling water.

'Double it,' I said. 'Remember those huge bowls your mama used to serve her pasta in? Eat, eat, she'd say, she would be horrified to see a portion so small, forget your fancy London ways, get back to your mama's kitchen,' I said.

He frowned, then shrugged, as if to say I was right, took another handful and threw it in, then reached for a bunch of basil and started tearing at it.

I leaned on the counter watching him and he suddenly stopped and said, 'I tear the basil because she doesn't like metal, it affects her taste if you use knife.'

'You knew what I was going to ask,' I smiled, and felt that old connection again, as fleeting as ever, but it was still there.

While he cooked, I made notes, so I could include highlights on the menu, and also in any press releases, as Gianni told me about the temperatures he was using to fry the steaks. Then, with several spoonfuls of cream, crushed peppercorns and a few dramatic sprinkles of spices thrown from a great height, he made a peppercorn sauce. The steam from the pan mushroomed into the air, filling the kitchen with a tangy, savoury aroma, laced with garlic.

I picked up my phone and snapped a picture of him cooking, mad hair, swirling steam, his hand high throwing pepper onto the pan, making it sizzle.

'That looks great!' I said, my mouth salivating as he threw salt over his shoulder in deference to the devil.

'A cliché, but the peasants love peppercorns with their steak,' he said, with a twinkle in his eye.

'Gianni,' I said, warningly, 'remember your promise that you won't be rude to or about people?'

He shrugged and from across the counter offered me a taste from the spoon, which felt very intimate and familiar.

'That's delicious.' I almost added 'babe' and then remembered how embarrassing that would have been, but how easy it was to slip back into the old dynamics. 'It's simple food and people will love it.'

'I have the squid ink shortbread with sea slug paté,' he started.

My heart sank. 'You know what, Gianni, I don't think we need it.' I waited for the rant, the rail against the world, the shouting, but instead he just laughed.

'I joke with you,' he said as he continued to laugh.

'Ah, you must tell me when you joke,' I said. 'I'm not used to it.' He'd certainly started to melt a little. Perhaps he felt better after talking the evening before, he certainly seemed more relaxed, sharing his feelings with me had finally cleared the air somehow. We were both easier in each other's company, like we'd stepped out of the marriage and the impending divorce and all the baggage that brought with it – and we both were beginning to understand each other again.

It may have just been the heat, but he was definitely glowing. Cooking enlivened him, his cheeks were pink from the oven warmth and his eyes lit up into that familiar amber fire I'd seen so many times before when his enthusiasm for dishes from home lit him from within. As someone who often seemed out of place in society, Gianni was always comfortable in a kitchen, and this was quite a kitchen!

I watched in awe as Gianni barked words, and Marco did as he asked without acknowledging his instructions, and it all came together. It was like a dance, the two of them doing their own moves gracefully, dipping and swerving, never colliding. One swooped across the stove grinding pepper, just avoiding the other as he leaned over to reach for a pan. Marco lugged boiling water across to the sink, narrowly avoiding a scalding incident as Gianni moved swiftly in the opposite direction. It was pure culinary choreography, and ultimately reached a climax in large plates of steaming food.

Marco immediately set off washing up like he'd been born to this and I was about to grab a fork and start sampling, when Gianni said, 'No, the dining room, we aren't at home now.' He'd obviously felt the same familiarity of the two of us in the kitchen reliving the past.

'I want you to taste and test and we will talk, in the best seat in the house,' he said, as we carried a tray each into the dining room. He seemed to be so much more cheerful and agreeable than I'd ever seen him as we took the window table and he sat down opposite me to eat.

He and Marco had made an array of small dishes, all winter ingredients, all local, and all looking delicious. Once I'd established the portions would be bigger 'on the night', I tucked in, feeling now like it was me judging him on *Masterchef*, as Gianni eagerly watched me eat, waiting for my comments. As I took my first bite, my taste buds were overwhelmed. It was delicious, just like those meals Gianni had used to cook for me, but if possible, even better.

'Mmm this casserole is lovely, but it's richer and has more depth than mine, what is your secret?' I asked (I could hear myself relaxing into flirting mode and desperately trying to stop, but there was something in his food that made me feel warm and... well, flirty).

'A secret is a secret,' he responded with a twinkle in his eyes, a smile playing on his lips; like someone I didn't know, he was different, in a good way. This felt weird, yet wonderful, like a first date, as though we were discovering each other for the first time. I could see this amused him.

'Gianni, you have to tell me your secret,' I said again.

'Okay, okay, but it has to be between just you and me,' he said this in a low voice, leaning across the table his face quite close to mine. I held my breath, and felt a frisson in my chest, and it wasn't anything to do with the secret ingredient. In fact, sod the secret ingredient, I was suddenly longing for him to kiss me and roll me around on the countertop – which if nothing else may have provoked a reaction from Marco – or not?

We were both facing each other across the counter, his breath on my face, I could almost feel the whiskers, the warmth of his lips close to mine. The dynamic between us was changing again, the past was being healed, all the resentments and perceived slights and misunderstandings bundled up in red ribbons and offered back to us like a Christmas gift. And I felt myself being drawn to him, like that first Christmas when he handed me little Snowflake in the doorway of Harrods.

'Coffee,' he whispered into my ear, his hot breath on my lobe; my whole body felt like it was disintegrating. 'My secret ingredient... is brewed... leftover... coffee.'

'I'd never have guessed,' I almost whispered, never taking my eyes from his. What was going on here? Were we actually flirting like teenagers after the failure of fourteen years of marriage?

'It geeves richness and layers of the flavour,' he said, looking into my eyes, his own revealing a secret and welcoming me in. And just when I found myself there, he spoke again. 'Not too much,' he added, his lips moving slowly, his voice still rich with the promise of late nights, red wine and smoky Italian bars. My eyes followed his fingers as he indicated a small portion between finger and thumb. 'Coffee should only enhance, not dominate.' I recalled those fingers brushing my lips, my breasts, moving down my body and... I had to stop thinking and try to concentrate on what he was saying.

'Not dominate,' I repeated, not thinking about the way candlelight made his eyes glitter like Christmas tinsel.

With that he sat back, pleased with his performance, leaving me with my eyes no doubt shining at him. God he was good. If I'd smoked I'd have laid down on the counter and lit a post-coital cigarette.

And as we sat in the window, the stark, white table throwing up light onto our faces and showing the colours and textures of the dishes, I saw a different man to the one I thought I knew. Perhaps he wasn't the arrogant, annoying, superficial man I'd considered him to be in recent years. The soft centre was still in there, but perhaps it had just been buried by the sad things that had happened to us.

'So, what other secrets do you have?' I asked, wanting to know more about this new Gianni.

'No secrets,' he smiled, 'not from you, Chloe.'

And my heart was filled up with something quite delicious and intoxicating – it felt like hope.

'It's all about theatre with you, isn't it?' I said, recovering myself quickly. 'There's so much more to you than meets the eye.'

'Isn't everyone more than what we see?'

'Yes, but everything you do is a performance, and last night I saw the old Gianni for the first time in a long time. I saw the vulnerable, kind, loving man I married.'

'You flatter me,' he answered, and the look on his face said it all, he was delighted by my compliment. 'I should be an actor,' he added, 'I have the talent.'

'Ah now you're back to performance, Gianni,' I said with a smile.

'I always perform, it hides the sadness,' he sighed.

'I know, I think I'm beginning to understand what drove us apart, it wasn't just about babies – it was the way we reacted to the hurt.'

'You are right… your hurt was so deep I couldn't reach inside and smooth it over. I couldn't touch you or make it better, and it killed me.'

'And I thought you were detaching yourself from me. I thought you were starting to move away from me because I couldn't give you what you wanted: a family.'

'We were our family, and no one else could give me anything, I only wanted you and whatever came with you, better or worse.'

I felt a deep sadness as always when thinking about our past, but this time I was also filled with a little sparkle. Gianni was everything I'd hoped he'd be when I first began to fall in love, he hadn't deserted me or chosen an alternative, he just hadn't been able to articulate his emotions and show me how much he cared back then. Gianni had continued to love me and I'd walked away, and now I didn't want to, but what did this mean?

Moving onto a dessert plate, he gently cracked the surface of the chocolate heart. The ice cream centre revealed itself and deep cherry liquor wept onto the white plate.

'This is me when you leave,' he said, gesturing towards the plate, his playfulness now replaced by melancholy.

'So why didn't you tell me, why didn't you beg me to come home, call me and tell me how you felt?'

'Because I think you have the lover, that you're having ride of your life with…'

'Gianni, I left because we were both unhappy, but you always come back to this. I think you find it easier to believe I left you for someone else than believe something was wrong with us.'

'Perhaps, but I couldn't walk away from us, and you did and I can't understand…'

'That was our problem, we'd grown so apart we didn't understand each other any more, and when we turned around to look for each other – we'd gone.'

I looked into his face, and I wanted to see the fire in his eyes again. We'd been through so much, and instead of our pain bringing us closer it had torn us apart. I knew he didn't want to dwell on the past and he'd never found talking about emotions easy, but this was a kind of breakthrough that we were addressing our marriage breakdown. I'd thought this was all over, that we were in the past, but I wasn't so sure any more, and if this wasn't all done, did I really want it all over again?

I put my spoon into the mess of chocolate and cherries and brought it to my lips as he watched me intently. The taste was exquisite, the pleasure of warm chocolate and the pain of sour cherries danced on my tongue.

'Chloe, the food, look how beautiful she is, it needs the light,' he said, pointing at the deep scarlet juice on my plate. It was time to move on from our conversation for now, and take it to a more comfortable space… food.

'Exactly, I agree, we need big house lights to see the food, but softer lighting to eat – I have an idea.' I stopped mid-sentence to appreciate another mouthful of sour cherries and chocolate, before continuing. 'Let's tell big porkies to the press, they've used you over the years for great stories about smashing plates and throwing things at customers, so this time, let's use them. We'll tell them you come from an acting dynasty,' I said, holding up my arms in a grand gesture and he smiled, he liked this. 'Your mother was an amazing cook, but also an actress, and you're a culinary phenomenon who loves theatre,' I joked, but he nodded sagely, in agreement. 'So when you do an interview with the local paper…'

'You mean with the ass pig who criticised my food?'

'The very same. Then let's say you turn the lights up for the beginning of each course, like theatre lights. And just like in the theatre, the audience/ customers can see their seats, see what they're eating, then the lights go down for the performance.'

Being Gianni, he loved the drama of this idea and clapped his hands together. It felt like he was back, *we* were back, his talent and my ideas coming together again.

'I've never seen you do that before,' I smiled. 'It makes a pleasant change from the Gianni shrug.'

'I apologise, I'm not the fun to be with person.'

'No, I'd like to say you blow hot and cold, but you just blow cold and freezing!'

He was looking at me, and without taking his eyes from mine he took a sip of his wine. 'I am happy here now, with this food, and I have my restaurant…' he started.

'Good, I'm glad you feel that your life is coming together,' I said, wondering for a brief moment about his real life, and how that was coming together. Was he single again? Was there still a redhead sweeping through with her endless legs and no doubt gymnastic ability in the bedroom? But I reminded myself quickly this was not my business any more, and yet I couldn't resist a little prod for information.

'So you're happy in all areas of your life?' I asked, blatantly.

'I am, and I have the very good reason for it.'

To my surprise, my heart dipped slightly, well it was more of a swoop followed by instant nausea. Not the redhead?

'Yes I am very happy in all the areas, because I have made a note of the names of the people who give me the one-star reviews on the Tripping Advisor and I will hunt them down and then I will kill them,' he said.

I was alarmed for a moment, but to my relief, he laughed.

'I fool you with the jokes, ah? Gianni isn't always so sad and boring, you know I can have the funs too.'

I took a large gulp of wine and smiled at him, glad he didn't put his happiness down to another woman. I swallowed the wine and returned to the chocolate heart, which was a little like my own... broken and messy. Could it ever be mended?

Oh, but the dishes Gianni served me that evening were exquisite, and despite his inner sadness I knew he was invigorated just by the quality of his cooking. The flavours were amazing, vegetables were crisp and fresh alongside little bowls of warming, aromatic stews, thick, juicy steaks smothered in jaw-achingly tasty sauces. The salads were herby with clever dressings that tasted of sunshine and Christmas in one mouthful.

Gianni needed someone to tell him how good his food was, because though he'd never admit it, his ego had taken quite a battering. What happened with us had made him feel like a failure and then his business had taken a hit too.

'I pull out the fingers eh?'

'Yes, you've definitely pulled your finger out,' I smiled, taking a bite of steak that was cooked to perfection and melted in my mouth along with a rich, salty Stilton sauce that made my mouth tingle.

And the puddings... 'Oh my God, I have never tasted baked apples like this before,' I sighed, pushing the chocolate heart aside to bite into warm, sweet fruit soaked in fig syrup and dancing with cinnamon cream. 'It's Christmas on a plate,' I said as I nibbled on white chocolate and cranberry bread and butter pudding, and Eton Winter Mess. 'This is so delicious and as long as the portions are big enough for grown-ups, you have a winner.'

Once I'd finished and we'd discussed each dish in detail, the pros and cons, the cost and profit and ultimately the tastes, I sat back. I was feeling more relaxed in his company than I had for a long time. He seemed miles away and I didn't feel comfortable continuing in silence, so I said: 'You're always very quiet Gianni, you never give much away.'

'I give too much,' he said, and I wondered what he meant, so I kept talking, hoping to tease some more out of him.

'Are you talking about us?'

He nodded, 'I give you everything, Chloe, and still you walk away… and now we have the lovely time together it makes me sad.'

'Me too,' I said, looking away. 'I'm sorry I hurt you, Gianni,' I said, gently, 'I was so wrapped up in my own emotions, my hormones were all over the place and…'

'I have the hormones too, you know,' he said, a little joke.

I smiled, and touched his hand. 'I know, and I just wish we'd talked back then, before it was too late… do you think it's too late, Gianni?'

'I don't know if it is too late, Chloe…' he started, and my heart landed on the shiny white floor. I was surprised at how disappointed I was at his half-hearted reaction to 'us'. Had I hoped he might be overcome, declare his undying love and we'd live happily ever after? Had I misread the vague and confusing signals?

He was about to add something, he looked awkward and I couldn't help but wonder if there was someone else after all, when Marco whipped open the secret door. He'd been washing up in the kitchen and I'd almost forgotten he was there, and gasped as he stormed past us, through the restaurant, opened the outer door, slammed it and disappeared into the night.

'Has he just walked out?' I said, panicking now that Gianni had lost his only member of staff.

'Yes, why you ask me you saw him?'

'Yes, I saw him leave, but he didn't say goodnight. Has he just left his job, is he angry?'

'No, why should he be?'

'He just walked out... without saying goodbye.'

'Chloe, what do you want him to do? You want the kissing on the cheeks and the thank yous. He has finished his work, he leaves to go home. Why take up more time saying goodbye?'

'Oh I'm sorry, I forgot we are in the Gianni Callidori restaurant of HR excellence where workers are cherished,' I said.

'I pay him, what more does you want, I give him a big kiss at the end of his shift?'

I rolled my eyes. Marco had burst the bubble, and it was probably as well. I'd had a few drinks, and it wasn't wise to start talking about regrets and asking if it was too late for us. I wasn't even sure of my own feelings, what did I want? And yet, there was something about the past couple of days that had drawn me in. I'd enjoyed being together, working for the same goals, and I loved that 'us against the world' feeling. Had he felt it too, or had Gianni moved on? Was I being naïve to think we could have that again? Now clearly wasn't the time, and I would see how I felt in the cold light of day when I was sober before I went digging around in his tied-up bag of feelings.

'So what next for the restaurant?' I asked, a rhetorical question, it was a segue back onto safer ground. 'I reckon we'll have to get leaflets printed and start dropping them off everywhere.'

'Oh so vulgar.'

'No it's not, it's what most restaurants do or you could buy a page in the local paper.'

'I won't be paying for them to feature my food, they are lucky to have me here.' We were back to grumpy Gianni, gone was the soft, loving one I'd fallen for once upon a time.

'Okay so in that case we need to get the paper on board. First you have to make up to the critic you upset… the one you attacked. Then you do a competition, and hopefully they'll put it in the paper, offer a prize… something simple like "what's the bird everyone eats at Christmas"?'

'Seagull?'

'No,' I said wearily.

'Holy mackerel, I was joking,' he said, unsmiling.

'Oh, please tell me when you're going to make a joke because as I said before it isn't obvious.'

He smiled.

'Anyway, as your prize you can offer a romantic Christmas dinner for two over the festive period.'

'But everyone will say the answer is the sodding turkey and then I have to give away the hundreds of bloody tables.'

'Are you joking again?'

'No.'

'Okay, so of course everyone will say "the sodding turkey", but that will hook them in because they'll think, that's easy and lots of people will enter. And you ask them to pop a postcard through the door with the answer on and then you pick one at random… or you tweet it,' I added, thinking of Roberta's tweets for the cafe.

Then I smiled to myself as I remembered Fred from the chippy thinking all his birthdays had come at once with what he thought was a tweeted invite to a Christmas orgy.

'You are pretty when you smile,' he said, suddenly.

'Thanks,' I nodded my head. He'd never been one for compliments and this was a big thing, but now I wasn't sure if I was reading too much into it all. Did he want more, or was this just Gianni trying to say what he thought I wanted him to? He still confused me, perhaps he always would. 'I'm just trying to think of free publicity, even the Ice Cream Cafe have a publicity manager, she seems to know all about Instagram and Twitter,' I said, trying to drag myself away from the intimate and move back onto the business level.

'I don't have the Twitter, my publicity manager Kim does all that.'

'Not any more apparently, you haven't tweeted for weeks,' I said scrolling down my phone on his Twitter timeline.

'Ah.'

'Did you upset her?' I asked, already knowing the answer and cringing while I waited for it.

'She has no manners.'

'Oh, that must have been awful for you to work with someone who was impolite,' I said.

He nodded, seriously. Even after all those years with me, there were times when he still didn't get sarcasm, I couldn't decide if it was due to the language or the lack of self-insight. Gianni was a lost cause... problem was, I'd always been a sucker for a lost cause.

'You can be my publicity manager,' he announced, like he was bestowing a great gift to me.

'Gianni, I'm your *events* manager, but I'll do what I can.' And I went through some ideas about posting photos of his food, asking others to do the same. Then I showed him TripAdvisor, which in hindsight probably wasn't the smartest move on my part as some of his guests had already commented, and it wasn't good. This resulted in a twenty-minute rant which ran along the lines of 'anyone posting a review on Advisor Trip is an ass idiot, and should be killed.' This diatribe included lots of swear words in English and Italian and much gesticulation which wasn't ideal as we were sitting at the table in the window and people were passing by as they left the pub. Given the unforgiving lighting nothing was left to interpretation and it was clear how the owner of Il Bacio was feeling that evening. And I was sure I would be reading about it on Twitter shortly.

'God Gianni, is this my life? We started like this at Harrods, am I destined to be in a bloody shop window with you ranting as you get lathered up over nothing?'

'I not lathering up, I just have the standards and people cannot say such things on the Advisor Trip.'

I ignored this and moved on: 'You wanted my advice, so here it is in four points and you won't like any of them. Number one – be nice, number two – serve the stuff you gave to me tonight, number three – make this place look like Christmas, and number four – be bloody nice. I'm sure it will all work out,' I said, not completely convinced. I went back to the cottage that evening wanting to push Gianni and the restaurant to the back of my mind, but all I could think about was decorating that lovely white space. I hadn't wanted to celebrate Christmas this year, but neither had I wanted to reignite feelings for my stroppy ex. And both Christmas and Gianni were seeping in like the melted snow under the door. It wasn't like I'd told him I had feelings for him, and it wasn't like I was going to stuff the cottage with tinsel and start singing 'Oh Little Town of Bethlehem', but there was, I'll admit a little part of me beginning to wobble – on both counts.

Christmas and Gianni went together for me – we met at Christmas and were married at Christmas and for those early years Christmases were magical because of him. Even now, since we'd split, every time I heard a carol on the radio, or spotted a Christmas tree when I was out and about, my tummy would turn over and I'd think of him. Was I missing the twinkle of fairy lights and the wreath on the door, or was I missing Christmas with Gianni?

Chapter Twelve

A Pink Pomeranian and a Hunky Russian Dancer

The next day I worked from home and late afternoon went out for a walk along the front. The waves were somersaulting onto the beach, the spray and the snow tickling my face as I marched along, loving the fresh, tingling cold in the air. I was about to pop in to John's Deli when I bumped into Roberta from the cafe, she was wrapped up warm in several brightly coloured scarves and a big pink coat. She was walking a gorgeous, fluffy little dog, who was also wrapped up warm in a pink snow suit with boots.

I had to stop and say hello. 'She's gorgeous,' I cooed, bending down to stroke the dog.

'This is Delilah,' Roberta said proudly. 'One of the girls she is, we inherited her, and she took such a shine to me we're inseparable.'

'Oh I can imagine,' I said, stroking her and thinking of Snowflake and how much I still missed her.

'She's a Pomeranian, thinks she's a St Bernard though,' she smiled. 'Such a strong feisty little girl, aren't you Delilah?' she said, as the little dog twirled and wagged her tail in agreement. 'I'm thinking of making her a stage costume to match my Beyoncé outfit.'

'Well why not?' I said, thinking how easily I was slipping into the craziness around here – and I liked it.

'Yes we're going to sew our stage costumes tonight, aren't we Delilah,' she said, picking up the little dog who I'm sure had false eyelashes on. 'And we're watching *Strictly Come Dancing* with something spicy, and I'm not talking about that hunky Russian dancer,' she laughed.

We discussed the pitfalls of dating a Russian and she told me she'd tweeted Putin but apparently his English wasn't very good. 'I do worry about what he'll do next,' she sighed. 'Oh Chloe, the world's a scary place these days, what with him and Trump – and don't get me started on Syria… you didn't get stuff like that going on when lovely Angela Rippon read the news.'

We lamented the loss of lovely Angela from the BBC evening news for a while and then Roberta said she had to get off she was late to her yoga class.

'Does Delilah do yoga too?' I asked, jokingly.

'Of course she does,' she said in all seriousness. 'Delilah's downward dog is legendary,' she called back as she rushed off down the road. I watched her go, smiling to myself and hoping I would be half that energetic and excited about life at the age of seventy-nine, before heading off to John's Deli.

Inside the shop, delicious Christmas hampers filled with lovely and unusual things waylaid me in the doorway as I caressed the jars of home-made fig jam, the huge Christmas pudding packed with nuts and soaked vine fruits, a Christmas cake, moist and delicious topped with achingly sweet icing and thick, nutty marzipan.

I was reminded of last year's Christmas cake, left uneaten. Gianni had come home from work very late on Christmas Eve. He was always late, but it was 3 a.m. and he was drunk and it was, for me, the final straw. We used to make Christmas Eve a special time for just the two of us, but as this had fallen by the wayside in recent years I had suggested we try to make the effort last year. I still wanted to rekindle what we'd had even then and I'd flown in from a work trip to be there for Christmas Eve. I'd asked Gianni if he could be with me when I put the three special baubles on the tree, two pink and one blue for the babies we'd lost. This was a little ritual I'd carried out for years, sometimes with him, sometimes alone and for me it was a small way of remembering them in happiness rather than loss. Little things like this were important to me, they were all I had and Gianni knew this; he also knew that our time together was precious and it hurt me that he hadn't come home early, or sober, there was no excuse. He tried to explain, slurring slightly and saying he couldn't bear to watch as I cried again, but I was too upset to listen.

I told him I was lonely and unhappy and I wanted out of the stagnant marriage. Even in his drunken stupor he'd been shocked, I'd talked about leaving before, but now I was determined. Cherry had moved to Australia the week before, but had left me the keys for her flat so I could keep an eye on things before the new owners took over. So I walked out into the night, and left him behind, like I felt he'd left me behind.

Now I could see that I'd overreacted, the alcohol had loosened his tongue, he was hurting too but I'd been too wrapped up in my own pain to listen. I could now see it clearly – it wasn't about him pulling away from me, it was about me refusing to face up to the fact that he knew he would also remain childless and he hurt just as much as I did.

I'd wanted to return to that place where we'd once been so happy, and wished more than anything that he'd just talked to me, told me how he felt, and hung on a little longer. But thinking about it now, I probably wouldn't have heard him. I'd become so obsessed with having a child I'd pushed everything and everyone away, especially Gianni. Then when I finally faced up to the fact that children weren't my destiny, my work took up most of my time and I shut Gianni out again. We were both hiding from each other and on the rare occasions we were home at the same time, we'd both be busy burying our heads in the sand, and thinking about work, when really we should have been concentrating on what was happening between us.

I headed home from the deli and by the time I got back was so cold I ran a bath pouring Jo Malone Pomegranate Noir oil into the running water, the aroma rising from the steam made me think life wasn't too bad. Looking back there were moments over those past few months when I'd wished Gianni far away, but now all I wanted was to have him near me again. Seeing Gianni again, and spending time with him, had stirred up emotions I'd tried to bury, and I still needed to be gentle with myself. So I would start by lighting candles around my bath and truly relaxing, allowing the warmth to seep into my pores and heal all the hurt.

Later, I sat on the sofa in my robe when my phone rang. I hoped it might be Gianni, I hoped he might have let his guard down and said he was missing me, but I was horrified to see it was Nigel. Nerdy Nigel, as Cherry called him. God no I didn't need him now, I recalled his desperation at the tube station and felt guilty that he might still be spending Christmas alone. But I couldn't possibly answer, so I pushed the phone under a cushion and poured myself a large glass of red. It was early, but I needed this and was just about to take a large sip, when my phone buzzed again. I left it and picked up my book, but when it had rung about ten times more in as many minutes I felt it might be necessary to pick it up and tell Nigel the score.

'Look, Nigel, I'm sorry, I don't want to go out with you any more and I'm spending Christmas alone,' I snapped.

The other end of the phone was complete silence, and I wondered if perhaps I'd been a bit harsh when someone said, 'Is this Chloe?' In a thick Italian accent.

'Oh Gianni… I thought you were…'

'Yes?' His tone reminded me of how he'd been the first time we'd met after I'd left, and gone was all the warmth and fun of the night before.

'It wasn't… he isn't… It's Nigel, he's just a stalker,' I said like that would make perfect sense.

'I have nothing to do with your personal life…' he started.

'Oh Gianni, don't be like that, I told you I haven't got another man, honestly,' I said. Apart from the fact that this was the truth, I didn't want to hurt him.

'I am not your husband any more therefore it is none of my business.'

He was clearly sulking and as childish as it was I have to confess to feeling slightly pleased that the idea of me with another man was making him cross. And I saw her in my mind's eye, long, tumbling red locks, perfect bone structure, her eyes on his.

'I know you're not my husband... which is why I don't need to lie about having a boyfriend,' I said, trying hard to push away the vague sexual images now popping into my head of Gianni with that beautiful woman. 'Anyway, I am not interested in your lover, I need your help,' he said. 'I have no staff and you've been around the town telling everyone about the restaurant and this afternoon everyone books for the dinners.'

'Oh you mean the Ice Cream Cafe Christmas do? Don't blame me for finding you customers,' I laughed. 'The girls from the cafe promised to spread the word, so I can't take all the credit.'

He just groaned.

'How many guests have booked?'

'Fifteen bloody people.'

'Oh God, I thought you were going to say forty or fifty.'

'You can sit there with the smiling, but me and Marco will be up to our bloody tits in peasant food, so who will serve?' He was so grumpy, I wanted to giggle. I suppose technically this was my fault and I couldn't leave him in the lurch, even though my job spec had once more been extended this time from events manager to waitress – make that general dogsbody. But I knew that if the restaurant is going to work I had to do all that I could until we found more staff.

'You have to be here Chloe, the first guests are booked in at eight, so you need to be moving your arses,' he was saying down the phone.

'Okay, okay, I'll... my *arses* will be there as soon as they can.'

It was now 5 p.m., so hopefully everything could be ready when the guests arrived. While Gianni and Marco were in the kitchen I could work my magic on the Christmas decor and try at least to make the restaurant look inviting. Hopefully this would go some way to satisfying the customers and I would pre-empt any anger from guests who weren't served as quickly as they might expect with a little white lie and say our staff were ill with flu and to bear with us. So I quickly got dressed and leapt in the car, feeling excited for the first time in a long while.

On arrival at the restaurant, Gianni greeted me with his usual non-committal half-smile, which was more than I got from Marco, who was already hard at it. Gianni was clearly still sulking about the fact he thought I'd left him for Nigel. 'Where do you want me?' I asked, and all I got was a 'Tables, the bloody tables need to be set.'

I wasn't going to pander to his sulking, he could think what he liked, I knew the truth and I also knew that once we were in the thick of things he'd forget what he'd been sulking about. Having said that, I was desperate to ask him about the redhead, but it seemed even pettier than his presumptions about Nigel. It wasn't like he'd ever mentioned her, I'd only ever seen one photo on Facebook, so perhaps it had been a fleeting thing and was all over before it began? I hoped so, and now wasn't the time to lay on a counter attack about who was seeing whom.

I put all the cutlery and glasses on a trolley and headed out into the restaurant, where I abandoned them immediately and opened up my bags of decorations. I spread them all out on a couple of the large white tables and within minutes I was dressing the huge windows.

After at least an hour of window dressing, I started on the ceiling decorations, standing on chairs, balancing on tables, almost landing on my bum several times. And as I fixed the sparkly ornaments at angles with the restaurant lights so they'd glisten, I also placed the candles on the tables so I knew where the ornaments would have most effect when the candles were lit. I kept standing back, walking in and out of the restaurant so I could see what would greet the customers when they walked in.

By 7 p.m., I felt like I had created the Winter Wonderland I'd always envisaged from the first moment I saw this place. I stepped outside into the freezing night and gazed through the windows, knowing I'd achieved the right balance of sparkle and Christmas without overdoing it. The restaurant still looked clean and white but now it was less 'operating theatre' and more 'Narnia'. I was gazing from the outside in, pleased with myself, when I saw Gianni enter the dining room. I stood on the pavement, waiting for him to notice me and rush out to thank me… okay the fantasy didn't stretch that far, but I couldn't wait to see the delight on his face.

I watched him look around, a little bemused, and I smiled through the window. But the more he looked around, the more grumpy his face seemed to be, though that couldn't possibly be the case, could it?

I didn't want to hang around outside in the freezing cold any longer, and something about his furrowed brow was telling me he might not be as delighted as I'd hoped.

'What the bloody hell have you done?' was his opening gambit as I carefully opened the door and peeped in.

'It's lovely… isn't it?' I tried.

'It's like the bloody Vegas in here.'

'It's not Vegas, it's Christmas, I've made it look all Christmassy.' Was this man blind?

'Christmas at bloody Jamie's.' I knew this was an insult, he was insanely jealous of all TV chefs (particularly Jamie Oliver) and loved an opportunity to knock them.

'I was only trying to bring Christmas to the place… I thought the customers would appreciate it.'

'If you have any more ideas of turning this into a grotto please ask me first.'

I was about to give him a piece of my mind when he stormed towards what he thought was the kitchen door, pushed his whole bodyweight into the wall and ended up smacking his face into it. I laughed, watching him feel around the wall looking for a way in.

'Serves you right,' I called after him as he eventually found the opening, and then followed him through into the kitchen to get my coat.

'Where are you going, we open in less than an hour?' he said, as I grabbed my coat and headed for the kitchen door.

I turned quickly. 'I've just spent two hours creating sodding Narnia in that room. It says "Christmas" but in a way that is stylish and simple and reflects the class of your new Christmas menu.

Jamie Oliver would weep for that dining room, Gordon Ramsay would go down on his knees before me – but you, you just turn into Mr Grump.'

'You turn my restaurant into bloody grotto.'

'I'm not putting up with this… with you, you grumpy sod!'

I set off for the kitchen door and a grand dramatic exit, but what I thought was the door turned out to be the bloody wall and I did exactly what Gianni had done moments before and smacked my face on the concrete. It wasn't so funny this time, but I recovered quickly.

'And that,' I hissed, pointing at a vague area, near the door, 'is ridiculous!'

I finally found the opening and shot through it, a little faster than intended as I slipped on the bloody polished white tiles, but managed not to land on my face on the shiny floor. I manoeuvred across the dining room awkwardly, aware that any gathering of momentum would lead to a nasty injury and me piled in a heap just as the first guests arrived. Negotiating the treacherous floor, I suddenly felt a strong arm take mine and twirl me round, which knocked me slightly off balance and I fell into Gianni. I was face first in his chef whites, and breathing in that strong, familiar scent of masculine cleanness laced with juniper and smoke. I was suddenly torn between anger and intoxication, I'd never felt so conflicted. My head said shout at him and storm off and my pheromones told me to stick around a while and have a good old sniff.

'Chloe, why you so angry with me?'

'Because you hurt me, and you don't even realise you're doing it,' I said, still leaning into him, which was quite unnecessary on a practical basis but felt good. He was so tall and big, and I had this urge to put my arms around his waist and push my face into his chest and breathe him in like I used to. He felt strong and safe and I wanted to stay in his arms for ever, but then I remembered why I had been storming out in the first place and the phero-mones lost their effect. 'I worked hard to make this look festive,' I said pulling away from him and gesturing at the white, sparkly decorations, which looked so magical, glistening and twinkling around the room.

'But you get all shouty ass in my face because I don't say it is the most beautiful…'

'No, that isn't it. I do my very best, I worked so hard, wanting to please you and make you happy and all you do is insult me,' I said, close to tears. I was upset and angry and I felt so unappreciated, a feeling I'd grown accustomed to during our marriage. 'Gianni, don't you understand, I feel like I've failed you, and I just wanted to prove to you that I'm not a failure at everything.'

'I don't say you are the failure… I just…'

'Don't you understand? Even now, I want to make everything right, I want to make it up to you…' The dam had opened and I was just spilling everything that I'd kept locked up for so long.

'You want to make it up to me for leaving?' he asked, confused and a little surprised by my sudden outpouring.

'No, I want to make it up to you because I let you down. I couldn't give you a child… I can never give you what you want, and now I even fail with the Christmas decorations,' I said and he put his arm around me as I burst into floods of tears. 'I used to be able to get it right. Gianni's restaurant was covered in cheap tinsel every Christmas. You loved it, you'd carve a nativity into panettone and I'd spend hours on a ladder hanging strings of fairy lights in every colour,' I said, tears still streaming down my cheeks.

His eyes lit up, 'And I'd make the mulled wine and then we say Buon Natale!'

I nodded, 'Yes and we'd talk about how one day our children would put the star on top of the tree…' I smiled, and instead of feeling a lump in my throat, I felt warm and happy, because he was the only one I could share this with – and he was here with me.

'And wake us up at dawn to go downstairs to see what Babbo Natale had brought in his sleigh,' he smiled.

'And when I lost the first baby we said it's okay, we have all the time in the world. We'll enjoy another Christmas on our own because by next Christmas we might be three? And the next Christmas we put the same baubles up on the tree and there were no little hands to help us, no excited little faces holding tinsel and wondering when Father Christmas would arrive. And then you opened the new restaurant and I had the final miscarriage. That Christmas I filled the car with our cardboard boxes stuffed with decorations and the wonky ladder from home as always. You were busy but eventually you joined me and we decorated the tree together. But it wasn't the same, there was no excitement, no hope and we didn't talk about next year, or the year after, because we couldn't bear to see the emptiness ahead. Suddenly I was older and it was too late – we didn't have all the time in the world any more.

'Gianni, you had your restaurant and it filled your life but I'd been left behind trying to get pregnant, obsessing about a child until I could think of nothing else, just sit and wait for my useless womb to kick in.'

At this he touched my hand. 'Chloe, I wanted the children, God knows this. But I couldn't see you go through the loss again. Every time the odds were against us, I would rather have you, and none of the children. I wanted it to stop – we couldn't keep trying again and again for something we couldn't have, it was giving you so much of the hurt and every time it happened a little bit of us died,' he said, tears filling his eyes.

'I can see that now, but at the time I think I was a bit crazy. And to finally say "no more" was the hardest thing for me; I felt useless, there was nothing I could do, no one needed me. I couldn't even do what I was made for – to have our baby.'

'Oh Chloe, I am so sorry that it was like all this for you.., I felt so helpless too.'

'I can see now that you'd probably almost given up on me.'

'Never,' he said with such conviction it caught me by surprise.

'I was wretched and unreasonable and I had to get out of the marriage to see myself, to see what I'd become.' 'I'm so sorry… I am idiot, I was so wrapping up in the new restaurant I lost you.'

'I'm just trying to explain things from my side, how I felt and why I did what I did, because I didn't understand myself at the time – leaving our marriage for a while helped me become more objective, like I was looking through a window at the two of us and seeing what happened. I had to find my own place in the world. To realise that I wasn't any less of a woman because I couldn't have a child, but I had to readjust because I wasn't who I thought I was going to be. I wanted to be the best mum in the world, but once I realised this wasn't going to happen, I wanted to be the best something else – so like you, I threw myself into my career and buried all the pain.'

'How could you ever have loved a bloody stupido ass like me, Chloe,' he said, bashing his fist on his forehead.

'Look, I haven't told you all this so you'll beat yourself up. God knows we've both been doing that to ourselves for long enough. I just wanted you to realise how much you can still hurt me. I'm not sure I realised it myself until tonight – until you called my Winter Wonderland "bloody Vegas".'

'It's beautiful…'

'Oh you don't have to say that,' I sighed, it was meaningless now. I wiped my eyes, and straightened up, I had to get a grip, this wasn't like me to wallow in misery. 'The simple fact is that I worked bloody hard on this lot and I'd like some appreciation,' I said in a brighter, more assertive tone.

'It's very bloody good,' he said, 'I mean it Chloe, I have so long with the money people I lose sight of what my restaurant needs. You bring me the sparkle… I missed it,' he said, leading me back to the kitchen, where he poured me wine and looked into my eyes.

My insides felt like warm chocolate. 'It's all I ever wanted, to bring you the sparkle,' I said, gesturing around the room. 'You know, you are still the most beautiful woman I ever saw,' he said. But before I could enjoy this, Marco appeared in the kitchen with a huge sack of potatoes and plonked it on the counter between us. 'Get a room,' he muttered, the look on his face suggested he was witnessing something truly horrific.

I blushed and told Gianni to get on with peeling the vegetables, but we were both smiling now, and he reached out and caught my hand. We both stood in the kitchen, with pans bubbling and water running, but for a brief moment, we looked into each other's eyes, and time stood still.

Chapter Thirteen

First Guests and Last Dances

Just before 8 p.m. the first guests began to arrive. They were a mixed bunch, and I couldn't help but wonder if they were here having heard of Gianni's Kobe beef fight rather than the good food on offer. Then at 8.30 I saw some familiar faces, Ella and Roberta turned up along with Sue in sequins and the glamorous older blonde, who I discovered was Gina, the co-owner of the Ice Cream Cafe.

'Oh isn't it just fabulous, like an ice palace,' Sue said, as I showed them to a large, circular table.

'Yes, from the outside it looks quite clinical, but once you're inside it's like Narnia,' Ella gasped as I guided them to their table.

'Will there be Italian food on the menu?' Roberta asked. 'You see we're a big Italian family.'

'I'm sure we can do something special for you,' I said, 'it won't be a problem, after all, the chef is Italian.'

'Oh Mamma mia!' she clasped her hands together. 'Sue tells me he's a big, brooding Italian who takes no prisoners.' She pushed out her chest, clearly wanting details.

'Mmm something like that,' I smiled. 'I just hope he behaves himself tonight.'

'Ooh yes, I hear he's very naughty,' Roberta said, with a wink.

I smiled and took their order while welcoming another group of guests. I kept telling everyone we were short-staffed and warned them politely things may be a little delayed but we would do our best. Everyone seemed quite understanding and took their seats, while I kept replenishing drinks, I was hoping they'd be so drunk they wouldn't care how long it took for their food to arrive. And landing in the kitchen through the invisible door (on which I'd placed a glittery star so the staff and I could find it – much to Gianni's annoyance), I was greeted with the news that the oven was playing up.

'She will ruin everything,' Gianni was saying, kicking the oven, which actually had the miraculous effect of starting it up.

'Holy cows – quick before she bloody dies again,' Gianni was shouting as he and Marco began desperately piling stuff in like they were shovelling coal into a furnace. Despite the oven being on the blink, it was hot with tension in the kitchen as Gianni had managed to acquire two trainees who seemed to be getting in the way. I could feel the pressure mounting and went back into the dining room before someone blew up.

With nothing ready to be served, I went about replenishing drinks – again, but after forty-five minutes one or two of the customers began asking where the food was. I was keen to replenish their glasses and explain how the chef was 'a perfectionist', and though it might take a little longer, the wait was worth it. My heart was in my mouth, hoping to God Gianni delivered what he was capable of and we could get through the night without any dramas or complaints and someone writing a damning essay on TripAdvisor. Meanwhile, Ella and the girls were quite the opposite, happy to keep reordering drinks and inventing their own cocktails.

'I want an Italian Stallion,' Roberta said, when I went to their table to take the drinks order.

'Oh I'm not sure what that is,' I said.

'It isn't a drink, I just want one,' she roared laughing and Sue slapped her on the back while Gina, the cool blonde, rolled her eyes.

'I spent the night with Sylvester Stallone once,' she said, 'now he *was* an Italian stallion.'

'Wow, well if one of your film star friends ever comes to Appledore you must bring them here for dinner,' I said. I wasn't sure if Gina really was as close to all these starry people as she implied, but the PR girl in me was keen to make the most of it if she was.

'Actually, Roberto Riviera is in town after the holidays,' she said. I gasped, apart from the fact he was one of Gianni's favourite actors, the prospect of having him within a twenty-mile radius of this restaurant would be wonderful for our publicity. I could see the headlines now, 'Italian Film Star Dines at Il Bacio', it was giving me goosebumps, just imagining the photos of Gianni and Roberto clinking glasses over a plate of pasta.

'I remember him in *Loveless Nights*,' Sue sighed, looking all dreamy, 'he must be in his seventies now, but he's still gorgeous.'

'Well I would,' said Roberta, winking at me.

'I would too,' Sue nudged her, and they both giggled like schoolgirls.

'I think Roberto would love it here,' Gina was saying, looking around the restaurant approvingly. I was intrigued and very excited, Roberto Rivera was a huge Hollywood star, he ran around with Al Pacino and Robert De Niro, if we could get someone like him to the restaurant it would be amazing; so I probed a little more.

'Is he actually coming here, to Appledore?' I asked, almost unable to believe this.

'Yeah, he's staying with me, we go back a long way,' Gina said. 'I knew him before he was Roberto Riviera and boy did we have a blast,' she was smiling at the memory. 'He's coming over for New Year, says he wants to spend some quality time with me, I said "Honey, it's been twenty-five years, it's about time."' She pursed her red lips and I could see her sitting on a bar stool in downtown LA drinking martinis and flirting with him.

'Gianni, my husband… the owner, he's a huge fan. Please bring him over for a meal on us when he's here,' I said, trying not to sound too desperate.

'Sure honey,' she said. I didn't feel I could push it any more, I still wasn't sure if she was exaggerating about how well she knew him, and if indeed he would be here for New Year. I vowed to keep my fingers crossed and took their drinks orders promising them their food was on its way.

'Don't you worry about us we'll be fine,' Ella said, ordering a Christmas Fizz and a Sex on the Italian Beach for her mum.

'I'll have an Italian Stallion,' Gina said, cool as a cucumber. I laughed, she was obviously picking up on Roberta's joke.

'Ah, but what will you have to drink?' I laughed, joining in.

'An Italian Stallion,' she repeated like I was mad. 'Vermouth, whisky, Campari and lemon... with a dash of Angostura bitters.'

'Oh... right. Sounds delicious,' I said.

'Roberto's favourite drink,' she smiled, 'he mixed it for me every night in his Malibu beach house.'

'I bet he did,' Roberta said, with an eye roll as she beckoned me over. 'Now Chloe, as a businesswoman myself I understand how staffing can have an impact,' she said. 'But if the natives get restless, I'm more than happy to sing... I have a huge repertoire dear.'

'Oh don't you just,' monotoned Gina. I detected a little prickly banter between these two and wondered what the history was between the niece and the aunt, but Roberta now had me in her grip and was holding onto my arm and telling me what she was prepared to do.

'I do Beyonce, Madonna... let me see... oh yes, I do an uncanny Celine Dion, and with a bit of notice I *am* Rihanna. I just need more time for the hairdo and the thong can be a bit of a trial,' she added in a whisper.

From the corner of my eye I saw Ella looking slightly alarmed, 'I'm sure Chloe's fine Mum, they don't need a floor show tonight,' she said gently, giving me a look. I got the message that this may not quite be the real thing – but if the worst came to the worst I'd have been prepared to give anything a go that night, and if the rumblings from the kitchen got any louder, Roberta's Beyonce might be just what the doctor ordered.

'Oh Roberta has an amazing voice, she can soothe the salvage beast all right,' Sue misquoted, nodding enthusiastically.

'Yes Bananarama are back,' Roberta said, 'me, Sue and Gina are dead ringers, you'd think it was them. And Robert De Niro's still waiting,' she winked, 'so just give me a shout if you need some musical entertainment.'

'Fabulous,' I said, and went to the next table, trying not to smile at the prospect of a frazzled Gianni emerging from the kitchen to the spectacle of a geriatric Bananarama singing in his restaurant. He complained that a few baubles made it look like Vegas, God only knows how he'd react to a fake and ageing Sara, Keren and Siobhan – it would be less Bananarama and more banana fritter!

I was just apologising yet again for the delay, when the sound of shouting came from the kitchen. I talked loudly over it, and wished we had music I could turn up (Gianni point blank rejected background music – 'this is not a sodding supermarket!'), I was contemplating a rousing session of Christmas carols to hide the kitchen racket and as Beyoncé was apparently having a night off I was ready to take Bananarama up on their offer when the invisible door whipped open and someone (one of the new staff) stormed out through the restaurant swearing. I didn't know him, I hadn't got round to getting their names and it seemed I'd now have one less name to learn anyway.

'I hope that wasn't the chef,' someone said.

I smiled, acting as though it was perfectly acceptable for a staff member to leave swearing in the middle of service, but as the sound of pots and pans crashed in the background I knew this was going to take more than one of my smiles to cover up. Then, to my horror came Gianni's voice, 'pissing staff... pissing peasants', and another crash, 'holy arses'. I suddenly felt like a stewardess on a doomed flight, blindly reassuring everyone and pretending it was all lovely, but knowing we were going down.

'We'll be off to the chippy at this rate,' Sue was laughing as the Ice Cream Cafe table downed more cocktails and talked excitedly of Christmas, thankfully unfazed by the drama.

I didn't have too much time to dwell on this because there was now more shouting coming from the kitchen and I could see the guests at the other tables were rather alarmed. I discreetly disappeared through the secret door into the kitchen to be faced with a sustained torrent of abuse directed at an inanimate object.

'The bloody sodding oven she's gone again, she ruins me, bloody Germans, they are useless!' Gianni was running around like a headless chicken, and I was trying to calm him, which seemed to make him worse, so I just ignored him, as Marco was doing.

Gianni was now holding a tray of mulled plums shouting, 'my plums, my plums', and I could only imagine what the Ice Cream Cafe girls would make of that.

Marco, as usual, didn't flinch, but just walked over to the oven and hit it with a rolling pin, which seemed to set it off again.

The problem wasn't really the oven or the Germans as a race – though clearly there was an issue here with the electrics. The real problem was Gianni's inability to stay calm in a crisis… and having been used to having lots of staff and a soundproof kitchen he wasn't used to having to deal with the minutiae himself. Watching him sweat and curse and crash I think it was fair to say he still had a way to go before this was the perfect, relaxed dining experience.

'It's mortifying standing up in front of the guests while you scream and crash around, they can hear everything,' I said.

At this he seemed to calm down slightly.

'Look, Gianni, there are three ladies of a certain age out there, they are all lovely and very pissed. They have offered to stand up in your restaurant and do their version of Bananarama...'

'The banana people who sang about Robert De Niro?'

'The same... but not. Now I love Bananarama – but it would be a travesty – a loud travesty, loud enough to cover the bloody racket in here if they were to perform. I have no doubt it will be hilarious for all the wrong reasons, and if you continue to make all this noise and fuss I'll have no choice but to get the band back together. In this restaurant. Tonight.'

With that I swept through the invisible door like bloody Bette Davis and sashayed back into the restaurant, knowing we wouldn't hear a peep from him again.

I went back into the dining room, announced the first course, and turned up the lights as the one trainee left standing began bringing the plates through. I gave her a reassuring smile as I saw her hands noticeably quivering, I just prayed those plates made it to the tables in one piece. Then I ran into the kitchen, where the oven was now back on, but who knew for how long? I piled the plates on my arms, just like I used to all those years ago at Gianni's restaurant in Islington and headed for the 'invisible' door.

'I've not lost it,' I said over my shoulder, and Gianni laughed.

'You were born to be a waitress,' he replied, and I stuck out my tongue in mock indignation.

Once the starters had arrived, the lights were turned down so the guests could enjoy the 'performance' – and they certainly did, the compliments to the chef were flying and the food was cooked beautifully. And with a mild threat via Roberta of Gladys Knight and two of the Pips re-forming in about ten minutes if Gianni didn't make my ice cream girls 'a special pasta', he produced a stunning bowl of linguine and seafood sauce just for them, even though it wasn't on the menu.

'This is on the house,' I said, putting down the gigantic, Italian bowl of sumptuous pasta smothered in garlicky, seafood sauce as they gasped with delight.

'Oh no, really...' Ella protested.

'No, you've all made me feel so welcome at the cafe, you've all lifted my spirits this Christmas, and made me feel at home. I haven't felt that for a long time,' I smiled, as Roberta helped herself.

'This is delicious, I feel like I'm back in Sorrento, nibbling linguine, sipping limoncello and watching the boys go by,' I heard Roberta say as I ran back into the kitchen for more plates.

From the minute the food had started arriving on diners' tables I was running in and out of the kitchen non-stop. It felt like old times for me as I balanced armfuls of plates filled with pastas, garlic breads, delicious sauces, and casseroles with creamy mash. The portions were human-sized as opposed to doll's-house-sized and there wasn't a frazzled sweetbread, a monochrome timbale or a turkey gizzard in sight. Gianni's pasta dishes were the best he'd ever made and filled the air with basil and rosemary, the heady, savoury scent of the Mediterranean.

By the end of the third and final course, which was all served at the same time, we were exhausted. I kept smiling and eventually bid goodnight to twenty-five very happy customers, who all promised to come again and give us rave reviews, including Sue who promised to post a review about Gianni's 'wonderful garlic carburettor'!

Later, when all was quiet, Gianni actually thanked the new trainee and Marco (who growled) as they were leaving. He asked me to stay a while and we sat in the restaurant with a bottle of red wine.

'So how do you feel after your first official night?' I asked.

'I feel like things went well but the oven she pisses me off... those Germans are arses.'

'It's just teething problems, that's all,' I smiled.

'I need more staff, stupid ass trainee walks out tonight – will you come and work for a few nights, I pay you well?'

'Can I think about it?' Tonight had been special, it had reminded me of so much that was right about me and Gianni... but would recapturing the past just make me sad? Was I in danger of taking a backward step? 'Why can't you always be like this?' I asked suddenly.

'Because I feel the stress.'

'But you must admit once you'd calmed down it all went so much smoother, like it used to before you became the *enfant terrible*,' I giggled.

'I wasn't so bad.'

'All I'm saying is tonight was brilliant, once you'd put a lid on it, and I reckon if you do more nights like tonight you will have a success on your hands.'

'I like that you were here…' he suddenly said, before taking a sip of wine, but keeping his eyes on me.

'Why? You shouted at me during the starters.'

He smiled. 'You know I don't mean it, the bite is worse than the barking.'

'I think you mean the other way around, but I agree, you're a nice guy under all the anger, resentment and hate,' I said, waiting to see if he got my sarcasm.

He smiled, 'You tease me, but I have the passion, food makes me happy, and tonight made me very happy.'

I laughed. 'If yelling at everyone and swearing is happiness, God help us when you're sad.'

'Ah you tease.' I wasn't. 'But you understand how much it means to me, because you also have the passion. It beats here,' he said, thumping his chest.

'I do understand. And now you're back to being you; there's no hiding behind a mask and a list of fancy ingredients any more.'

He nodded, and I brushed my hand along his arm. I pretended this was for reassurance, but I just had this need to touch him, to let him know I felt the connection.

'I think you're a little scared… am I right?' I said gently, looking into his eyes.

'Chloe, I am always a leetle bit scared. That's why I came here to live by the sea.'

'I know, everything feels better living by the sea, doesn't it?' I know it was working for me, I'd felt so much better since being here away from the hustle and bustle. Even though the sea was a foreboding grey, just being near it and breathing in the crisp salty air had revitalised me, though I suspected that wasn't the only thing that had an effect on my well-being.

'I had to get away. I had no love... and what is life about if not about the love?'

He was right, and it made me think about what was important in my own life, and I had to agree, what was a career, a home, even a family, if you don't have love?

'So, what do you have here, now?' I asked.

'I have a home, in a flat above,' he gestured towards the ceiling. 'And I have work, if I can be keeping lids on and fingers out.'

'Yes I think that's the key,' I smiled. How ironic we were both in the same boat, we had what we needed, a roof over our heads and enough to live on – nothing more.

'Love is for another day,' he sighed. 'For now I have sea, candlelight and good wine, I just need the beautiful woman to share it with.'

'Are there any beautiful women here?' I asked, flirtatiously.

'No, I don't have that – but you're here instead.'

I looked at him in mock annoyance, and he broke into a smile.

'I was doing the joking, you tease me and I tease too.'

I whacked him on the arm in reprimand and laughed along. I was exhausted from the evening and the wine was making me feel very mellow. The snow was falling outside and my decorations were sparkling inside – and I couldn't help it, I felt a shimmer of Christmas.

'I was in the deli today and they have small Christmas hampers,' I said.

'Thank you for telling me that, Chloe.'

I rolled my eyes, my sarcasm was catching; 'I was thinking, that might be something you could do here in the restaurant? Make up some hampers with your own home-made mince pies and...'

'Mince pies? Who do you think I am bloody Mary Berry?'

'Please don't swear in the same sentence as that name, the woman is an icon, it's like saying "bloody Mary Magdalen".'

'At least Mary Madgdalen didn't put bloody cream into the spaghetti Bolognese like your Mary did,' he tutted, shook his head and crossed himself.

I laughed, and as we both sipped our wine in sync, we seemed to slip back into our own little worlds. I wondered if he was back in Gianni's Christmas Eve 2001, the ring in the bauble, the proposal followed by a million kisses.

'Will you stay for Christmas, Chloe?' he suddenly said into the silence. 'I need you here...'

I was touched, was he asking me to stay with him over Christmas? Was he asking for me to stay with him full stop? Our relationship was certainly on the up and the more time I spent with him the closer I felt, like when we were first together.

'I have to go back to London after Christmas,' I said, being sensible and going against my instincts which were confused to say the least. I loved it here, and I was enjoying his company, did I really have to go back straight after Christmas, could I stay a little longer?

'Okay, you leave after Christmas,' he said, immediately erasing my dilemma. 'But you'll stay and help with the restaurant until then?'

'Oh yes,' I said, disappointed. I'd thought he was asking me to stay with him for Christmas but clearly he only wanted me around to keep the restaurant on track.

He stood up. 'I have to go to the little men's room,' he said, and wandered through to the back of the restaurant to the toilets. I was going over our conversation in my head, and considering this new friendship/relationship. The lines were blurred, were we estranged lovers, old friends, or just colleagues? I was pondering this when suddenly Gianni's phone screamed into the silence, making me jump. It was on the table, face down, ringing and buzzing at the same time, creating its own little commotion and causing the wine to shudder in our glasses. I allowed myself a moment to calm down and let it ring for ages, relieved when it finally stopped. I went back to my thoughts, but then it bloody rang again and I realised that ringing twice after midnight must mean an emergency, and though I felt uncomfortable doing it, I reached over and picked it up. I intended to press the button and answer, but, glancing at the screen, my stomach did a somersault and I suddenly felt very sick. The face in the photo looking back at me was framed with red hair, the eyes were greener than the photo I'd seen on Facebook but I'd know her anywhere. Her name was Natalia, it was very late and she was clearly desperate to speak to Gianni.

I felt so stupid, so hurt and so angry, not to mention so very short and unattractive with my imperfect teeth and muddy brown eyes. Had I misread all the signals? Was he still in a relationship with this woman, and if he was what a hypocrite to be banging on about me and Nigel when he was banging Natalia.

I heard the door opening and he walked through the restaurant, still smiling, still intending to pick up where we left off as he flattered me into staying and working over Christmas for him. But in the few seconds it took for him to grab a second bottle of wine from behind the bar and stroll over to our table, I had come to my senses. Okay, so he was still seeing the beautiful redhead, who could blame him? And yet, I'd recently felt a vague resurrection of old feelings, a warmth I hadn't felt for a long time, and I had even begun to believe he was feeling this too.

'Your phone rang,' I said, as he sat down.

I searched his face for a reaction as he picked it up and looked to see who it was, but nothing, he just put the phone back down with his customary shrug.

'I think it may have been urgent,' I tried, desperate for a reaction, or even better for him to call her back and tell her he wasn't interested in her late-night musings.

'No, it isn't urgent,' he answered. This was followed by agonising silence. I wanted to ask a million questions, but I knew it wasn't fair on him. I was the one who'd walked out; he had been sad and lonely and was entitled to have someone else in his life.

'Is she your girlfriend?' I heard myself say, but he didn't respond, just put the bottle opener in the fresh cork and started to twist, while looking straight at me. He wasn't going to talk to me about her, and though it was like a physical pain to imagine him with someone else what right did I have to protest? We were separated and we were working together. Yes it had, in my mind, become a bit flirty, quite warm and easy and nice, but that was it. All the time this lovely woman was waiting for him, talking to him and sharing things with him that I used to. I imagined she was still in London, I supposed she'd eventually move to Appledore and they'd do all the things we'd planned – only they'd be far more successful. I'd always said he should find someone else, someone younger who could give him the family he so wanted, so I had to let this be.

'Do you remember the way you used to feel about me?' I said into the silence, gazing into his face, looking for a clue. Was he feeling the same flicker? I just wanted him to feel something this one last time, before he went back to his new life with another woman.

He ran his hand through his hair, then he looked at me, his eyes now soft. 'Yes, I remember the way you'd smile at me from the other side of the kitchen, catch my eye in the middle of a service, holding the piles of plates, wiping down tables. Your face would look up and I would see all the sunshine, it would be filling the room.'

I smiled, 'And I remember the way you'd look at me across a table, over a boiling pan, through the steam and chaos and swearing, and suddenly, I'd see you looking and the whole world stopped.' *And I loved you...* I almost whispered.

'I know,' he said. And for a moment I wondered if he was admitting his feelings too? But then he moved on. 'Another drink?' he asked, lifting the new bottle of wine to pour me another.

'I can't, but thank you...' I had to go before I did something I might regret, like try to kiss him or hurl myself at him across the table. The phone call tonight had made me aware of my strength of feelings, I'd been fooling myself that I could handle this. I still found him incredibly attractive and I'd never stopped loving him, but any kind of slip, a drunken kiss, a declaration made in the heat of the moment could have far-reaching consequences. I wasn't sure how serious this was for him with Natalia, and I didn't want to know, because even if he did still have feelings for me, where would that take us? Did he want to be with someone who was unable to give him what he wanted? And was I able to even consider stepping back into a mess of a marriage I'd walked away from a year ago?

I was confused and overwrought. He wasn't going to tell me about Natalia, he clearly felt it was none of my business and I now had to be a grown-up about this and move on. I said goodnight and he stood up and went to hug me. It may have just been the mood, the Christmas glitter, the memories, but I didn't want to let go, and I breathed in his spicy aftershave, felt the thick, coolness of his white shirt on my face and I wanted to bury my head in his chest.

'Chloe...' he said, catching my hand as I pulled away. 'You talk of my change, but you change too.'

'Really, how?'

'Today you're softer... kinder to me.'

'Was I ever unkind to you, Gianni?' I asked, horrified.

'Sometimes. It started around 2008, in between losing the baby and finding the molecular gastronomy.'

We both laughed. 'God you were bloody impossible,' I sighed, shaking my head.

'And you were bloody *very* impossible,' he said, still laughing.

'I think perhaps we make better friends, than spouses,' I said, not sure of this, but wanting a reaction.

'Perhaps you're right,' he agreed, which wasn't the reaction I'd wanted.

'I'd better go,' I said, picking up my coat from the back of the chair, suddenly disappointed.

'One minute, Chloe… stay there,' he said, his finger in the air as he ran towards the bar. Then he leaned over, pressed some switches and suddenly the dining room was filled with Frank Sinatra singing 'Have Yourself a Merry Little Christmas'. My heart felt all sweet and gooey and my eyes filled with tears as Frank filled the air with Christmas – and who we used to be.

Gianni ran back over to me and held out his hand. 'Dance?' he said.

I took his hand, just like I used to in our first restaurant when all the customers were gone and the chairs were piled on the tables and it was just us. Together we slowly glided across the shiny floor, melting into the music and each other, and I knew that even if he didn't love me, there had never been anyone else for me, and there never would be. And I kept asking myself, is this our last dance?

Chapter Fourteen

Christmas Goodies and Nosey Neighbours

I returned home that evening feeling confused. I'd hoped being here and working with Gianni would clear my head. I think subconsciously I'd hoped that spending time with the man who'd become so obnoxious and impossible would kill off any vestige of feeling I might still have for him. But the truth was that the old Gianni was still in there, the one who pulled back chairs for me to sit down, who valued his family, loved his food, told daft jokes and held me when we danced. And while I'd been travelling the world, it looked like someone else had discovered all his lovely traits too.

I was conflicted by my own feelings and his. Did he love someone else, did he want me back, or were we both just under the spell of Appledore and the past, carried away by the music and Christmas?

The truth was, that now I was wondering if I'd done the right thing in walking away from my marriage. He hadn't seemed too bothered by the phone call, he didn't call her back immediately and declare undying love, so was it just a fling? But I'd hurt him so much, even if Natalia had been a perfectly proportioned diversion he wouldn't want me back for fear I might walk out on him again. Gianni was all about pride, he couldn't bear rejection of any kind, and redheads aside, I may have thrown away any chance of future reconciliation when last year I'd said goodbye, and walked out into the snow.

Sitting in the car, snow now landing in fluffy thickness on the windscreen, I rested my head on the steering wheel, conflicted about where I was – and more to the point, where the hell I was going. Since I'd left Gianni I'd swung from one feeling to the next, sad that we'd let it all go, a lifetime slipping through our fingers like snow. I felt guilty about being the one to end it, but I'd had to make a stand and couldn't just keep my head down, working, living, cooking meals, paying bills. I felt my eyes prickling with tears and was overcome with a deep, cold sense of loss that started in the pit of my stomach and crept like frost through my veins. I should have taken some responsibility for the state we were in, and I should have tried to listen to him before walking out.

I suddenly felt very cold and realised I'd been sitting in the parked car for a few minutes and my toes were starting to freeze. I slowly climbed out, and walked up the snowy path to the cottage in a kind of daze. Gianni was right, I had changed and tonight I'd felt like my old self again. I'd loved the excitement of the restaurant, the anticipation of something new. I loved chatting to the guests, talking about the food, discussing the menus and, if I'm honest, I even enjoyed the problems, Gianni being the biggest one! Should I have stuck it out at the second restaurant with Gianni all those years ago instead of running away the minute things got tough? Instead of standing my ground and sticking by him, my problems conceiving and carrying a baby had affected my self-esteem, made me feel I had no self-worth as a woman. So I'd run away to my own career where I knew what I was doing, where I felt valued – and I could escape from the day-to-day problems of a relationship. I could see now I'd been as guilty as Gianni of burying my head in the sand and refusing to talk.

As soon as I opened the cottage door and walked in, I felt a little better, still confused, but calmer and within half an hour I'd made a fire.

It was after 2 a.m., and the only appropriate drink was hot chocolate, so I boiled milk as the fire began to crackle and fizz, and as the milk started to bubble I felt an inner sparkle start to ignite within me again. This place had a magical effect on me. I loved Appledore and its blustery walks, snowy streets and friendly people. I also loved this cottage with its lovely little nooks and crannies, the whitewashed walls, the black and white photos of Devon beaches and happy seaside summers. Gianni and I had such a shared history, no lovely girl with shampoo advertisement hair could ever take my place, could she? Our lives were entwined, our beautiful, bumpy life together had bonded us, spoiled us for anyone else, and this little cottage had been a place of hope, with its line of wellingtons in different sizes waiting to be claimed. And just because that had changed it didn't mean there was nothing here for me and I had to give up on a chance of happiness. Yes this had been a place we'd bought thinking about a future, picnics on the beach, summers spent on sand, blue skies and sunshine on our faces. Could it be that again?

Once the fire was set and warmth was beginning to seep into the room, I drank my steaming hot chocolate with cream and mallows. I sat in front of the now crackly flames, breathing in the smoke and sweet steam from the towering, fluffy-cream-topped drink. And as soon as those sweet, deep chocolate notes hit my nostrils, I immediately went back to that evening in the restaurant, me and Gianni working hard, creating, building another dream, dancing around the tables, a much happier place than I'd been in for a long time.

I was beginning to wonder if I needed the restaurant as much as it needed me, because I was actually feeling excited again. Yes I was enjoying my time with Gianni, the unexpected frisson I felt when I saw him, and the way his voice made me melt inside like marshmallows in hot chocolate. I also loved being at the beginning of a new venture in the way I had with the first restaurant – like my life was a white canvas. But what to paint on that white canvas was the question.

I thought again about Gianni and his pride. 'Pride comes before blood,' he always said, it was an Italian thing wrapped up in family and being a man therefore not being vulnerable, which was a contributing factor to the mess we'd got ourselves in. The even bigger problem was that I didn't have the courage to make any moves, because if I did and he rejected me I'd be so hurt. It would change the dynamic of our relationship and affect any kind of long-term friendship I might hope to have in the absence of something more. Appledore might have offered me the opportunity for a fresh start, but I wasn't prepared to sit around on the edge of his life and watch him meet and marry someone else. I had pride too, and with both of us being so stubborn neither of us would make the first move for fear of rejection. So as lovely as our time together had been, we were at stalemate again. Gianni hadn't said he wanted me to stay around after Christmas so perhaps the best thing to do was to enjoy this time together, head back to London after Christmas and get on with my own life.

The following morning was Christmas Eve and I awoke to a heavy knocking on the front door.

'I'm coming, calm down,' I shouted and once I'd put my robe on and staggered down the stairs I opened the front door, but no one was there. I looked down the path to see if anyone was around and was turning to go back in when I almost fell over a Christmas tree. Someone had left it on the step along with a basket filled with home-made Christmas goodies, the ones I'd been lusting after the previous day in John's Deli. A little bag of iced stars tied with a bow, another with two gingerbread men, a white box containing six mini mince pies, a bottle of red wine and a piece of Brie wrapped in greaseproof paper.

I took the basket inside and put it on the kitchen counter, delighted to see a little note attached from the sender, but I had a good idea who it was from. Gianni must have ordered it to be delivered because the note was typed.

Dear Chloe, happy Christmas. We're both on our own, so what about giving things another go? I thought it might be romantic to share this Christmas hamper. I could come over to the cottage and spend Christmas with you, I don't mind driving through the snow, you're worth it. X

I was amazed. So this thing with Natalia was nothing 'We're both on our own,' I read again, 'I thought it might be romantic' and 'you're worth it'. So Gianni had finally been able to put aside his pride and all the silly games and come clean about his real feelings – and my tummy was filled with tinsel.

This hamper, along with the Christmas tree, was obviously an acknowledgement from the past, of Christmas food we'd shared here and the time we'd carried that first Christmas tree through the cottage doors together.

I re-read the message, I was ecstatic, he obviously wasn't in any kind of relationship with the stunning redhead. That phone call I saw might have been her wanting him back, but he'd said 'No, I love my wife and we're going to share Christmas together, you can take your lustrous hair and your long legs and be away with you, because I'm back with the woman I love,' or something along those lines. The fact was that Gianni had been feeling exactly the same as I had, and when earlier in the evening, he'd said it was too late for us he had obviously been feeling unsure. But he'd had a chance to think about it and now he was *very* sure, inviting himself over, suggesting we share the hamper perhaps even thinking of the open fire and me naked on a picnic rug. I laughed at the thought – would this be the dramatic reconstruction of our energetic honeymoon wrapped together in front of an open fire? Or was I just getting completely carried away by it all?

I grabbed my phone and texted him, knowing he wouldn't respond.

Thanks for the Christmas gifts, please do come and share my fine Brie and tasty tarts in front of the fire this evening.

I kept it light, jokey, I wanted to be flirty without being over the top, because knowing Gianni there was every chance his tenuous grasp on the English language could read quite differently than his intentions, leaving me with egg on my face. Quail's egg in aspic to be precise!

I looked again at the note, rereading it over my breakfast of hot coffee and thickly buttered granary toast, imagining how the hamper-sharing evening would progress. He would arrive in a lovely smart, but casual suit, a white open-necked shirt, and when I opened the door we'd fall into each other and he'd carry me into the dining room between kisses. Okay maybe I was getting a bit ahead of myself but this was Christmas after all maybe I was due one miracle?

I caressed the lovely hamper, sniffed the mince pies, inadvertently hoovering up icing sugar, making me sneeze. At this point the door knocked again and I rushed to open it, thinking it might be Gianni come to surprise me early, perhaps he'd been waiting outside all the time. But when I opened the door it was an elderly lady, who introduced herself as Mrs Tunstall. She was wearing a hat and scarf and big coat with a hood, but I could just see her little face peeping out from under all the winter fabric.

'I came to tell you your Christmas tree's getting covered in snow. If you leave it out here it'll be ruined,' she said.

'Thank you, it's a gift from my husband,' I said, beaming. This was technically true, we were still married in the eyes of the law and after tonight it could be even more true. What a difference a hamper makes, just thinking about him as my husband now filled me with a lovely warmth rather than the emptiness it had done for the last year. 'He owns the new restaurant down the road.'

'Ah, the big knob from London who whacks people over the head with a leg of pork... I saw it on the Twitter.'

'Well, it wasn't quite like that,' I said defensively.

'Apparently he strangles them if he doesn't like what they say about his food. I retweeted *that*,' she said self-righteously, like it would change the bloody world.

Oh the joys of being in a small town, where everyone knew everyone else's business – talked about it – exaggerated it and sent it back out into the world with bells on.

'It... yes that's the restaurant... but it wasn't a leg of pork, it was a beef sausage,' I said, like it was okay for chefs to hit their customers with beef products but not pork.

'Only a sausage, she says,' she laughed and shook her head in disgust, and was now scrutinising me from under her hood. 'Are you on drugs?'

I bristled, implying one had to be high on bloody drugs to want the facts rather than local fantasy made me cross.

'He's an excellent chef... actually,' I said, aware this wasn't the first time I was defending Gianni in the sinking sand of public opinion. I was also a little discouraged on Gianni's behalf, because last night had been such a success I didn't want rumours and people's misconceptions being plastered all over social media and ruining his hard work.

But Mrs T was clearly a busybody and not happy with 'out of towners' and felt the need to share this with me. 'I've been on the local council for fifty years and I've met some people, but you Londoners think you can come down here with your legs of pork and your cocaine...'

What the hell was she going on about? Every village had one I suppose, but just my luck the Appledore eccentric lived next door.

'Mrs Tunstall, the local newspaper critic was being rude about the food... and it was only a sausage,' I repeated, reaffirming that sausages were perfectly acceptable weapons to use against one's restaurant customers. 'Goodness people round here do exaggerate,' I added in my poshest, most indignant voice. 'Now if you'll excuse me, I have a tree to decorate,' and with that I picked up the tree by the top sprigs and attempted to make a swift and dignified exit back into the cottage. However, this wasn't easy with six feet of Nordic spruce between my legs, and heaving a little too hard, I ended up on my back in the hall with the tree on top of me. Fortunately I was nimble, and my foot engaged quickly with the front door, slamming it and drawing a veil over the messy scene before Mrs T could get a shot of it and spread me across the Twittersphere.

I lay there for a few seconds, and started laughing to myself at the ridiculousness of it all. Eventually, I scrambled from under the beast, dragged it into the room and, using all my strength, hauled it to a standing position, then stood back and admired it. The scent of cool forests in winter now filled the room and even undressed without her baubles my tree looked magnificent. If

Gianni was coming round later to sample the hamper, it would be good to show him my appreciation by dressing the tree he'd bought me. So, once I'd checked the coast was clear, I set off down the snow-covered streets to the little shops where I'd bought the restaurant decorations earlier that week.

Chapter Fifteen

Mafia Men and Italian Stallions

Once I'd bought my tree decorations I decided to pop into the cafe where there seemed to be more staff than customers.

'Hello love,' called Roberta, who was wearing tinsel doodle boppers on her head and jiving at the jukebox. 'We're having a bit of a Christmas do, grab a drink!'

'Mum's still tipsy on last night's cocktails,' Ella said, from behind the counter. She was standing with Sue who was decked out in her usual vibrant colours, and today was accessorising with Christmas pudding earrings.

Meanwhile Gina was sitting on one of the stools at the counter vaping, it smelled of cinnamon and when I commented on it, she said: 'Christmas Surprise, honey, we all like a surprise at Christmas?' She looked at me, 'Are you okay? Is that snow under your nose or are you doing coke?'

'What?'

She opened her handbag and handed me a mirror. 'Sort it, honey, they don't look too fondly on class A drugs around here…

the last time I did coke I went to the ladies' and woke up in Corsica.'

Sue's ears pricked up at this and she was over, 'Oh love, I didn't have you down as one of those coke crackerheads.'

'I'm not,' I said, indignantly, worried Mrs Tunstall's gossip had already gone viral around town. I looked into Gina's proffered mirror and spotted a white stain of icing sugar under my nose. 'It's from the mince pies…' I laughed, 'I sniffed them.'

'Well as long as that's all you're sniffing,' Sue said, 'I don't believe in drugs, I mean it's up to you, it's your provocative…'

'It was mince pies, I was sniffing mince pies,' I stressed, realising the icing sugar under my nose was probably what nosey neighbour Mrs T was referring to when she'd mentioned cocaine. It would probably be all over town now.

'Well I've never heard of snorting mince pies,' Roberta said, hand on hip. 'I've heard of the Pizza Connection, but that was money and drug laundering in pizzerias back in the motherland. I knew some bad people from Sicily…' she started.

'Mum, stop telling everyone you're a friend of the Mafia, you're going to get yourself locked up. Alan Sugar won't let you on *The Apprentice* if he thinks you're involved with organised crime.'

'I just won't tell him, love,' Roberta said as she carried on wiping tables.

'Mum, the nearest you've ever been to the Godfather was at The Odeon,' Ella giggled.

'I know some Mafia men,' she said, indignantly.

'Al Pacino doesn't count, he's an actor, and you've never met him.'

'I have,' said Gina with a wicked smile, 'and he wasn't acting with me.' She took a long drag of her vape pen and the vapour swirled around her red lips. She was no spring chicken, but looked like a 1940s film star, all crossed legs and blonde hair, in tight designer suits. Everyone went quiet for a moment so I gently stepped in, 'Wasn't Al Pacino a friend of Roberto Riviera?' I asked, hoping to reintroduce the possibility of the star coming to Appledore and visiting the restaurant.

'Yeah… they fought over me once,' she said. 'Roberto won,' she added with a sly wink.

'I bet you're looking forward to seeing him, when he's here in the New Year?' I offered, hopefully.

'Can't wait babe… I'll bring him to meet you, just hope Al doesn't find out, Italians can be brutal.'

'Well, I can't say I've slept with Roberto Riviera or Al Pacino,' Roberta piped up, 'but I'm catnip with the red bloods down the Over Sixties Italian Club'. 'Those old boys are all ex mob, and they can't get enough of me, say I'm the spitting image of Sophia Loren.' She wasn't.

'They probably tell you they were Mafia so you'll go out with them,' Ella added.

'Ooh I hadn't thought of that. Italian girl problems,' Roberta sighed, like it was a burden to be adored, and carried on jiving to the music as she wiped tables.

'Do you speak Italian, Roberta?' I asked, wondering if it might make Gianni feel more at home if he could chat to someone in his native language.

'Si, si,' she said, both arms now in the air swaying. It was good enough for me, and I made a mental note that there was help in Italian if he should need it.

'Why do you want to know?' she asked, dancing towards me. 'Are you hoping to get that lovely big Italian chef into your bed for Christmas?'

'Mum please?' Ella said, looking at me with an awkward face.

'Oh she doesn't mind me asking, do you luvvie? I mean he's very handsome, but he's a piece of work isn't he, I mean all that waving his meat around and swearing. He's like that chef off the telly?'

'Ooh yes the sweary one, Gordon Ramsay,' Sue said, glistening under the cafe lights like a Christmas tree. 'You've got the hots for him then?'

'Gordon Ramsay?'

'No, the one you were married to, Giannininini... or something?'

'I don't know, we're not together at the moment.'

'Ooh I reckon there's a chance, I saw him gazing into your eyes when you first came in here,' Sue said, as I blushed. 'What's his star sign, love?' she asked, warming to the theme. 'I reckon he's an Aquarius... loyal, but with a dark twist, very moody with Venus rising. What do you think, Roberta?'

'I'm thinking big, hairy goat,' she said, looking at me thoughtfully, 'Capricorn on the cusp. Stubborn, yet dreamy, cold, yet capable. And brimming with Latin passions,' she giggled.

'He's a Leo,' I said, 'and I'm Taurus.'

Sue crossed herself, 'Sweet Jesus, it's a wonder you ever even kissed, let alone married. An ongoing battle between patience and passion… yours is the patience, his is the passion. It'll never last, love.'

'It didn't,' I said, though I hadn't put the failure of our marriage down to star signs until now.

'Ah who knows, the stars can sometimes surprise us. I hope it works out for you, sweetheart, I really do – we need a bit of a Christmas romance around here,' Sue sighed. 'If he's a Leo he's the kind of man who needs a woman, and once he gets the one, he's faithful to the end… Leos are very loyal, mark my words,' she winked.

'Well faithfulness would always come high on my list – but stubbornness is his problem, I'd like to talk about the possibility of trying again, but I don't know what his reaction would be,' I heard myself say out loud.

'Remember what happened with Liz Taylor and Richard Burton?' Gina said, from behind a cloud of 'Christmas Surprise'. 'They went down the aisle twice, big mistake, I told him too, but he wouldn't listen, couldn't resist her, like a moth to a flame.'

'We're still married, so we wouldn't need to get married again,' I said, hopefully, wondering why Liz and Richard's marriage failed twice, and if that could happen to us. I wondered idly if Gina had slept with Richard Burton and decided she probably had.

'Oh well, if it's what you want, why don't you just wrap yourself up in Christmas paper and lie under his tree. Then on Christmas morning when he comes downstairs jump up and shout happy Christmas,' Sue offered. 'I did that for my ex-husband once.'

'Yes, but his new wife was a bit pissed off,' Ella said. 'Remember the injunction?' she added.

'Oh, that was all a big overreaction on her part,' Sue said, wafting her hand away like it was nothing. 'She pretended to be scared, like she didn't expect me to jump up from under the tree on Christmas morning.'

Ella shrugged and gave me a wink.

'If I were you I'd go for it while that big Italian stallion is still single,' Roberta said. 'He might be your ex, but he's a handsome chap, all the girls will come running for him the minute they know he's free.'

I felt a little uneasy at this, and I saw the redhead in slow motion, shaking that lovely hair loose and laughing. In my face.

'How is he this morning after all that pan crashing?' Gina asked.

'Oh I don't know; I haven't seen him today…'

'Yeah honey, I'm sure,' she winked and blew out another swirly cloud of cinnamon vapour.

'No, honestly, nothing's happened between us since I came here, we just danced… last night, when everyone had gone.' There was a communal 'aaaah', and I was warmed by their obvious support.

I perched on a stool next to Gina. Ella was behind the counter wiping glasses and Roberta was still dancing when another girl came from the back kitchens with a huge tray filled with chocolate brownies. I recognised her from the restaurant the previous evening.

'I've baked these in case we get a rush on, but if we don't we can eat them all,' she smiled. 'It's okay, I'll just run to Scotland and back to work them off!'

Ella laughed at this, 'And back again, judging by the amount of chocolate in that recipe.'

'I made them with beetroot, so these babies are at least one of your five a day,' she added, smiling at me.

'This is Dani, our assistant manager,' Ella said, and Dani smiled and gave me a little wave.

'Sorry last night was a bit chaotic,' I said, 'I hope you enjoyed it in the end?'

'You mean your Italian having a big strop?' Roberta offered. 'Oh don't worry about it, us Italians are very hot-blooded, I understand, love… quite enjoyed it really, just wish he'd come and said hello.'

'He will next time, I promise. Last night was all a bit stressful with the oven and…'

'Oh don't be daft, these things happen, and the food was delicious,' Ella said.

'Yes he's a great chef, I'm just working on his customer care now,' I smiled.

'You'll never change him, men will be who they will be,' Gina said, rather cryptically. 'He'll shout and scream and you'll take him to bed in your best underwear and afterwards he'll be like a kitten, all soft and pliable, and you'll be able to get anything out of him. Diamonds, a Chanel bag… a designer vagina?' she added, like it was just another coveted accessory.

'No. He won't be seeing my best underwear, not for a while anyway,' I giggled.

'Famous last words, honey,' Gina laughed.

'It's his Mediterranean blood, the passion and the temper,' Roberta was saying. 'I'm just the same, but you have to make it work for you. But take my advice and next time he loses his shit in the middle of a busy service, make sure "someone" anonymously calls the local paper and lets the reporter know it's the same guy who attacked a man with a Japanese sausage – and hey presto, it's all over the local news again, you can't pay for publicity like that.'

I didn't plan to take her advice, but nodded enthusiastically, she was trying to help and was so delighted with her plan I couldn't knock it.

'Sue's had her share of hot chefs, haven't you, love?' Roberta said. 'She met one on eBay didn't you?'

'Oh I did. He was selling off his pasta utensils and we got chatting, said he was an Italian chef closing his restaurant. Turns out he was an escaped convict who'd burgled a restaurant. Mind you, I should have known when he put too much origami on my Bolognese, a real Italian wouldn't do that... but we live and learn don't we?' She smiled and everyone nodded sagely like she hadn't just said something completely bonkers. In spite of their whacky view of the world, I liked them; none of these women judged each other, and they welcomed me into their fold so readily.

'I've not been on many dates, never had a proper boyfriend until my husband,' I said, their warmth making me feel comfortable enough to share this. 'It all seems rather scary being out there, doesn't it?'

'Oh love, these three could all tell you about husbands and being single and toyboys and...'

'And Tinder...' Sue added.

And as the snow fell outside, we drank hot chocolate and 'the girls' shared their stories. It was like watching a wonderful moving, funny, tragic box set of women's lives. The stories involved love, betrayal, Hollywood film stars, divorce, being rinsed/loved/ abandoned on a roadside in Spain wearing only fake tattoos and bunny ears (Sue) and a mild, if dangerous flirtation with the mob on Twitter (Roberta). And as the late Christmas Eve afternoon turned to evening, fuelled by brownies, ice cream, and lots of laughs, we huddled together around the counter like girl guides at camp telling our stories. And as we laughed and told the stories of our loves and lives I felt like everything was coming together for me here – and I wondered if I could ever leave? But first I had to work out just what was happening with me and Gianni, and that was the tricky bit.

Chapter Sixteen

Paper Stars and Bloody Cheeses

I got back to the cottage as night fell, and closing the curtains I dressed the tree. I also filled jars with glitter and tea lights and spread fairy lights everywhere, even the kitchen, then cut out little paper stars, attached them to twine and strung them on the tree and around the windows. Aware I'd suddenly gone from 'Christmas doesn't live here' to full on 'Santa's grotto', I justified it by telling myself I was doing it for Gianni, my guest.

I prepared a small wine and cheese platter with a loaf of crusty bread and the cheese and home-made Christmas chutney from the hamper he'd sent me. I looked forward very much to sharing this together, it was so thoughtful and romantic. I also found it endearing that he'd used this as a way to reach me, to let me know how he felt. I'd hurt him so much he was scared to put himself out there and tell me how he felt — so he'd used the idea of sharing a hamper to break the ice. I was touched, and excited to see him.

By 7 p.m. there was no sign of him, and he hadn't responded to my text so I wasn't even sure if he was going to turn up. The restaurant was now closed until after Christmas, so it wasn't like he was busy, so I called him and was relieved when he picked up straight away.

'Hi, I have Christmas Eve ready and waiting,' I said, 'so come over whenever you're free.'

'Really? Is okay?'

'Yes, of course. I want you to come and share the hamper with me. We can eat the cheese and chutney and drink the wine and… talk. Oh and I've decorated my tree!'

'Ah well… that's good. I will be along soon then.'

I put my phone down and smiled at myself as I glanced in the mirror, but soon stopped smiling when I saw how flat my hair was from constant snow. On closer inspection, my face was also dry and a little ruddy from the cold and my eyes looked small and piggy. I wished I'd brought more suitable clothes with me. I hadn't thought to bring any nice underwear or low-cut dresses because I hadn't bargained on any kind of Christmas seduction, and my thermal vests were hardly the stuff of male fantasies. I quickly brushed my hair, applied some foundation, slicked on a little lipstick and immediately felt better. I pouted in the mirror, wondering if other people could see what I saw, an eighteen-year-old girl – in a forty-five-year-old body. When the hell did that happen?

At 7.30 there was a knock on the door and I rushed to open it. There was Gianni standing on the doorstep covered in snow, and I had to laugh. 'You look like a snowman… a yeti,' I said, gesturing for him to come into the hall as I closed the door behind him. He'd brought in a flurry of snow and chill and I shivered slightly as I walked him through into the living room. 'Da da,' I said, and pointed at the tree. He looked at it and smiled, which I guessed was as good as it ever got with Gianni and I reminded myself I had to manage my expectations.

'Follow me,' I said, walking into the kitchen. 'Voila!' I stood by the hamper like a gameshow hostess.

'Yes, very nice,' he said, still non-committal and quite under-whelmed by what he saw.

'So, let's drink wine, eat the contents and talk,' I said, feeling a little deflated at his mood.

I was puzzled, he wasn't the most effusive person, but he seemed almost indifferent and I'd expected a more positive reaction, especially as this had been his idea. 'This is what you wanted to do, isn't it Gianni?'

'I'm not so sure...'

'Oh have you changed your mind?' What the hell was going on here? Surely I hadn't misread the signals again?

'My mind is changing all the time, I have not the clue for this.'

'Well, let's just have a glass of wine,' I said, upset by this sudden backpedalling.

I needed a drink, so opened the bottle of red, and poured two glasses, while continuing to smile, but his reticence was making me feel more like a magician's assistant just before the knife-throwing act.

I had laid out the cheese and chutney, figs and bread on the kitchen counter, and I asked if he was hungry.

'No, I already ate.'

So why had he sent me a bloody hamper with a note to say let's get together tonight or words to that effect?

'Look if you'd rather be somewhere else?' I said, puzzled.

He looked at me; 'No but this is… I just bloody freak out… being in little cottage with the little bloody cheeses and you…'

What was his problem, me, the cottage or the cheese? 'Gianni, I thought you wanted to share the hamper and talk?' I said, confused.

'Yes, but hells balls Chloe, I want the big Tuscan cheeses, robust Puglian wines… not the little pissing cheeses from France…'

'If you had such a problem with the geography of the bloody cheeses perhaps you should have asked for Italian,' I snapped, tired of walking on eggshells. 'God Gianni, it's like dealing with a sulky teenager, what's wrong with you?'

'I am sad, coming here and seeing the tree and the little stars on the windows… I miss my old life… with you,' he said. It came from nowhere, out of the blue, and he looked at me, his face searching my expression. 'It's okay… you don't have to say anything,' he said.

'I miss our life too,' I echoed, relieved and happy that he felt the same, both sitting at the little kitchen table from our old life, thoughts flickering in the candlelight. I wanted this, I wanted him and I knew now that I'd always loved him and probably always would, but I didn't want to go back to what we had when I left. 'I miss the life we had at the beginning, not the one later on, where we lived separate lives,' I said into the silence.

He nodded and reached for my hand across the table. Two lonely people with a lifetime of mistakes back together on Christmas Eve.

'I told myself I wanted to be alone this Christmas…' I started. 'I thought it would be good to have some time and space to myself. I thought I could work with you and not feel anything, but the past keeps grabbing me and hauling me back, I don't know if it's being with you, being here – or just Christmas. Are you lonely?' I asked.

He looked straight at me. 'I teach myself to live without other people,' he said. 'It's better to be lonely than sad and allow them to trample over your feelings and destroy you.'

'Oh, that wasn't what I wanted for you. I just had to leave, I felt like it was over and I was so unhappy, so lonely…'

'But we were married, how could you be lonely?'

'You were never there.'

He nodded slowly and kept his eyes on mine.

Was it the candlelight, or were his eyes deep and warm in a red wine kind of way?

I looked into those eyes thinking how it was like we'd been washed up here in Appledore like two pebbles on the beach. I looked down at his hands now resting on the table, fingers entwined around the delicate stem of his glass and allowed my mind to contemplate the big hands, calloused from kitchen work. Those hands cajoled ingredients gently and skilfully into the tastiest, most sublime dishes; they manipulated pastry, tore leaves and firmly massaged oil over meats. I allowed myself to remember what those hands felt like on naked skin. My naked skin.

'I sometimes find things hard to say,' he said, the wine clearly softening him. 'But I am touched by everything you do.'

I was about to say something trivial, light-hearted when I saw he had tears in his eyes. I reached for his hand.

'I just… no one has ever done anything for a long time… for me. Just for me.'

Roberta was right when she'd described him as an Italian stallion. His hair was wavy, there was lots of it and, tonight, it was even wilder than usual. I'd seen it like this before many times, but seeing him through someone else's eyes I appreciated how handsome he was. What the hell was in this delicious Italian wine? I had to stop drinking now, because I was suddenly overcome with the desire to run my fingers through my estranged husband's hair, and who knew where that might lead.

'Gianni,' I said, and he stopped talking and looked at me.

'Did you know that Leo and Taurus are the most incompatible signs of the zodiac?'

'I don't believe it.'

'Neither do I,' I said.

There was definitely some magic in the air that Christmas Eve – I felt like an old-fashioned heroine, smiling coquettishly across the table, while aching to tame my man. I never wanted Gianni to lose his spark, his fiery temper, or his passion, but I also needed him to be kind and sensitive to me. I knew he could be rude and arrogant, but he was also vulnerable, and he needed me to be kind and sensitive too.

'Talk to me about Italy,' I said, like I used to when we were young. And as he talked, I tasted the fresh plum tomatoes from his family's Tuscan farm, sweet and savoury and juicy, ripened under an Italian sun. I breathed in the heady fragrance of the full and rounded reds from the nearby vineyard and ran barefoot through fields of bright yellow sunflowers. And some time later, I stood up to get more wine and he said, 'I'd better go.'

And the sweet tomatoes, the heady wine and the fields of sunflowers receded as my heart sank into the deep snow outside. I didn't want him to go, I'd hoped he might stay, that tonight on Christmas Eve in Appledore we'd give ourselves the benefit of the doubt and perhaps try again. But that wasn't to be, and I had to stop thinking about his beautiful hands and bare feet in sunflowers.

He stood to go and for the first time Gianni revealed a rather gallant side and walked behind me to move my chair. And as he headed into the hall pulling on his coat, I felt a tug inside my tummy, but despite what we'd shared these past few days, Gianni obviously wasn't feeling the same. I remembered the lovely green eyes, the urgent ringing of his phone, had this been an invitation to rekindle what we had, or a guilt hamper? Maybe friendship was all that was possible for us now and I had to try to accept that and let him go. I opened the front door and a blizzard was raging outside – the blast of cold air took my breath away as a huge pile of snow fell into the hall.

'Hell, that's just crazy out there,' I said, my mind spinning, I'd never seen snow like this.

Gianni stood on the doorstep half in and half out, apparently unsure whether to come back in and close the door or make a run for it.

'You'll never walk home in that,' I said, staring out, amazed and in awe at the curtain of snow barring access to the outside world. It was quite scary and beautiful at the same time, the cold night air turning everything to icicles and glittering frost.

'Sorry I have to go,' he said, 'you stand back so you don't get the snowing.'

With that he took a big step forward into the darkness and was immediately calf-deep in snow. He stopped and moved back into the doorway and just as he seemed to be setting off again, I touched his back with the flat of my hand and he came back into the cottage and stood in the hall looking down at me wordlessly.

'I can't go anywhere, I'm ass stuck here,' he said, holding out both hands helplessly.

I almost laughed out loud at this, I was also relieved he couldn't go, I felt we still had unfinished business, even if he didn't.

'Yep, looks like you're ass stuck here with me and the little bloody cheeses,' I smiled. I looked up at him, like a cat wanting to be stroked, and I couldn't help it, I instinctively leaned my head on his big, broad chest. I have no idea what made me do this strange, animal-like gesture. Perhaps my primal, sensual side had taken over?

Being here with Gianni in the cottage where our marriage had begun and remembering those early days when I could, at times of tiredness or stress, quite literally lean on my partner had obviously reared up, and it felt right. He was huge, about a foot taller and several stones heavier, plus he often worked out. I'd been reminded of this when he'd been hot in the kitchen and had taken off his white jacket to reveal those rather marvellous pectorals. I thought of them now as I leaned into him and had to stop myself from clutching them, they always felt so good.

He put his arms around me and I just continued to rest my head on his chest like I was checking for a heartbeat, and said, 'You will have to stay here.'

'A taxi?' he said.

My heart sank, why was he so desperate to avoid spending the night here with me?

'It's Christmas Eve, you can try, but it's not like London, you can't just put your hand out and flag a taxi down.' I was feeling rather silly, but as he'd made the first move with the hamper I'd foolishly assumed I was on safe ground to make physical contact. I clearly wasn't, so I moved my head from his chest. Finally free I looked him in the face. 'Oh God. Sorry, I hope I haven't come on a bit too strong, but we're still married and I just thought it would be easier if you stayed.' I don't mean with me in the same bed,' I added, embarrassing both of us in one sentence.

'No of course.' He went to the door again and I couldn't help but think he really didn't want to stay, not even in the spare room. I hoped for some reason I hadn't scared him off, but the fact he was now standing in the doorway desperate to make a run for it on what was probably the coldest night of the century wasn't the biggest ego boost. The wind was stronger now, the snow spiking down and underfoot it was probably impossible, but he looked at me one last time and said, 'I really do think it be the best if I go back tonight.'

I nodded, and it felt like my heart was breaking as I stood in the swirling snowy doorway watching him wading through snow one step at a time. Each step must have been such an effort it would take him ages to walk the couple of miles back to the restaurant. The fact he was prepared to wade through calf-deep snow in the dark on Christmas Eve told me all I needed to know. So much for sharing a bloody hamper. I watched him go and on he pushed, through the snow and hail and face-whipping wind, the sound of the sea crashing in the distance as he walked.

Before he disappeared into the darkness, I shouted 'happy Christmas,' and I could see him turn slightly and wave. And as I stepped back from the freezing, swirling weather, into warmth and sanctuary, I closed the door and felt irrationally sad, not to mention confused. Was there something Gianni hadn't mentioned… like that he was seeing someone else? Oh God, was he still with the redhead and I'd totally missed all the clues? Were the hamper, the lovely note, the Christmas tree and the softness around the eyes merely the fond gestures of a soon-to-be ex-husband? All I knew as I walked back into the kitchen was that my compulsion to touch him had to be reined in from now on, because whatever was going on with him, it wasn't the same as what was going on with me.

I felt the blood rush to my face as I relived the hall scene, me face deep in his chest like a bloody pet dog while he patted me and left. For God's sake, what I did was bordering on sexual harassment, you can't just lean on people and hope they'll reciprocate, even if they are your ex. I put the kettle on, no more wine for me – it made me do daft things and feel more intensely. Drinking that Chilean red had turned me into some kind of primal being, and I was stopping drinking as of now. If I wasn't careful I might find myself out in the snow sniffing out random men like a bloody wolf. But as I put my teabag in the cup I knew this wasn't about random men, it was about one man. And there was something about his eyes, his stand-offishness, his talent, his need to tell the truth in a world full of liars that made him special. And I wanted him… but perhaps I wasn't alone, and someone else now had his heart, and now it was too late?

Chapter Seventeen

Hormones, Memories and Lust

I drank my tea with a heavy heart, and even the sight of the lovely Christmas tree couldn't lift my spirits. Receiving that gorgeous hamper and the tree had given me a crazy idea that Gianni was making the first move to get back together, but clearly, I was wrong. He was so bloody handsome it was an easy road to take, falling for him all over again. And with no girlfriends around to talk sense and stop me from getting carried away, I'd turned the whole evening into some crazy Richard Burton and Elizabeth Taylor, 'let's do it all again, darling' date in my head.

Meanwhile, Gianni was oblivious to the stirrings he'd caused by his kind gift. To him it was just a hamper, it meant nothing, just a basket of figs and fancy cheese with no strings or promises. Any normal person would have realised this straight away, but not me. I was too overrun by hormones, memories and lust.

I wandered around the cottage at a loss. It was Christmas Eve, and usually I'd be defrosting the turkey and peeling carrots, surrounded by wrapping paper. The ham would be covered in marmalade, sweet and salty and pink, waiting in the fridge after a long glistening shift in a hot oven. The kitchen would smell of cloves and Gianni would be creating a magnificent pasta sauce and singing along to music while hurling salt over his left shoulder to keep the devil away.

It wasn't like I hadn't experienced snowy Christmas solitude, but now I missed noise, chaos, other voices. His voice. So I turned on the TV. It was Midnight Mass, and echoing carols filled the room with Christmas, like fragrant pine. I breathed it in and opened another bottle of red (okay so I'd given up on my vow to stop drinking, made half an hour before), Gianni and I had already drunk one and I thought again about the terrible weather and how he'd left, wanting to face that rather than spend the night with me. I sat down, hugging my glass and 'Once in Royal David's City' started up and I felt my heart swell with the season. How could I hope to escape this? Christmas was in my DNA, my parents had always made it special for their only child. All three of us would decorate the house in early December, and every year we'd use the same baubles on the tree, but we'd ring the changes. Mum and I would make paper angels, we'd save jam jars for tealights and stick cloves into oranges to make Christmas pomanders. We didn't have much money, but it was always special and it was those Christmas creations that sparked my love of the season. I'd always thought I'd pass on those family traditions, making paper chains and tealight jars with my own kids, and by the time 'Deck the Halls' had started on Midnight Mass I was crying and singing at the same time. Loudly.

I was just giving everything to the fa la la la la la la la la when I saw the silhouette of a man at the window – and it definitely wasn't Father Christmas. So as if my life wasn't going downhill enough, a madman was now preparing to enter the premises and accost me. The hairs on the back of my neck stood on end and I was rooted to the chair, but then I heard something at the front door and I leapt across the room, grabbed an old cricket bat I'd seen behind the sofa and went into the hall. I could see the silhouette, loitering, the shadow of a face peering in through the little window. 'GO AWAY I'M CALLING THE POLICE!' I screamed, as the fa la la las continued on the screen and the man began banging hard on the window. The louder he banged, the louder I screamed and the louder those halls were decked with bloody holly. Then, slowly but surely, the figure at the window materialised.

I moved towards the window, cautiously holding the cricket bat at my side, just in case it was a murderer who struck on Christmas Eve – I really had to stop reading those murder stories. And the nearer I got to the window, the more foolish I felt. It was Gianni, back from his snow hike, his face at the window begging to come in from the cold, like Cathy to my Heathcliff. Okay this probably wasn't the best comparison given what happened in *Wuthering Heights* – in fact they make Liz and Richard's second marriage look like a roaring success.

'I knew you wouldn't get far in that weather,' I said the cricket bat still in one hand as I opened the door, the blast of cold hitting me in the face.

'You playing the cricket?'

'No,' I said, too fragile to explain and ushering him in while putting the bat back where I found it.

'My feet they ache and I have the balls of an old man,' was his opening gambit as he landed in the hall, a flurry of snow and winter around him like an aura.

'Too much information,' I said, my Christmas bubble was well and truly burst – one minute you're singing along with the choir from King's College, eyes full of tinsel and fire, the next you're starring in *Scary Movie*. My heart was still beating wildly and it had nothing to do with romance – when a man chooses to head out into the freezing tundra rather than risk a night in your spare bed, you have to adjust your expectations.

'I stay here a little while until the snowing stops.' He was already planning his escape; did he have a romantic arrangement with someone else this Christmas?

'The snowing won't stop tonight,' I said. I'd checked the weather report, it was brutal for at least another twenty-four hours, roads were closed, train lines were down and no one was going anywhere – especially Gianni, even if he did want out. 'Stay in the spare room?' I said, standing well back from him and trying not to make it sound anything more than it was. I knew rejection when I saw it and I wasn't going there again.

'Ah I don't think I can stay…'

'Look, when I leaned against you before… it wasn't because I was trying to… touch you or anything,' I said, hoping this would be enough explanation.

But he stood with his head slightly to one side, waiting for a more substantial justification for my earlier shenanigans.

'I just had to lean on something and you were there. You're big and solid and you were always good to lean on… you said you missed me and I thought it'd be okay, I don't know – call it for old times' sake or something.'

'For laughing out loud Chloe, I don't know what to say to you. I don't know if I can trust my own feelings, or yours,' he added.

'You mean for crying out loud,' I automatically corrected him, like it mattered at this juncture. 'Look, let's have a Christmas Day armistice Gianni and just shelter here until the storm subsides?' I suggested.

He agreed, and I went into the kitchen to make us both a mug of cocoa.

'Take off your wet things, if you put your jumper by the fire it'll be dry by morning,' I said. 'The weather's so much more raw by the sea isn't it?' I called through from the kitchen.

'Yes and the bitch is frozen up, hard and cold all day.'

'Yeah,' I smiled to myself at this. 'I'd been hoping to have lots of lovely long walks, but it's just been so cold I've not walked nearly as much as I wanted to,' I was saying as I walked into the living room with two steaming mugs.

He'd taken off his coat and jumper and was sitting on one of the sofas; for a second I wasn't sure whether to sit next to him or take the other sofa. But then I thought, *sod it, this is my husband, I can sit next to him if I want to*, and I wanted to. But as I sat down I almost spilled my cocoa because it seemed he'd also taken off his jeans which were lying by the fire, and was sitting there in boxer shorts. He looked as yummy as steaming hot chocolate with melting marshmallows and fluffy cream, but I tried not to look below the waist. Being Italian, stripping off was something he always did easily. I'd often thought it must be the warm climate, the hot blood, aware I was stereotyping but not sure what else to put it down to. Sometimes it had been like living with Magic Mike', the way he abandoned his threads and wandered around the house half naked. I sat on the edge of the sofa and handed him his mug, trying not to look down at his thighs, now exposed beneath cotton striped boxers. I remembered them only too well.

'My balls hurt,' he announced for a second time.

What the hell was this? He plays it cool all night then twenty minutes in the snow and he's stripping down to his boxers and talking about his balls. Perhaps I'd dismissed the romantic element a little too briskly after all? But I decided to ignore this comment, I wasn't going there again, I'd already been rebuffed once tonight. So we sat together in front of the fire the flames dancing in our eyes as we both stared into it – with me trying not to let my eyes wander south anywhere near his apparent problem area.

I was just beginning to relax and settle down with my drink when he suddenly started making groaning noises. I looked over to see him grabbing one of his feet in a weird yoga type movement.

I hoped I wasn't in strange territory and he'd acquired new sexual appetites while we'd been apart, I didn't even know he could get his leg in that position.

'Gianni, I nearly spilled my cocoa,' I said, sounding very unsexy. He was now rocking backwards and forwards and now lifting his other leg up, until he was in a weird Lotus Position.

'My feets balls they kill me from the walking,' he said.

'Oh your balls… you mean the *balls* of your feet?'

'Yes,' he said, like I was being stupid, and hoisted up his other thigh again. This he did with some vigour, almost causing a wardrobe malfunction around the crotch area and I had to look away while he adjusted himself. 'So, are you spending Christmas Day alone?' he asked.

I studied my drink, so my eyes didn't happen on anything they shouldn't. 'Yes.'

He sipped his cocoa, oblivious to the drama his boxers were causing in my head.

'And you?' I asked, hoping if he did have an assignation with the redhead he didn't tell me. I couldn't take that, not on Christmas Eve, our wedding anniversary.

'Alone, yes.'

'Oh, I assumed you'd be spending Christmas with someone special,' I said, trying to find out without sounding bitter but personifying the woman scorned. It all made sense now, he was touching my cheek and dancing with me, but that's all it was nothing more, he was saving himself for her – I'd read too much into it.

'You seem upset,' he said.

'Not at all. But I don't know why you don't just tell me. I saw her Gianni… the girl with red hair… in the photo, at the awards… she called you, the other night.'

'Ahhh, yes, Natalia,' he said, 'she is lovely girl.'

I thought I might just cry. 'So are you together, is this why you don't want to stay here with me, because you're with her?'

He was laughing, his head was down, which I thought was a bit cruel, Gianni had never been cruel.

'What's so funny?' I snapped, about to burst into tears.

'Holy mackerel Chloe, you think I have the girlfriend?'

'I saw the photo of you and her… draped across you,' I said, trying not to sound bitter, and not achieving it.

'I not going out with anyone.'

'So who is she?'

'No one… In fact, I am giving up all the women.

'Even Natalia?'

'Yes, she has the boyfriend.'

'She was unfaithful?'

He was looking at me, laughter dancing in his eyes.

'It's not funny, Gianni.'

'She is just my friend.'

'I'm sorry. But "just my friend" doesn't call after midnight.'

'Okay I stop the teasing you ass basket. She was hired by Kim, my crazy publicity manager – Natalia is a model, we pay her to go to the awards, it was all for the publicity.'

My heart did a little dance, well, a big dance actually and I wanted to hug him, but I resisted – we'd been there already.

'Oh, so she wasn't your girlfriend?'

He shook his head, but I still wasn't satisfied. 'So why was she calling you on your mobile, at midnight?'

'She was calling from LA, where she lives – it was afternoon there, she calls to say she is getting married and she won't be playing my girlfriend for the events any more.'

'Really?' I felt rather stupid.

'Did it make you jealous, Chloe… I hope so,' he winked, and I just rolled my eyes. I felt very silly but I wasn't giving him the satisfaction of letting him know, because he'd tease me for ever.

'So if you don't have a girlfriend – why are you so against spending the night here, with me – not even with me, I mean in the spare room?' I suddenly heard myself say.

'Because I have to protect Gianni, I can't let you come back and then leave me again.

'I understand, but I think I know what I want now… you weren't there for me Gianni.'

'I was, I leave work early to pick you up from airport when you were away working, I leave awards ceremony because you have the crisis with your car. You cry in the night and I am by your side, I dry your tears and I make the big bowl of pasta to make you feel better at 4 o'clock in the morning.'

I looked at him for a moment as I saw these memories through his eyes for the first time. He was right; in his own way he had always been there for me, but he gave me physical comfort when I really wanted to talk and share how we both felt with each other.

'I think we just didn't ever realise what the other needed,' I said, aware that I hadn't been there for him either.

'But what about the *Star Trek* man who talks to you on Face-book, does he give you what you need?'

So he'd been stalking my Facebook too? I was rather pleased, it meant he cared, but alarmed that he'd spotted Mr Spock's ears, I thought I'd cropped them out. 'Oh Nigel, he's lovely, but he's not anything. I went for a few drinks with him, but it came to nothing.'

'You try to make me jealous?'

'No. Well okay a little… I saw the photo of you with Natalia and assumed you'd moved on, so I wanted you to see that I had.

'You can't be so sure you won't go back with him though. Is it really all over, because I couldn't be with you if you have the lover and you leave me again.'

My heart did a hopeful flutter, 'Is he the reason you didn't want to stay tonight? Nigel? Is he the reason you've been blowing hot and cold since I came here?'

'I never blow on the hot or cold.'

'I mean is that why you're giving me mixed messages, one minute I think you want to get back together, the next I'm getting negative vibes?'

He nodded. 'I might mix the messaging, but I want to be with you, Chloe. I came to Appledore to escape you, but you were everywhere, I see you sitting on the little benches, laughing on the bitch. And when you finally come here, I know I love you all over again. For me you are the only one…'

I was consumed with joy, how could two people feel so much and not communicate their feelings? We were both so damaged, so hurt we'd been unable to reach out – and I really wished now I'd never bigged Nigel up on social media. I'd been so psycho for a while after seeing Gianni in the photo with the beautiful Natalia I put up with Nigel so I could post selfies of us, sometimes even tagged him when he wasn't there in photos of cocktails for two. No wonder Nigel was confused, Gianni wasn't the only one who'd been blowing hot and cold, poor Nigel must have wondered what the hell I was up to when I'd only been out with him a few times, and one of those was to a bloody Star Wars Convention.

Looking at Gianni now, I believed him when he said I was the only one. I felt a stirring of passion for my husband that I hadn't felt for a while – when a man strips off and sits on your sofa you tend to see them with fresh eyes. Until recently I'd seen Gianni through a veil of irritation, but discovering he was single and now sitting next to me with wet, tousled hair and boxer shorts was quite a different proposition.

'Have you loved anyone since me?' I dared to ask. If we were communicating then we needed to get everything out there if we had a chance of any kind of relationship in the future.

'Yes.'

My heart almost stopped. 'A woman?'

'No a goat, they live in my village in Tuscany, I see her in the summer, eet was only a holiday romance,' he rolled his eyes.

I giggled. 'I was just checking. Are you in love now?'

'I think so.'

'Is she still in your life?' I said hopefully.

'She is.'

'Is she gorgeous?' I giggled, willing him to just take me in his arms and kiss me.

'She's beautiful and a lovely person too, very kind and caring...' He was staring into the fire, then he turned to look at me.

'This woman, the one you love, do you think she loves you?'

'She did, but she could be a son of a monkey and she had no idea at first how bloody good I was in bed. And once she realised that I had the Italian passion and I loved her, that was it... we were the happy ever afters.'

I giggled. 'Do you think they could ever have the happy ever afters again?

'Yes, I think so... if she could stay and love me again.'

'She does,' I said, in an almost whisper. And I thought about how different this Christmas Eve was to the year before when I'd left. Back then I thought there was nothing for us but here we were, we'd found our way back to each other.

He put his empty cocoa mug on the floor and held both my hands.

'I should never have walked out on you, but you shouldn't have let me go, Gianni.'

'I know, I hit my head against the wall and say you stupid bloody bugger you had bad ass everything and you let her walk away.'

'I should have talked to you... do you hate me for leaving?'

'No, do you hate me for not coming after you?'

'No, I needed the time alone. But now I'm glad I came back here, where we could get to know each other all over again without the big restaurant and all the pressures.' I didn't know if it was down to fate, but I was with the right man in the right place at the right time – and in Gianni's words, how 'bad ass monkeys arses' was that?

I couldn't help thinking how ironic it was that we were finally able to communicate about our feelings, away from home, away from the marriage. But it made me realise that being married could sometimes be an obstacle to being in love.

'My heart she broke every day,' he continued. 'I bake the iced cakes for when you come home because they are your favourite and I wanted to give you everything that made you happy. But you never came home, and the iced cakes they go hard and stale and start to crack like my heart,' he said, gently caressing both my hands with his.

Ending a marriage is like a death, but here now, in the dying embers of the fire, I felt a flicker of something new igniting inside me. I was surprised, but pleasantly so when Gianni leaned over and took my face in both his hands. I felt the intensity of him. The fire now in his eyes, I lost myself in the flames, forgetting the hurt and the emptiness, and soon his lips were on mine.

This was the Gianni I knew, strange, yet familiar, even his smell was slightly different. He was fiery and passionate, and so were his kisses, his tongue pushing gently but firmly into my mouth until I thought I might explode. And after a while, just kissing and giggling and holding each other, he pushed me gently back on the sofa and asked me in a husky voice if I was okay. I nodded and pulled him onto me, taking his boxer shorts down and running my hands along his bare skin. I wanted him more than I'd ever wanted anything. It was wonderful to discover we were still capable of such feelings, like finding a Christmas gift under the tree and slowly opening it to reveal an amazing surprise. This wasn't my husband making love to me, this was the man I'd fallen in love with years before, and I loved the thrill of this new flesh on mine, this hot and strange desire taking me somewhere I'd never been before. Christmas was here and as we reached a crescendo I heard his cries of ecstasy and the sound of the King's College singers bringing it home with a stirring performance of 'Hark the Herald Angels Sing'.

Chapter Eighteen

The Force Awakens

The next morning I looked across at the other pillow, expecting to see those sleepy eyes, that tousled hair and the whiskery face of an unshaven man. But he'd gone. What happened? I really thought we'd worked everything out last night but had Gianni had a sudden change of heart?

I put my robe on and marvelled at the fact there was still a snow storm whipping around out there. Gianni must have been very keen to leave my bed this morning if he'd headed back in that. Only I could have a one-night stand with my husband, who then scarpers in the morning without even a goodbye. It might have been nice if he'd stuck around, at least to say happy Christmas.

We were both so keen to go to bed we hadn't really firmed up arrangements re the marriage. Were we together or not? I hoped so, but his absence was speaking volumes.

I wandered into the kitchen to put the kettle on and dropped a tea-bag into a mug, unable to think straight, desperately trying to work out what was going on. But as the kettle boiled I heard the door open and someone walk in, I was alone, in my robe, so my first instinct was to grab the cricket bat again and head into the hall. I didn't breathe, just clutched the bat, ready to whack whoever tried to overpower me, but he was inside, walking heavily down the hall. I hadn't heard him shut the door behind him, so he could escape quickly, but before I had a chance to brandish my bat he entered the living room to do his evil. I leapt forward with the bat, and he dropped whatever he was carrying. It was Gianni... and at his feet was a pile of croissants.

'Why you always carry a cricket bat in this house?' he said, looking at the croissants, but before I could pick them up, he grabbed me around the waist and my arms flung around his neck and we kissed.

'Gianni, I thought you'd gone,' I said, pulling away, relieved, almost tearful, but laughing at my ridiculousness.

'I wanted to bring you the breakfast in bed, because you make me feel so good, so happy. I surprise you with warm croissants from the restaurant. We should have them with real Italian coffee, but you only have the instant shit in the jar.'

'What a lovely thing to say...'

'About the instant shit in the jar?'

'No that I make you feel good, happy. Because you make me feel happy too,' I said.

Then he leaned in and whispered in my ear: 'You were desperate to be in the bed with me last night, yes?'

'Steady on, I wasn't desperate,' I laughed, now desperate to have sex with him again. I pushed him away playfully, feeling a little hot under the collar. 'What about you and me?' I asked.

'It's simple, we are back together, no?'

'I would love that, but how will it work?'

'What do you mean?'

'Well you live here now and I have a flat in London.'

'You move here we run the restaurant together – it won't work without you, Chloe. We live happily ever after.'

He was saying just what I wanted to hear, and I had held this in my heart like a secret, never daring to hope. To stay here with Gianni and run the restaurant would be what we'd always dreamed of, and a magical and very happy ending to our story.

'Am I ready for this… are *we* ready for this?' I asked.

'I've been ready for you to come home for a long time,' he said.

I smiled. 'I only came home for your iced cakes,' I said.

'You are the son of a monkey,' he laughed, and we kissed again and within seconds were rolling about naked on warm croissant crumbs. I was suddenly so reckless I didn't even worry about the butter in the bread staining the rug, I just enjoyed wild, abandoned sex on the floor. Then he carried me to the small dining table, and clearing it with one hand, lay me down on the Christmas tablecloth and made love to me. I'd never experienced anything like this before, and when it was all over I gasped, with pleasure of course, but also surprise.

'We've never… had sex like that before,' I said, as I climbed off the table, wrapping the tablecloth around me.

'We had all of the baggage in the past,' he said. 'This is a new Gianni and Chloe.'

He was right, this was our second chance and we were so lucky to be given the opportunity to get it right this time.

He smiled and took my hand, leading me to the sofa where we snuggled up together, he caressed my cheek with his hand. 'You make me want to be creative with you, I want to make love to you everywhere, and anywhere,' he sighed. I felt like a door had been opened onto something completely new, something I'd never even glimpsed before. Intimacy had been a part of my marriage, but it wasn't at the core and always accompanied by some inhibition from me. I was Gianni's wife, but sex became a way of trying to conceive and for a while became a chore for both of us, the spontaneity had gone and when I realised we couldn't have children, I didn't want sex any more. But now all that had changed and we were together because we wanted to be with no agendas, no pressure, just the two of us making it on our own.

Sitting on the sofa, dressed in a tablecloth, my legs still throbbing from my table action, I remembered something I'd buried, a lovely memory of our honeymoon, while staying here. We were walking along the beach hand in hand and I'd had this uncontrollable urge to make love to him and when we kissed it was me wanting to take it further. It was December, there was no one about and I suggested we walk a little further down the beach and find somewhere private, and he looked at me, like I'd given him the most wonderful gift, and he grabbed me by the hand and we ran along the beach, both looking for a sand dune, a sea wall. And when we found a shelter, we covered ourselves in his big coat, I climbed on top of him and we made love. That was who I used to be, before all the complications and disappointments, when I knew who I was, not a wife, not a wannabe, never be mum, just me, Chloe.

And I thought about my life, the twists and turns, the good times and bad. I wasn't pregnant, nor would I ever be, but I was with a man who I now knew only gives his heart away once. We would never have everything we'd ever wanted, but we had each other, and that was enough. I felt cherished again.

Gianni was warmer than ever and seemed to relax even more, kissing me gently on the cheek, running his fingers along my arm, following me into the kitchen when I made tea because he wanted to be near me. And I felt the same.

Then my phone rang, and as I picked it up we both saw the name on the screen. It was Nigel.

'No, I don't believe the ass butt he call you now, here?'

'Calm down. Maybe he just wants to wish me a happy Christmas?' I said, clicking the red button to stop the phone ringing.

He was looking at me with a sulky face.

'Oh don't be such a baby, Gianni. Look I'd better pick up or he'll just keep ringing, he's a bit bonkers and he might even turn up on the doorstep!' I joked, pressing the accept button as Gianni muttered something about camels' arses.

'Hi Nigel, this is a difficult time,' I said.

'Oh, I'm sorry.'

'No, it's fine.' I felt a bit mean fobbing him off on Christmas Day, he was probably lonely, and I had to do this gently.

'I just wanted to say happy Christmas, and check you got the hamper?' I heard him say, and for a moment I had no idea what he was talking about. Then it all suddenly started to make a weird kind of sense.

'You mean the hamper from the local deli... here?' I looked at Gianni, who was just staring ahead, a frown on his face. Oh God, so it wasn't a Christmas gift from Gianni after all.

'Oh... yes, I did, it was lovely, thank you,' I said, recovering quickly. 'And the Christmas tree... you sent that too?'

'Yeah as one deli owner to another I called him up and asked John's Deli to send their best Christmas hamper and a tree to the beautiful lady in Seagull Cottage. I had no address, it was all a bit vague, just glad it reached you.'

'It was a lovely surprise,' I said. 'Thank you so much.'

Gianni was still nearby muttering curses and listening, watching unsmiling.

'So, what about it? How about me coming down to Devon and sharing that hamper with you?' Nigel was saying. 'I'm ready to set off now if you like, I could be there by teatime?'

'Oh that's sweet but...'

'Chloe, three words... *The Force Awakens.*'

'Oh yes that sounds great, but...'

'Don't even try to resist, I have it in my hand as I speak.'

'Oh God... what?' I said, horrified, I hadn't expected the call to take this turn.

'I am holding... wait for it... a brand new copy of the collector's edition in – you guessed it, 3D!'

'Oh...' I breathed a sigh of relief, and glancing over at Gianni gave him a smile, and he eventually smiled back. And Nigel kept on talking.

'I originally watched the film when it came out,' he was saying, 'and have to say I was disappointed, so I left it a year and decided to watch it again with a fresh mind.' Gianni was now holding out his hands in a 'What the hell?' gesture and I smiled again and blew him a kiss.

'I'm sorry Nigel, but I'm not free, I'm not single any more, I've got back with my husband… I loved him all along. I suppose you could say I've had my force awakened.'

I turned off my phone and Gianni took me in his arms. 'No more stalkers,' he whispered in my ear, and then he lifted me up and carried me up the stairs, to the honeymoon bedroom where our story had begun.

This wasn't how I'd expected our story to end, but what a wonderful ending it was. The two of us thrown together by fate and the kind of love some people are never lucky enough to experience. We now had a future together, it was exciting, filled with hope and happiness. We'd once let our marriage melt in our hands like snowflakes, but that wasn't going to happen again because we both knew what we had, and what we might lose, and neither of us wanted to lose it again. I should have thanked Nigel really, because if it hadn't been for him sending that hamper I might never have invited Gianni round and been so honest and uninhibited about my feelings. We'd both been scared of rejection again and both too proud and too stubborn to put ourselves out there and make a move, it needed an outside force and in Nigel-speak – may that force always be with us.

Epilogue

It was New Year's Eve and I was driving to the restaurant from Seagull Cottage. There were a few tables booked in the restaurant that evening, and it was great to finally be open, life excited me again, and I hadn't felt that for a long time. Business had picked up really quickly after Christmas and it had a lot to do with the wonderful food and service Il Bacio was now providing. It may also have been helped by a little PR work from me when I contacted the press. I took Roberta's advice, held my breath and called the local newspaper about 'the sausage incident'. I said Gianni wanted to apologise to the critic he'd 'attacked' and after a sprinkling of charm and flattery from me, the critic agreed to turn up and be photographed (and apologised to). The next day the paper carried a photograph of both men brandishing large sausages in a humorous way – it was PR gold. It was the week between Christmas and New Year and there wasn't much news around so it went everywhere. Even the TV news turned up for the story and before we knew it we were everywhere – and completely booked up until February.

❄ ❄ ❄

I drove along the front at Appledore, the snow still around in drifts, a memory of Christmas and the new sparkle in my life. I drove slowly, taking in the early evening flurry of waves, lost in the dark greys and whites along the shoreline. The beach would soon emerge from the snow and by spring there'd be blue skies and big, fluffy white clouds – and I'd be here to see it all, because London was my past, and here was my future now. The sky was drawing in, and it would soon be a black, frosty winter's night but it was New Year's Eve and there was a tingle of excitement in the air.

This was my new beginning and I wasn't going to let it slip through my fingers this time. I'd accepted that life didn't always bring everything you want, but if you were patient it might give you what you need – and a little extra. I climbed from the car and was treated to a sparkle of fireworks exploding like little stars in the black sky and I was grateful for everything I had.

Stepping onto the pavement, I kicked the leftover snow, and suddenly became aware that the restaurant was in darkness. This seemed strange, so I went up to the window and peered in. There were definitely no lights on inside, and no movement either, which didn't make sense because I'd booked the staff to be here myself. I pressed my face against the window and was about to start banging on the door, when it opened and Gianni appeared.

'Ahh finally you here?' he said. I was momentarily distracted by his beautiful eyes that lit up when he saw me. I would never get bored with that.

'Gianni, what's happened, why is the restaurant closed?'

He shrugged and gestured for me to enter. 'Come in and I will explain,' he said, and in those few seconds as I walked into darkness, I imagined all the things that might have gone wrong since Gianni left the cottage this morning: bankruptcy, food poisoning and another food critic bashed over the head with his own dinner flashed before my eyes as I stepped into the dining room.

'SUPRISE!'

The lights came up and I couldn't believe it; so many smiles, so many people! I recognised some as new friends, others as familiar faces, but they were all smiling and it seemed they were all here for me. I looked at Gianni in amazement, and he smiled warmly, touching my arm. He grabbed a couple of flutes of cold champagne from a passing waitress.

All the girls from the Ice Cream Cafe were here, including Delilah the Pomeranian (in a sparkly red dress, accessorised with several strings of pearls). All of Appledore must have been there. I saw the man from the deli with his wife, and even spotted Fred from the chippy, who only had eyes for Roberta. There were other new faces from the village too – my village, and they were raising a glass of fizz to me. I beamed back at them all, amazed and confused, then looked at Gianni whose arm was around my waist.

'You said I had to get people to like me,' he whispered in my ear. 'It's been bloody hell – I've been very sodding busy for the last couple of days. But Chloe tells me if I smile they will smile back, and she was right, I think some of these monkey asses actually like me now.' Aware that people were waiting for some kind of announcement, he turned back to the crowd and said, 'Happy New Year everyone and thank you for coming! As you all know this is a surprise party for my wife Chloe, who thought we were open for business tonight but we're not. This is a party night for our new friends, and Mr and Mrs Callidori welcome you!' He turned to me, 'I wanted to do this for you because you have done so much for me, and I think I don't say thank you enough.' I had to catch my breath, everything I'd ever wanted was here now and this was the Italian icing on my cake. Everyone said aaah and I smiled and glowed and couldn't believe how lucky I was. 'So, thank you Chloe for everything,' he concluded, 'you turn up out of the grey when I needed you and I shout and call everybody names and still you stay. I am a holy ass, but you are my queen – thank you for giving me the second chance… to second chances!' He raised his glass as he looked into my eyes and everyone repeated his phrase.

'TO SECOND CHANCES!'

I clasped my arms around his waist and he kissed me and it seemed he couldn't wait to show me how hard he'd worked for the party. I was so touched that he'd go to all this trouble, but I knew the biggest thing for Gianni must have been to approach all these people – and be nice to them.

'You must really love me,' I said.

'I do. I even got the bad ass into the party spirits, just for you,' he pointed to the corner where 'DJ Marco' was now bouncing out some tunes, which made me laugh because he looked so uncomfortable in this happy setting.

Gianni and I clinked glasses, just as Roberta ran over to tell me she'd been booked to 'do Madonna' as the cabaret.

'We wanted Italian with a modern twist, just like the menu, didn't we my torta di dolcezza?' she said to Gianni affectionately.

'Yes, my darling, we did, and you will be bellissimo.' He added, 'There will be a standing ovation for your "Like a Virgin",' he then blew her a kiss.

I just stood back and watched in awe. Was this Gianni, my husband, the man who in most social situations had all the charm of a tasered bear? I reckoned the sea air had softened him, and I wasn't complaining.

'But I'm not the star attraction tonight am I, Gianni?' Roberta said, with a wink.

'No, we have the very special guest, I have been as excited as a chimpanzee,' he said, grabbing my arm and taking me over to Gina. She was wearing a sparkly black full-length knock 'em dead gown and her hair was coiled in big blonde curls. She had her back to us as we walked towards her and as she turned to greet us I was amazed and delighted to see a craggy, very handsome, and familiar face. It was the Hollywood film star Roberto Riviera, here in the flesh, just as she'd promised. I couldn't speak. I'd worked with celebrities before, but he was A+ list and I felt weak at the knees as he turned to Gianni and I and smiled.

'My dear Chloe, I'm delighted to meet you,' he said, shaking my hand. I still couldn't speak, I just gazed at him like he'd just stepped out of a film and I was in the cinema audience. His hair was steely grey, his skin golden, and his eyes still the chocolate brown that once broke a million hearts. He was charming and warm and he and Gianni had obviously bonded in the hour he'd been here – arriving from LAX and coming straight to the restaurant on Gina's strict instructions. Once I got my voice back, we talked about Hollywood (as you do) and he shared funny stories and titbits of gossip and I asked him all about his friendships with 'Al and Robert'. He lit up the room with his perfect teeth and his LA glamour and I invited him to dine with us the following evening.

'Oh your husband has already kindly extended an invitation to dinner,' he said.

Gina snuggled next to him, 'And Roberto would be happy to have some photos taken with Gianni in the restaurant, won't you my love?'

He touched his head with hers and judging by the sexual chemistry, these two had quite a lot to catch up on.

I was now the new co-owner of a seaside restaurant with my husband, and you can take the girl out of PR but you can't take PR out of the girl, and I wasn't letting this slip through my fingers. So I asked politely if Roberto would mind a TV crew turning up from the local news. 'Why not?' he said, delighted at the prospect. Mind you, the way Gina was looking at him over her glass I reckoned he had other delightful prospects to look forward to before the evening was out.

❄ ❄ ❄

It's hard to describe how I felt that New Year's Eve, it was like I had caught my dream against the odds, and I was starting all over again.

'I can't thank you enough for tonight – and appreciate just how hard this has been for you,' I said to Gianni when we were finally alone for a moment.

'Yes it is beeg strain to be nice, I understand now what you mean when you say it is not easy and it is bloody hard. But I like most of these people in the room tonight, so I will keep going until I don't.'

I laughed, who knew when that would be? But I figured if Fred from the chippy called him 'Pedro' again – we might just find out.

The rest of the evening was wonderful, Ella had brought her kids and their partners and Roberta had a handsome silver fox on her arm who was apparently something to do with 'The Mob'. Sue also had a gentleman with her and when I said he looked nice she agreed, but added, 'I like him, but I don't want him to take me for granite – I've been there too many times, sweetheart.'

Meanwhile my husband continued his charm offensive and the only dubious moment was when he put his arm around me and told the man from the deli, 'I am glad to be near the bitch again.' I made a mental note to insist he work on his pronunciation in the New Year, it didn't matter how friendly he was, there were plenty of opportunities for beach references while we lived here and I didn't want any more trouble.

After the buffet was finished, Roberta appeared and the 'floor show' started. Roberta had changed into a red, spangly dress to match Delilah's and they walked into the middle of the room like it was Caesars Palace, Las Vegas, with hooting and cheering and much bowing from the two 'stars'. Roberta set off and her singing (and Delilah's accompanying a cappella barking) was surprisingly good, a strong voice and the kind of flexible moves a woman half her age would find hard. She was mesmerising, and positively shimmered and, as Gianni had predicted, her 'Like a Virgin' brought the house down. She later tweeted photos and a video to Madonna, but unfortunately was a little confused with 'The

Twitter' and inadvertently sent it to 'Madonna House' instead. This turned out to be 'a Catholic community of priests dedicated to serving and loving Jesus Christ'. And he alone knows what the priests made of a seventy-nine-year-old woman and a dog, dressed in scarlet with a million strands of pearls jumping up and down, singing about being 'touched for the very first time'.

After spending a wonderful New Year's Eve with lovely new friends, delicious food, fine wine, laughter, the whole restaurant set off to the beach at midnight where we held hands and sang 'Auld Lang Syne'. It was a clear night and we stood beneath a million stars and exploding fireworks and my husband took me in his arms and kissed me, until my heart was mended.

Eventually, everyone left and we waved goodbye to them on the step of the restaurant, promising to get together again soon. And when they'd all gone, Gianni beckoned me back inside and led me into the kitchens through a proper door that you could see – it had a handle and everything, and the CCTV cameras were also gone.

'No more barriers?' I said.

'No more barriers,' he repeated, leading me upstairs to the little flat above.

'I thought we were staying at the cottage,' I said, disappointed. 'I don't want to sleep upstairs over the restaurant, it will take over our lives like it used to.'

'Yes of course we will always live at the cottage, and we'll have Sundays off and we'll cook for each other and have our own life too. Ella told me about these things called "date nights",' he said, looking at me uncertainly, seeking my approval.

'Date nights are good,' I smiled, kissing him on the cheek.

The girls had been teaching him well, and I looked forward very much to getting to know them more.

We reached the top of the stairs and he opened the door to the flat and I followed him in. And there, in the corner of the tiny kitchen, was a little pet bed and two tiny bowls with food and water in. I turned to him, 'What's this?'

'Take a look,' he said, and I walked over to the pink bed crowded with baby covers and inside was the cutest little white kitten.

I looked up at him, tears in my eyes, 'Oh Gianni.'

'Snowflake 2,' he said, and lifting her gently from the cat bed, he handed her to me as he had all those years ago.

'Welcome to our family, little one,' I said, carefully taking her from him. Her tiny pink mouth opened as if she was saying hello in her scratchy baby animal cry.

Gianni put her inside his coat as he had all those years ago with the first Snowflake and as he held open the door of the restaurant for me to leave, we both looked back at what we'd created. This was the place we now called ours. I watched him turn out all the lights, Snowflake at his chest, me on his arm and I realised that sometimes two people are meant to be for ever, and to make it work, they have to say goodbye first, and find each other all over again.

Stepping out onto the road, the wintry night was cold and clear, the last few fireworks exploding over the sea, their sparkle guiding our little family home. Who knew what this next year would bring, but for now I was with the man I loved, in the place I loved, with our little white kitten. I had all I needed right here and whatever happened, I wasn't leaving any time soon.

A Letter from Sue Watson

Thank you so much for reading *Snowflakes, Iced Cakes and Second Chances*. I hope you enjoyed being back in Appledore for Chloe and Gianni's story and that the snow, sparkle and hot chocolate made you feel all Christmassy.

If you enjoyed this book and would like to read more I'll let you know when my next one is released if you sign up by clicking the link here: www.bookouture.com/sue-watson

I promise I won't share your email address with anyone, and I'll only send you an email when I have a new book out. I'd also love it if you could take a few moments to leave a review.

If you want to taste Christmas in a dish do try Chloe's Christmas Crumble, it is delicious, simple and so easy – let me know what you think!

Happy Christmas!

Love, Sue x

www.suewatsonbooks.com/

 Sue-Watson-Books

 @suewatsonwriter

Chloe's Christmas Crumble

This is a hearty, warming pudding with no sea slugs in sight!

A simple and delicious dessert to serve around Christmas. When combined with cinnamon and poached in mulled wine, the plums in this crumble taste like pure, unadulterated Christmas. The topping can also be varied by adding orange zest, chopped nuts, flaked almonds or a sprinkling of brown sugar. Another way to make this dish even *more* festive is to add rum sauce or brandy cream, turning a simple crumble into a Christmas or New Year dinner party pudding.

Ingredients *(Serves 6 people)*

Fruit Filling:

- ❋ 1oz (28g) butter
- ❋ 1kg plums
- ❋ 2 cloves
- ❋ 3 teaspoons cinnamon
- ❋ 150ml (5floz) mulled wine or cranberry/raspberry juice
- ❋ 2 tablespoons muscovado (or soft brown) sugar
- ❋ 2–3 teaspoons orange zest

Crumble Topping:

* ❋ 8oz (225g) plain flour
* ❋ 3oz (85g) butter at room temperature
* ❋ 3-4oz 75–110g) soft brown sugar
* ❋ 1 teaspoon cinnamon

Method

Pre-heat the oven to Gas Mark 4, 350F, 180C.

Put the butter into a pan and add the muscovado or brown sugar, warm on a moderate heat until the butter has melted and the sugar dissolved. Now slowly add the mulled wine, trying not to stir the liquid too much as this will make the syrup grainy. Next add the sliced plums and cinnamon and cook gently for between 5–10 minutes until the plums have absorbed some of the fluid and are sitting in a syrup. Now put the syrup and fruit into an oven-proof dish and set aside.

Measure the butter and flour and place in a large mixing bowl. Rub the butter into the flour with your fingertips until it is evenly distributed and has a breadcrumb texture. Add the sugar and cinnamon and combine into the flour and butter mix. With a large spoon, transfer the topping to the fruit, laying it evenly until it is all used up. Now add any extra topping you desire, orange zest, chopped nuts, flaked almonds or brown sugar, sprinkling liberally on the top of the crumble.

Bake for 30–40 minutes, until the topping is tinged with golden brown and the fruit is bubbling. Allow to cool a little, then add custard, cream, rum sauce or brandy cream... or, if you've had enough of all that festive indulgence, just eat it with nothing on – Gianni does!

Acknowledgements

Happy Christmas and iced cakes as always to Oliver Rhodes, Claire Bord, Jessie Botterill, Kim Nash, Emily Ruston, Jade Craddock and the rest of the Bookouture team, who weave their magic with my words and turn them into books.

Thanks to all my blogger friends who take the time to read and review my books. I can't thank you enough for your kindness, support and enthusiasm – you keep me going through the snow.

Love and sparkle to all my family and friends, you inspire me in so many ways and make every season feel a lot like Christmas!